GLASS GIRLS

GLASS GIRLS

A NOVEL

DANIE SHOKOOHI

GILLIAN FLYNN BOOKS
A zando IMPRINT
NEW YORK

zando

Gillian Flynn Books is an imprint of Zando.
zandoprojects.com

First Edition: June 2025

Design by Neuwirth & Associates, Inc.
Cover design by Katie Anderson
Cover art: (woman behind glass) Nic Skerten / Trevillion Images; (border) AlyonaZhitnaya/Shutterstock.com; (stain) Alexander Yurkevich/Shutterstock.com; (splatter) Lee Charlie/Shutterstock.com

Library of Congress Control Number: 2025934832

978-1-63893-190-4 (hardcover)
978-1-63893-191-1 (ebook)

10 9 8 7 6 5 4 3 2 1
Manufactured in the United States of America

TO NIC AND ELLA,
my beloved siblings,
who have taught me how deep
the well of love can go.

This
Is a mean task, this business
Of burying oneself before one
Is dead.

—BRIGIT PEGEEN KELLY

Without a functioning Broca's area, you cannot put your thoughts and feelings into words. Our scans showed that Broca's area went offline whenever a flashback was triggered. In other words, we had visual proof that the effects of trauma are not necessarily different from—and can overlap with—the effects of physical lesions like strokes . . . Even years later traumatized people often have enormous difficulty telling other people what has happened to them . . . Trauma by nature drives us to the edge of comprehension, cutting us off from language based on common experience or an imaginable past.

—BESSEL VAN DER KOLK

GLASS GIRLS

A Lifetime Ago . . .

ONCE UPON A TIME, when Isabeau and Bronwyn Glass were still small enough to share the top bunk of the camper, in the years before Killian's birth, before they moved into the Little House, back further still, before their mother met Frank, before they'd even heard of Kirtland, Ohio, their mother would tell them a bedtime story.

It was only a bedtime story in the sense that their mother told it to them after she'd tucked Beau and Bronwyn in for the night. The girls knew bedtime stories were meant to be sweet and soothing, an escape and a dream, but their mother's story offered no such paltry comfort. It was meant, instead, to teach a lesson, and so she saved it for when Beau and Bronwyn had behaved exceptionally poorly—or after she had read their tarot cards and foreseen their misdeeds.

Night was when their mother was at her most dangerous, most capable of hurting them. The crackling overhead bulbs in the camper would camouflage her—dull the red in her hair, blur the sharpness of her freckles. She'd unfasten her many gold bangles, which jangled as she walked, and wipe the scarlet lipstick from her mouth. Without it, she'd look plucked, as fragile in her baggy t-shirt as a newly hatched crane. Their mother would smile through her story, but the smile, Beau knew, was an anglerfish, meant to lull them into complacency. At a single peep or whimper, she would snap her children into her mouth and gnash them up, bones and all. On their mother, softness was always a threat.

The version of the story Beau remembers best, the one her mother told most often, began like this: "Once there was a girl who cut off her shadow.

"The girl did it for love. She'd found herself with child, but her lover had refused to marry her. For she was the kind of girl like us, strange and marvelous. She could spell charms to bring down the rain and bake prosperity into pies, and she was born with the special gift of whispering the plants to harvest and the flowers to bloom. The lover named her magic a sickness, called her gift 'dark' and 'devilish.' That's often the way with men, my darlings—they will love you for your power and yet fear what you can do with it.

"Though the girl would likely have done better raising her child alone in the woods—as I did with you—she loved him. But because she refused to give her idiot lover up, and because everyone knows that all manner of wonders live in your shadow, she decided, instead, to do a brave and stupid thing—she decided to cut it off.

"The girl packed a flint in the pocket of her dress, and she searched deep into the heart of the forest until she found the place where the oldest and wisest oak tree lived. The girl knelt between its gnarled roots and bowed her copper head to the dirt. 'Old Oak, Old Oak,' she whispered, 'how can I cut my magic out?'

"The tree told the girl, 'Young One, do not ask me for such a terrible thing.'

"Twice more the girl asked the oak, and twice more the oak denied her. But the girl was quick and the girl was clever and the girl pulled the flint from the pocket of her dress and told the tree, 'Old Oak, Old Oak, tell me how to cut the magic out, or I will burn you down to a withered old stump.'

"The Old Oak trembled and blustered and begged, but the girl was resolute with the child stirring inside her. At last, his fear overcame his wisdom. 'Young One, it is not such a simple task to cut your shadow out,' he said. The Old Oak told her then of the place where the forgotten gods had buried a knife so sharp it could carve a shadow free from the balls of a human's feet. 'But,' he cautioned, 'if you want to keep the magic gone, you must cut a rune spell into your heels and fill the wound with a paste of angelica and dill, burned to ash on a full moon. You must pack it into the trough of the wound in order to make the scar raise properly, for this is a ritual that can only be completed once.'

"I could tell you of the struggles she underwent to find this knife, of the sheerness of the cliff faces and the stalactite teeth of the caves, of her bleeding nail beds and the blisters on her palms—but some pains must belong to us alone. For all her ordeals, the girl found it at last, and on the new moon, she scraped her shadow clean off and cut the bind runes in its place.

"She wept and bled and thought she might go mad with the loss of it, but then she remembered her lover. Now he will marry me, she thought. She hobbled to him, her footprints bloodied with the evidence of her love. And though the lover had once feared her for her magic, he could no longer love the cloven part of her that remained.

"And that's why we must never question our gifts, not for anyone." Their mother would touch each of their cheeks, her hands blade-cold. "It is madness, my little loves, to buckle to the whims of a world that prioritizes happiness over power. Our gifts may be dark, and they may be dangerous, but without them, we'd be pathetically ordinary."

Then, their mother would flick off the lights, leaving the girls holding hands in the dark, shushing each other whenever one would try to speak, afraid she would hear them—afraid she would come back.

ONE

As Alice Haserot stares at the twin lines of the pregnancy test, her hands shake. She checks the booklet again; the test is still positive.

She slumps to the bathroom floor, digs her fingers into the fronds of the rug as if they can ground her. It's February—most benign of all the months. The shortest, the youngest sister, filled with the bygone slush of January's pristine snows. Month of nothing all that important, month of candy hearts staining the dirty mounds in the parking lots an artificial red, month of the last few stubborn Christmas lights coming down. Nothing bad is supposed to happen in February.

She needs to tell her boyfriend. She doesn't like calling Eli her boyfriend—it sounds juvenile and tenderhearted—but he loves the term, so she indulges him. She met Eli two years ago on a dating app. Alice asked him out because he looked like a magazine ad for a wristwatch, glossy and crisp, and that's what she'd thought she was looking for at the time. Their first date was to an ice cream shop, her pick. After Eli paid for her sundae, he admitted he was lactose intolerant but had been too nervous to suggest somewhere else. In person, he had a prettiness she wanted to touch, to see if he was as delicate as he looked.

They'd talked about kids on that first date. She was thirty-two then, and at thirty-two kids weren't theoretical. She'd been relieved when he said he didn't want any. Good, she thought. Not a worry here. Yet here she is, two years later, trapped in the bathroom with this damning piece of plastic.

Except, this is no time for Alice to be pregnant. Not ever, but especially not today. Alice had known that even as she pulled the test from its plastic wrapper. Susan, Eli's mother, lands in two hours, and Susan already dislikes her. Alice spent her morning in a frenzy of rubbing alcohol and wood polish, because when Alice gets anxious, she cleans. "It's okay," Eli said, gently prying a dish rag loose from her grip, "Mom doesn't really like me either." But Alice doesn't handle being disliked well, so she polished the kitchen faucet, reorganized bookshelves, washed the windows—anything to calm the rabbitlike pounding of her heart.

The test was like that, she supposed—another tick off her to-do list before she cleaned the bathroom. She was late and worried about it, so she'd decided to pee on the stick to stop fretting. She'd considered every possible outcome except the one in which she might actually be pregnant.

Alice has only lived with Eli for a month and a half now. She still hesitates before she touches his things, bunches herself up when she moves through the doorways to avoid intruding on his space. She hadn't wanted to move to Saginaw, but Eli, an architect, designed this house himself. How could her rented condo compete?

It isn't even that she dislikes the house—she could never dislike a place Eli designed—but she wouldn't have picked it herself. The house backs onto a park, which itself breaches a nature preserve. "There are predators in the woods," Eli warned her. The occasional timber wolf or bobcat, but mostly coyotes. In fact, the week Alice moved in, a pack of them attacked a neighbor's dog, still attached to its owner's leash. It was one of those soft-mouthed spaniels, all long red and white fur and black teddy bear eyes; big enough that it fought back. It didn't win. Alice tries not to consider this an omen.

So it doesn't feel like home yet. Maybe it could, if she let it. She taps the pregnancy test with her forefinger, testing its solidity, its smoothness, its strange warmth.

Beneath her, the garage door vibrates. Eli, returning from the grocery store. Alice wipes her face with the back of her hands. She needs to tell him. Of course, she does—it's the right thing to do. At the last moment, she hesitates, hand on the doorknob. Then Alice wraps the pregnancy test in a cocoon of toilet paper and buries it in the trash can under the sink. She tells herself motherhood, with her condition, is impossible. She tells herself she feels nothing.

Downstairs, Eli is standing on the other side of the kitchen island, surrounded by a sea of plastic bags—shredded coconut, candied pineapple, macadamia nuts. He's been making his own trail mix for as long as Alice has known him. It's one of the few residues of his eating disorder that they still allow. Eli almost died in his early twenties, goofing around while perched on the thick metal railing of a trolley bridge. He fell nineteen feet, shattering his rib cage on the half-submerged rocks below. His chest is half scar tissue, half metal. He emerged from his hospital bed weak limbed and shaking, treats his body like an animal that might spook. The result was orthorexia nervosa, an excessive preoccupation with exercise and eating healthy food—the words all far too mild for the way his near-death stalks him.

"You're staring." Eli clasps the jar and gives it a practiced shake. "Do you want to try this? It's a new recipe."

He will be the type of father who sends his kids to school with carefully calibrated sandwiches, she thinks. Their child will trade grained bread for Fruit Roll-Ups. But this thought is in bad faith. There will be no child.

"Alice?" Eli focuses on her, the jar open and extended.

She realizes she hasn't answered. "That's okay. I'm going to slice up a lemon in a minute."

Eli frowns, setting the jar on the counter. Alice shelves the cashew milk, but when she returns, Eli reaches out. His fingers graze her wrist, coarse with salt and sugar. "What's wrong?"

"Nothing. I'm just nervous. Your mom's particular." Alice doesn't like lying to him, so this isn't a lie, not precisely. His mother thrives on her own difficulty, and it's her first visit since she moved to Scottsdale last year. Susan picked the most impossibly busy week to visit, last minute of course. Alice about sold her soul to wrangle the time off: She had to reschedule all her clients at the hair salon, which means a week of twelve-hour days when she returns, and one woman who wants Alice to achieve the improbable miracle of dark brown to white-blond. Eli has been on and off the phone all morning with his own new and particularly difficult client, a Dow Chemical exec who is insisting on breaking ground for his new house before the snow has even begun to thaw. They had to beg Susan to take the connecting flight to Saginaw; she wanted to be picked up in Detroit, a three-hour round-trip drive.

"We could send her to a hotel." Eli flattens his palms on the counter, leans over them. "I'm only kind of joking. We could, if you want. Give me a reason."

"It's okay," Alice says, because she can manage Susan. The bigger problem is growing inside her. She has observed over the years, with some horrified fascination, the way some of her Facebook friends post about their babies as produce. *Today, our daughter is the size of a pea. Today, she's a cashew, next week a strawberry.* An entire grocery store inside them. That loose macadamia nut on the counter—is what lives inside her that big yet? Or is it a grain of rice? Is she a week late? Closer to two? She knows nothing about pregnancy, hasn't been tracking her cycle, procrastinated taking the test. Even now—maybe especially now—it's difficult for Alice to consider pregnancy as anything other than the act of being consumed.

"Do you want to talk about it?" Eli grazes her knuckle, startling her. She pulls away without meaning to.

"We don't need to talk about everything, do we?"

He hesitates and then forces a stiff smile. "I guess not."

She shouldn't get so defensive when Eli fusses like this. Before him, no one woke her from nightmares. No one handed her glasses of ice water before bed or kissed her teenage cutting scars or hounded her until she quit smoking. It's her own fault that being taken care of makes her feel so exposed.

The lemon's waxy rind is bright in her palm. Alice loves lemon slices dipped in sugar. She imagines them as sunshine, warm and painful and sweet. Something that will cleanse her entirely, so she will not have to consider the failure of her body, will not have to confess what it's done. Is it cruel to tell him now, with his mother hurtling through the air toward him? It might be, but will he forgive her for waiting until Susan leaves? For all that he needs a gentle hand, Eli doesn't like being handled gently.

Alice hesitates. "Eli." She hates the smallness of her voice. Eli leans toward her, but then his cell phone rings.

He fishes the phone from his pocket and squashes it against his ear as he pours a bag of cashews into the trail mix jar. "Hi, Mom," he says.

The lemon rolls across the granite counter and stills against a bag of Brazil nuts.

"Everything's almost ready for you. We can't wait." Eli follows the lemon's path and looks up at Alice, grimacing. He sets the phone on speaker as Susan complains about her layover—she's been trapped in the airport all day, tired and hungry; why is the Detroit airport massive; she despises regional flights, next time they have to pick her up; she ate an overpriced meal at an awful, greasy restaurant; she has heartburn; she can't possibly handle the salt in Chinese takeout now, it's entirely out of the question. Alice could almost laugh. With Susan, there's always some urgent inconvenience.

As Susan drones, Eli shrinks over the counter, massaging his temples. "I got back from the grocery store fifteen minutes ago and we're right in the middle of meal-prepping for the rest of the week."

"God, will you give the meal-prepping a break. Every time I talk to you, you're meal-prepping." Through the phone, Alice can sense Susan bristling, the pursing of her lips, the setting of her jaw. Alice has a sixth sense for difficult mothers.

"We agreed on delivery." Eli passes a hand over his face. They are three months into his latest recovery, but changing meals around still presents a significant stressor. "Would you rather do sushi?"

"What if Alice cooks?" Susan says. "How about that beef? The one with the wine sauce and those cranberries? I've been craving it for ages. Do it for your mom? Please?"

"Be reasonable, Mom. I can't ask Alice to drop everything last minute because you have a craving."

"Why not?" There's a rustle on the other end of the line, as if Susan scraped the speaker against her coat. "If Alice minds cooking, she'll say something. Ask her."

When Eli is flustered, he reddens in swatches—his cheeks, forehead, the curve of his neck, right where the blond hair curls under the lobe of his ear. And if Alice doesn't do something to mediate, he's liable to spiral out for the rest of the night. The two of them will snipe at each other for hours, until Eli finally collapses into bed in a fit of piqued and bitter exhaustion, and Susan gripes about his inflexibility for the rest of the trip. Of course, Alice also has more selfish reasons to buckle to Susan's whims, this mundane emergency presenting an opportunity for escape. She reaches across the counter and wrenches the phone away.

"Hi Susan." Alice avoids Eli's gaze—instead, she focuses on the sink, on the dull light glaring off the faucet. "Beef and cranberry sauce is a great idea. In fact, it's perfect for a chilly day like this. I'm glad you thought of it."

"Oh. Good." Point to Alice. Susan clearly didn't anticipate that she was on speaker. "Well, I'm looking forward to it."

When Eli ends the call, they stare at each other from across the kitchen. Alice sucks in her cheeks and bites down. If she moves, she'll crack and tell him everything.

Eli breaks the silence first. He turns to the fridge and pulls out a bottle of Vernors. "What was that about?" The bottle hisses in his hands.

Alice counts to five in her head and leans forward on the counter. She knows she can't hide behind it, but its slim coverage offers her a certain comfort. "This'll make it easier to say no to other things later this week."

"You don't have to humor her. I really don't want you to, actually. My therapist said I need to set boundaries."

Alice knows.

"I don't think I should go back to the grocery store." The barely contained panic in his voice gives Alice pause. He's picking at the wrapper on his bottle. A substitute, so he won't pick his skin. Alice knows this about him, just as she knows that he wants a reason to be upset with himself when he's actually upset with her. She can't tell him about the test, not now.

"I'll go." Alice nudges past him to reach the junk drawer, from which she pulls a small yellow notepad and a pen.

Eli blinks once, then twice. "You hate the grocery store."

Alice scribbles down the ingredients, holding the pen so tightly it leaves a red indent on her middle finger. "That's why you'll fold the laundry and chop the vegetables."

"Why do you want to go to the store?"

Alice shrugs in a way she hopes is casual. "I need some air. Last chance and all." She rips the page out of the notepad. The ink smears, staining her thumb. Almost free.

"Let me call her back." Eli peers at her. "I'll tell her we're ordering delivery. I meant it, about the boundaries."

Alice tosses the notepad and pen back into the junk drawer and pushes it shut with her hip. "It won't take that long." Alice cups his jaw, pelts the soft corner of his mouth with kisses until reluctantly, he smiles. "I'll be home in half an hour."

This is how Alice finds herself in the posh co-op off Gratiot Road, lifting cans of jellied cranberries, one a hand, trying to determine through touch whether Ocean Spray or organic will offend Susan less. Resolutely, she sets the Ocean Spray back on the shelf. There's still buttermilk and sirloin to agonize over. Hopefully, Eli will set the table with the good dishes. Eli always remembers the outline of what he's supposed to do, but never the particulars of it: He forgets the coupons during checkout, washes the dishes but forgets to wipe the counters. Alice fishes her phone from her purse and finds his contact. She types, *bougie plates for dinner please?* and adds a kissy face emoji. As she tucks her phone into the pocket of her purse, the back of her neck prickles.

She looks behind her. A woman, painfully thin, is watching her from the threshold of the aisle. The woman is still, but in her stillness, her skin quivers like a deer's. Her fingers graze the chap of her lips. The nails are long and thickly lined with dirt. Her gaze, wide and wild, locks onto Alice's. Her mouth parts into what could be called a smile if Alice were feeling generous. It forms creases at the edges of her eyes.

Something in Alice's belly clenches. She almost recognizes the woman, but at the last moment, she chooses not to because the woman is impossible. Alice has spent so long telling herself the Family can't find her that even now, with this woman staring at her, Alice tells herself that plenty of people have silver eyes and hair as red as Alice's own. Alice is overreacting.

The woman whispers something low and impossible to catch. Then, loud as a keening, "Beau!"

A few stray shoppers turn their heads. A young mother glares up from her floral-printed diaper bag before trudging toward another aisle. Alice's sweaty palms tighten uselessly around the handle of her cart. Suddenly, the narrow woman stutters into motion. She takes long steps down the aisle. Her stride exposes the thin thread of her leggings, holes studded up to the knee like constellations. Dried mud caulks the length of her bedraggled coat. The woman pushes carts and shoppers out of her way, does not excuse herself. Alice needs to move. Her feet are frozen to the tile.

The woman has mistaken her identity. The shouted name is coincidental. The Family can't find her, not now, not after so many years. This is a mistake. All Alice must do is explain. Instead, Alice finally turns tail. She presses hard against the cart, speeding up to round the corner of the aisle, but the narrow woman is faster. She tugs hard on Alice's elbow, sends her stumbling back. "For fuck's sake, Isabeau."

It's the Isabeau that does it, that clarifies the narrow woman into her older sister, Bronwyn. Panic gathers low in Alice's diaphragm. She yanks against Bronwyn's grip, but like a finger trap, pulling only tightens it. Bronwyn tugs her close enough that their noses almost touch. She smells like stale cigarettes and unwashed bodies. "You didn't recognize me? Really?" Alice's periphery blurs, and the world distills into the self-satisfied brightness of Bronwyn's eyes. Bronwyn is laughing. "I could tell it was you even from behind."

Alice's heart pounds a dizzy rhythm in her temples. "Please don't do this."

"Do you know how long it took me to find you? How long I've looked?"

"Let me go. I need to go. Please." Alice should be struggling. She should be pulling her arm free and screaming instead of whispering like this. Someone in this goddamn grocery store would help her. Even now, a woman near the canned fruits keeps ogling them, her eyebrows tight with concern. Stop looking at the fucking mandarins and help me, Alice thinks. But the woman tosses her cans into her cart, rounds the corner, and disappears.

"It's real important. I wouldn't have come looking if it wasn't," Bronwyn is saying. "Beau, please. Hear me out."

"Eli's mother is coming tonight, and I need buttermilk." Alice hears the pitiful words coming from her mouth but she's unable to stop them. She's already shed her body like a rind. Her brain speeds through the connective tissue of panic—if Bronwyn is here, in Michigan, it means Gisele could be, too, and that sends Alice into a fresh terror. It's been sixteen years since Alice last laid eyes on her sister—what else could Bronwyn want from her, if not to hunt her down for their mother? She needs to leave before it's too late, before they steal her back. "Let me go."

"Come on, Isabeau. You can spare a minute. I thought you'd appreciate that I didn't swing by that McMansion you live in." Bronwyn grins and deep in her mouth she's missing a tooth. She looks even more like their mother than she did when they were teenagers. "You've done real well for yourself. I didn't expect that."

"Does she know I'm here?"

"Who?" Bronwyn's grip softens and Alice sees her freedom. She punches and her aim is good. She catches Bronwyn in the collarbone, the place she broke it falling out of a tree the year she turned twelve. Bronwyn yelps and staggers back, her hands jerking up to protect herself, but Alice is already running. She abandons her cart and her cranberries and her sister. She runs like the stupid scared rabbit she is, runs all the way back to her car. Behind her, Bronwyn shouts her old name. "Please, Isabeau. Please." It rings in her ears the whole drive home.

TWO

Age Six

ONCE, ALICE HAD A BROTHER, and sixteen years ago, he died.

Killian's death was genetic, in a way. Hereditary. Call it, perhaps, an illness. Call it, even, a curse—the girls for the gift, and the boys for the grave. "Never birth a boy," their mother used to say, though not when Killian might overhear. "Better to cut the baby from your belly than watch him live and die before you."

If the Family must be called something, they might as well be called witches. Not the wave a wand and bibbidy-bobbidy-boo sort, but the inherited kind. Casters of small magic who could coax abundance from unpolished rounds of citrine and prevent lightning strikes by hanging garlands of acorns across the windows. Theirs was a power that required careful practice and the study of folk knowledge to master. Their spells could only be cast if you knew the energies that lived in inanimate things. Bronwyn used to call it Wicca, only less lovey-lovey and more juice.

Though of course the word *witch* offers its own imprecisions, doesn't explain the gifts. Even now, Alice finds it hard to separate the two, to parse where the witching stopped and the gifts began, though the gifts did seem to be more of a specialization, a talent no one else could replicate. If the witching gave them magic generally, the gifts were a distillation of their particular skill set. Any witch worth her salt could throw some herbs together in a spell jar, but only an Herbalist could grow a lemon tree outside in the middle of winter. Their mother used to theorize that a girl's gift came from the core of her personality, the pinnacle of who she was for better and for worse. Whether the gift shaped the girl or the girl shaped the gift, Alice still couldn't say, but she'd never come to a better explanation.

The gift usually manifested when a girl turned four or five. The later it came, the stronger it would be. Only for daughters. Their sons died, without exception, before their nineteenth birthdays. That was their family's origin story, hundreds of years old, if not more. "The first witch made a terrible bargain with the old gods in a ritual we no longer know," their mother had once explained. "She asked for the power to change her life, in exchange for any price. And the price they demanded was her boys." So their family had always known Killian would die young—they just hadn't known how or when. This is a reality Alice must live with if she keeps her baby. If she should birth a boy.

If Alice finds it hard to pry the gift from the witching, it's even harder to pick out which parts of her are Alice, and which are Isabeau. Only that they're different—and Beau is dead. But what happened in the Little House belongs to Beau. Maybe this encounter with Bronwyn has called Beau back. Alice can feel Beau stirring in the ground.

The early years of Alice's life were as nomadic as they were best forgotten. These were the lean years of the early '90s, when a witch was a taboo and mostly impoverished thing to be, before the commercialization of New Age stores. They couldn't afford to live off witching in any one place for longer than a month, and so their mother would set up the next job, and the next, and the next, and they bounced around the country between occult hubs where clients could be recommended or poached or lured by newspaper ads. They lived as far north as Maine in the fall, and as south as Virginia in the winter, and once they even made it out to Colorado. In the spring, their mother drove up through Tennessee, chasing the Renaissance faires, where she read tarot in lilac tents.

Gisele was an Oracle, a term she insisted was far lovelier than Seer or Prophet. Her gift was fortune-telling—she could read the glittering web of possible futures, each permutation of fate drifting behind a person's shoulder like silk, and she specialized in stitching them to the fabric of reality, using tarot the way a spider used thread. Though, of course, fate was permeable, changing with the choices people made, and her gift required perfect knowledge of her subject to shift those futures onto the paths she wanted. Practically, this meant that for every five things she got right, she got another two wrong and lied about the rest.

The ruining of their lives could have begun in an infinitude of places, but if Alice had to pinpoint a precise moment, it would be the May they stayed on Mrs. Hunter's land on the outskirts of Salem, Missouri. Alice was already six, but sometimes she thinks her memories begin there—in the damp smell of earth overturned in the garden and the glint of the sun off the dew on purple coneflowers. In the evenings, Alice's mother poked bonfires to life, the sunset burnishing their red hair to burning gold. Most afternoons, Mrs. Hunter came swaying up the walk, carrying a steaming potpie to trade for a reading.

It started after one of those readings, with Alice in her appointed place in the top bunk to deter the more scandalous questions Mrs. Hunter asked about her neighbors ("Best watch for Isabeau's sensitive ears," Gisele would say). That day, it was about a woman in Mrs. Hunter's church group. Gisele managed to hold the client smile of concerned tenderness until Mrs. Hunter shut the door in a puff of lavender perfume. Then she sagged at the camper's foldout table, pinching the bridge of her nose. "Shit, shit, shit," she whispered. "Mrs. Hunter is going to ruin that poor woman."

Gisele hated mining the cards for gossip. She found it undignified, and doing so always ripped something out of her, but Mrs. Hunter gave them a generous rental on the land. It was one of the few times in Alice's life that her mother seemed unable to tell someone no.

"Gisele?" Their mother always insisted on being called by her first name. "What's a cuckold?"

"Never you mind." Gisele sighed and settled in her seat. A trickle of sweat trailed down her temple, disappearing under the curve of her jaw. "It's not your place to fuss after other people's business unless you want to grow up into a gossipy old biddy like Mrs. Hunter." Gisele reached for the cloth condiment basket in the middle of the table and sprinkled a few grains of salt into her palm. "Why am I salting the cards, Beau?"

"Salt clears energy. Like raw quartz and rosemary smoke." With Gisele, an incomplete answer was almost always worse than a wrong one. Precision was important in rituals—magic worked through sympathetic connections with the natural world and a single imprecise correspondence could destroy an entire spell. "Mrs. Hunter's energy seems sticky today."

"Don't go telling her that." Gisele chewed the corner of her mouth as she angled the cards into the light pouring through the window, squinting at the glare bouncing off the laminate.

A single card slipped free of the deck. It floated to the floor and landed face up. The Four of Wands. A couple, their clasped hands twined with ivy, stood in front of a blazing hearth. As Gisele's fingertips grazed the card, she yanked back as if burned. "Oh," she gasped. "What's this?"

Even now, Alice believes Gisele's deck possesses its own separate snarling power. The things we love contain us, and Gisele had painted the deck herself as a teenager. The images were based off the classic Rider-Waite-Smith deck but lacked the cohesion of the tarot decks Alice had seen sold in stores. All the suits were strangely mismatched in different art styles—the impressionistic Cups in baleful blue-gray watercolors, and the postmodernist Coins in frenzied smears of gold leaf and gauche. On the back of each, the hook of a crescent moon glinted over an inky darkness. The laminate clicked like pincers, and when shuffled, the occasional card slipped free with a hiss. When Gisele wasn't using them, she kept them wrapped tight with a black leather cord and placed them in a velvet pouch, as if at any moment, the cards might struggle free and bind futures of their own.

As Gisele swiped the Four of Wands from the floor, the card shivered between her fingers. "Oh," she said again. A flush warmed the pale skin between her collarbones.

Alice started to say her mother's name, but Gisele silenced her with the sharp angle of an eyebrow. Gisele propped the Four of Wands against the condiment basket, then spread the remaining cards face down across the table in a neat line.

It never boded well when Gisele read her own future. It always indicated a certain desperation, an inherent dissatisfaction that would spur her into episodes of manic chaos. The last time had been a month prior in Gloucester. They'd lingered too long for a man who'd treated them to milkshakes and capped the night by backhanding Gisele for supposedly flirting with the waiter. For an hour, she'd sat on the camper roof, chain-smoking menthols with a bag of frozen peas pressed to her black eye, flipping card after card. Whatever Gisele read in those cards sent her fleeing so fast and so far through the night that she'd almost run the camper off the road. Alice had woken to a crack of pain at the crown of her head, Bronwyn's elbows and knees crushing her against the wall, screaming as the camper lurched toward the median. Gisele had wept afterward, holding them to her, promising she'd never risk them for a man ever again, she'd never forgive herself, her poor little loves.

Now, in Salem, Gisele caressed the air above the cards, from left to right. She lingered near the end of the line, before she pulled the Chariot free, then the Lovers. Something brittle settled in Alice's chest. "What's that?" She scooted closer to the edge of the bed, clutching her stuffed antelope tight to her chest, shielded by its felted horns.

Gisele glanced up, her gaze soft and unfocused. "A thread. A rare, almost impossible, singular thread where we will be so happy. Oh, Beau, we will meet the man of my dreams, and we will all be so happy." She laughed, then slapped a hand over her mouth as the pebble of fear in Alice's center sunk deeper, rippling.

Alice always struggles to think of Gisele as young, but her mother was only twenty-six that year. Young enough to believe that this rare and almost impossible future could be a promise. Perhaps all ruinings begin this way: with a promise and an impossibility.

The cards held the promise. The impossibility came when Bronwyn returned home that afternoon from playing in the woods. Gisele paced the camper, bobbing near the screen door like a flittering moth. Every twenty minutes or so, she stepped outside to light a cigarette and pace the length of the camper.

Bronwyn was a Diviner, and her gift worked like a magnet—or maybe a leash. Bronwyn could find anyone or anything so long as she could follow their energy trail. Gisele had called it an energy lock. When Bronwyn had first started tracking lost keys and missing dolls, and rotating like a compass to find their mother in the grocery store at age four, their mother had sighed. "It'll be a gift like mine," she'd said. "It'll take practice to do it well."

When eight-year-old Bronwyn burst in, dirt mottled and grass stained, Gisele caught her by the shoulder and passed her the Four of Wands. "What do you see?"

"Is that a trick question?" Bronwyn looked at Gisele, then down at the card. Alice bit the tip of her tongue. Bronwyn should know better than to talk back when their mother took that tone. "What do you want me to do with this?"

"I need you to track an energy lock. Obviously. It should go to a man. I can See him, but it would be a tricky thing to find him without you." Gisele snapped her fingers in front of Bronwyn's face. "Now, please. For once, make yourself useful."

Bronwyn trembled as she held the card. She rotated, first to the right, then to the left, again and again, but each time she swiveled, she was drawn back to Gisele. "It goes to you."

Gisele tightened her grip on the table. "Try harder."

Bronwyn stared into the card so intently that her eyes crossed. Finally, Bronwyn gasped and dropped the card, shrank back into herself. "There aren't any other energy locks. I'm sorry, I'm sorry, I'm sorry."

Gisele smiled as she bent to retrieve the Four of Wands. She smiled as she squeezed Bronwyn's shoulder, smiled while she dug her thumb into Bronwyn's collarbone. Smiled wider when Bronwyn sobbed in pain.

"Useless," Gisele hissed. When she released her grip, Bronwyn's knees buckled, and she fell to the floor. "I suppose I'll have to do it myself, like everything else."

Later that night, Alice woke to Gisele standing at the kitchen table, ghoulish by candlelight, stringing red and orange beads onto an oiled black cord. She knotted a metal heart at the end, which she brought briefly to her lips. "Bring me to my lover," Gisele whispered, her face raw with hope. "For their happiness, let me find him." As she dangled the string, the heart swung faster and faster still.

It took Gisele eleven days to find the place where happiness lived. Gisele hung the cord from the rearview mirror and drove along to its directions. Location spells do work, but sluggishly. They don't possess the same precision as a map, can't conform to highways or interstates or even roads. The little metal heart hanging from the end did little more than swing in the right direction, and spin in circles if Gisele took a wrong turn.

That was the thing about magic. You could only cast with the knowledge you possessed, and, unlike the ease of the gifts, the Family's magic required intensive years of focus and training. The simple fact was Gisele simply didn't have very much.

What could Alice say of those days other than they passed? They bled into other ordeals in the camper: forcing down canned chicken and peas for dinner, the dusty smell of road thick in their clothes. Gisele tearing her hair and snapping that they would lose their chance to find him, this man who would change their lives. Every few hours, she'd pull over at a truck stop to draw a card from the tarot deck and adjust their future. One time, she trotted to the vending machine and returned with three bags of pretzels. "If we stop for dinner," she explained, "we'll get caught in traffic. Eat up." Another time, they killed half the day playing on a swing set because "Otherwise we would get into a minor fender bender, and we don't have the time to wait on car repairs." There was a timeline at play, a plan, but only if they arrived in time to lure the man in. Alice dreamt that the camper would careen over a cliff or into a semi that would crunch its metal around them, burst their innards like pinched bugs.

And then, one uncharacteristically misty morning in late May, when the fog seeped from the tree trunks across the veiled asphalt, Gisele drove them into a pinprick suburb of Cleveland called Kirtland, Ohio, a place so small that it and the adjacent towns of Mentor and Willoughby went unmarked on the scrunched road map Gisele kept balled up in the glove box. The fog curled around the gabled rooftops, rapped its knuckles against the camper's windows as if trying to warn them away. As they crossed into the city limits, the location spell gave a final wild swing and stilled.

Gisele placed an ad in the local paper the same afternoon they arrived—*Gisele Glass, Psychic Services, Cash Only*—but she didn't accept most of the clients who sought her out. The ad was a lure for the mysterious man, a means to an end. "I'll know when it's him," she explained to the girls after she'd sent away the fifth client. "I'll feel it in my bones, and I don't want to be busy with a silly love reading for some middle-aged twit when he comes."

The only love readings she concerned herself with were her own. She wasted those early days at the kitchen table, flipping cards and scrawling notes across a legal pad, and from that legal pad, changes manifested. "He likes a tidy home," Gisele announced one day, and suddenly, she spent the late afternoons prettying the camper. She scrubbed the walls free of skid marks and scratches, washed the dishes after dinner, scolded Alice and Bronwyn into arranging their toys like strangers in a queue. Soon, even their skin smelled like off-brand Pine-Sol.

Another day, Gisele decided he loved fresh flowers and returned home with a dollar store vase. She carried gardening shears in her purse so she could liberate flowers from around the neighborhood. She nailed a set of rusty wind chimes above the camper door. She wore too much perfume; she stopped smoking; she painted her nails yellow, then gray; she wove small bells into her braid. By then, Bronwyn and Alice had been eating canned peaches for a week, sticky with hope for a future that procrastinated its appearance. Alice still longs to rip that legal pad apart.

"He's coming, little loves," Gisele promised, patting their heads or pinching their ears—depending on what mood they caught her in. "He'll be here so soon. So soon."

Bronwyn lapped the last of the peach syrup from the last of the cans, her tongue as small and slow as a cat's. "He better hurry."

Happiness finally arrived a week after Alice's seventh birthday. It was a scorching afternoon in June, and outside, the cicadas hummed loud and insistently, and cardinals thrummed in the tree branches. A single knock came at the camper door, and a man poked his head inside. He couldn't have been more than forty, but the sun-pressed lines on his face made him look older. As he stepped inside, he removed the baseball cap from his graying head and held it gingerly in the center of his chest. He glanced around uneasily, as if trying to figure out how he arrived there. His name was Frank, and he was looking for the lady who read cards.

Their mother rose from the kitchen table, her expression twisted with hope, fear, and a tinge—Alice would later realize—of disappointment. Probably, Gisele had been expecting a beautiful man whose face would break her heart, and no one could ever accuse Frank of that. But Gisele composed herself quickly, straightened her shoulders, and granted him that kind client smile. "How lucky—you found me." Gisele shooed Alice and Bronwyn out to play, then the door swung shut.

It was too hot to do much of anything, so the girls climbed the camper and sprawled on the beach towels they'd smuggled up there back in May. The metal frame smoldered Alice's back, even through the terry cloth. "Do you think it's him?" Alice asked once they settled in with a box of Red Vines. Now Alice never saw a box of them without thinking of Kirtland. A few weeks earlier, Bronwyn had gotten hungry enough to master the invisibility glamour Gisele had taught them. It was meant to distract the eye from the caster, rendering them unobservable. Every few days Bronwyn snuck into the gas station down the street to steal food, peacock ore, silver topaz, and calcite—all clenched in one fist. She'd return, red-faced, with their stolen necessities tucked into her bag: Red Vines and orange soda and canned chicken noodle soup.

"Do you think it's him?" Alice asked again, cocking her head toward her sister. "He looks—nice."

"Who cares if he's nice as long as we get out of here soon?" Bronwyn shrugged, her mouth twisting. "He looks old."

"His reading's taking forever. That's a good sign, right?"

"Maybe she'll make enough to buy us Burger King tonight." Bronwyn swatted away a mosquito buzzing near her shoulder, and for a time they sank into the humidity of the afternoon, drowsing in the alternating cool of the breeze and heat of the sun. Then Bronwyn asked, "You think there are more of us?"

"What do you mean?"

"The gifts, Dumb-Beau. We can't be the only ones."

Alice sat up and yelped as she placed her hand on the searing metal. Bronwyn clapped a damp and salty palm over Alice's mouth, hissing for her to be quiet. Alice tried to bite her, but her teeth slid off Bronwyn's skin. Bronwyn gave her a dark look as she wiped Alice's spit on the hem of her t-shirt.

"You aren't supposed to bite."

"You started it. You grabbed my mouth."

"Don't be such a baby." Bronwyn held out her hand, and Alice passed her the candy box.

"If there are more of us—" Candy stuck in Alice's throat, and she swallowed before continuing. "Then why doesn't Gisele talk about them?"

Bronwyn lay back on the towel, and her hair spread out like a corona around her pink face. "What if something bad happened to her because of the gifts?"

"Like having a boy bad? Or like how Gisele won't talk about her mom bad?" Alice and Bronwyn had long ago concluded that Gisele's family was gone. They knew about the picture in her wallet—twelve-year-old Gisele, gap-toothed and grinning, tucked in between four beaming ginger boys, all of whom had died bloody and young. Only occasionally could Gisele even bring herself to say their names, and only ever as a lesson. The girls were not to be left alone with plastic bags—their uncle Declan had suffocated in one when he was a toddler. Gisele saved for months to afford allergy panels because Isaiah, then sixteen, had eaten zucchini for the first time, and when his throat had closed, he'd driven into oncoming traffic. They weren't allowed to go trick-or-treating because Connell had fallen on the hem of his costume and cracked his head on someone's concrete steps. David had been the worst. Their mother could not speak of David, except when commanding them to stay indoors when it stormed.

Their grandmother, hovering nearby, had been scratched from the photograph. Only a hint of red hair and a flash of skin were still visible. Questions about her were the easiest way to send their mother into a rage, throwing pots and pans in a teeth-aching clatter around the small kitchen, screaming, "What, am I not enough for you? Could you possibly desire more?" She'd throw open the camper door so hard it would leave a chip in the doorframe. "I'll treat you like that woman treated me and then you'll appreciate what you have."

Bronwyn yanked another Red Vine from the box. She pulled a bite free like a fox savaging a rabbit. "What if gifts can be as bad as the curse? Like the girl who had to cut off her shadow?"

"That's stupid," Alice scoffed. "The gifts are never bad."

Bronwyn sat up, wrinkling her nose. "I bet your gift will be bad, Dumb-Beau. I bet it'll be stupid and horrible and it'll make you grow horns and spider legs."

"Take that back!" Alice yelled, but as she lunged for her sister, the camper door swung open. Bronwyn pushed Alice's head down out of sight.

Frank ducked to avoid the wind chimes as he exited, Gisele a few steps behind. Her blouse slipped off her freckled white shoulder, exposing the thin strap of a black bra, the red trough it dug into her skin. As she descended the camper steps, her hair blew back with the wind, and in the gold light of near dusk, their mother appeared sad and beautiful, as if she could cup the world between her palms and drink from it. When Frank turned back, he was grinning, uncertainty gone. "Will you be here again tomorrow?"

"I suspect I'll be here for a long time, Frank." Gisele tucked a strand of hair behind her ear, and Frank raised a hand in farewell and fled. Gisele watched in the entryway until Frank drove out of sight. Then, without looking up, Gisele said, "Clean up for dinner." The door shut behind her with a gentle click.

They moved into Frank's house at the end of the summer, after the whirlwind of a courthouse wedding.

Frank called it the Little House as a joke because there was nothing little about it. Alice is sure he never meant the name to stick, but Gisele had nodded. "Our little house," she repeated, easing into a dreamy smile. "My little house." And so, the Little House it became.

In fact, the Little House contained more rooms than people, and if Frank hadn't inherited it from his parents, they'd never have been able to afford anything like it. It was a proper home, beautiful even from the outside, where pinkish spirea bushes bloomed along the flagstone walk up to the fairy-tale green door, and the Japanese maple spilled its maroon leaves over the front steps. Bees bobbed like lazy drunks into one flower, then another, and hummingbirds frequented the petunias in the window box. Frank worked as a landscaper and knew how to dress a building.

Of course, that didn't change the fact that, inside, the Little House was moldering. On that first day they saw the house, Gisele's face grew hot and red as she thumbed the sagging upholstery of the living room couches. When Frank showed them the fissures in the crown molding, her hand shook in Alice's. None of the doors in the Little House locked, not even on the bathrooms, and they wouldn't shut without being slammed. The doors all tilted open of their own accord, toward the slope of the floors. Even the windowsills slanted left, like poorly hung paintings. The Little House ingested drafts and consumed sound and resisted all attempts to clean or modernize it. *Nothing can move me*, the House seemed to say. *I'll swallow you whole.*

Some houses are destined to sour. Frank's parents had bought the Little House toward the end of their lives, when the real estate market was good and their salaries, as a schoolteacher and an airline pilot, held actual spending power. There'd been a bloody fight over the inheritance—Frank, single and childless, had been named in the will, while his older sister contested that she and her flock of children could better use the space. Frank had gone to Gisele for a tarot reading over this legal battle. With a little help from her magic, the verdict later came down in his favor.

On that first day they saw the house, when Frank noticed Gisele's face, he crossed the space between them and kneaded her shoulder. "Hey, hey. It's a beginning, all right? We'll make it our own."

Gisele nodded, but she toed the dingy blue carpet with the tip of her shoe. Vulnerability didn't become Gisele—she wasn't a small woman, in stature or nature. She didn't like disappointment and she didn't tolerate emotionality—retribution came quickly and decisively to the source of both. The tension in her mother's body sent a spike of anxiety through Alice's spine. She tugged at Gisele's sleeve, but Gisele flung her off, the movement attracting Frank's attention.

"Do you want to pick out your bedroom, Beau?" Frank's hand encompassed her shoulder, warm and comforting. Alice shook her head. "I set up a playset for you guys with a slide and some swings. Do you want to check it out?" Alice shook her head again. Frank knelt to Alice's eye level and peered at her until she giggled nervously. "It's a big change, huh?"

Gisele squeezed Alice's wrist until the bones ground together. "But you're thankful for everything Frank is doing for us, right, Isabeau?"

Alice flinched but managed to bite back a whimper. "Thank you for sharing your house with us, Frank."

As Frank glanced between them, his smile dimmed. "Hey," he said at last. "Why don't we grab your sister, and I'll show the two of you the creek out back? You can play out there while your mom and I bring the boxes in. Would you like that?"

Gisele gave the slightest nod, so Alice nodded, too, a puppet, a shadow of her mother's wanting.

Frank guided the girls to the mouth of a half-disappeared trail thick with long grass that tickled their ankles, walking until they emerged from the woods into a clearing rounded by tall oaks and maples. The creek lay cradled between the gentle slope of leafy banks, the water murky and tempting with salamanders. Frank adjusted the fit of his baseball cap. He was often uncertain around Alice and Bronwyn—fussed about letting them eat too much sugar, still held their hands when crossing streets, as if such things mattered in the scope of how they'd been brought up. The attempted interventions made Alice and Bronwyn exceedingly fond of him. "We have a couple of rules about the creek, so everyone can play safely, okay?" He rattled off the obvious ones: Don't come here alone; don't go into the water without an adult, you could slip on the rocks; don't dirty your nice, clean clothes; and most importantly, don't wander off the path. "You could get lost," he added solemnly.

Alice burst into giggles, and Bronwyn jutted out her hip, arching one eyebrow in perfect mimic of their mother. "How do you expect us to get lost?"

"You don't know the landmarks out here yet, and people sometimes lose their way in the woods." Frank trailed off, rubbing his neck as he glanced between them.

"Then give me your hat." Bronwyn wiggled her fingers and Alice covered her smile behind the scoop collar of her shirt.

"What do you need my hat for?" He raised a protective hand to the brim.

"Uh, so I can find the way back? My gift only works if I'm holding something you own."

Frank swallowed thickly. "Oh," he said. "Slipped my mind, I guess." But he didn't take the hat off. "Guess I'll leave you to it, then."

As Bronwyn bounded toward the creek, Alice smiled at Frank. "You'll get used to it."

It seemed a certainty then, but it's a wonder to Alice now that he ever did. He accepted them and their oddness so readily, surprising Gisele with bundles of dried herbs in place of flowers, slipping citrine worry stones into her and Bronwyn's backpacks on the morning of their SATs. She wonders if Eli could cope half as well.

On that first day at the Little House, everything was new and old and strange. In the woods, the girls decapitated wildflowers with sticks, made note of which trees would make for good climbing, and then returned to the playset to watch the progression of boxes. They sat knee to knee in the captain's nest of the slide, spinning the maple copters littered across the wood.

"Do you think Frank is a good man?" Alice asked.

"Mhmm." Bronwyn squinted at a spider spinning a cocoon around a struggling bee above them. "He bought us a playset. He's letting us live in his house. *Of course*, he's a good man, Dumb-Beau."

"I mean," Alice hesitated. "I mean, do you think he's a good dad?"

The maple copter slipped out of Bronwyn's grip. "Why?" she asked, her voice sharp. "Do you want him to be our dad?"

"I know he's not *our* dad. I'm not an idiot."

"Who cares about our dad?" Bronwyn nodded toward the house, where Frank was carrying a box to the open garage door. "What do we even remember about him anyway?"

Gisele treated questions about their father in much the same vein as she treated questions about her childhood—yelling, slammed doors, chasing them with an open palm. Bronwyn insisted that he'd smelled like mint ice cream. Alice recalled, faint as a dream, a blond man humming "Scarborough Fair" as she'd toddled around the playpen in the back of the camper. But they possessed nothing else from their father, not even something as small as a name.

"Yes." Bronwyn's voice barely carried over the hum of cicadas and the late summer breeze. "I want him to be our dad. We'll be happy here. Don't you think?"

Gisele stood behind the glass porch door with her hand covering her mouth. Alice couldn't figure out if she was about to laugh or cry. "He's soft," Alice said.

"But that's good, Beau. He's nice."

Alice shook her head. "Not with Gisele. He won't keep her in line."

"What's that supposed to mean?"

"It means," Alice said slowly, "he won't make a good dad." These were hold-their-breath days, fragile days, days where the wrong word or a strong breeze could set the future off course. If Alice held herself still as an insect trapped in amber, then maybe the cards would keep their promise.

In October, only a handful of months after they'd moved in and long before they unpacked the final few boxes of winter clothes, Gisele announced that they were expecting a new baby. A girl, Gisele said, according to the ultrasound image, so they would be keeping it.

As the baby grew, Gisele became something unfamiliar, as if some tender stranger had slid into her skin. There were no more gruesome lessons masqueraded as bedtime stories, no more screaming or pots thrown. She softened, playing tea party with Alice and braiding Bronwyn's hair, giggling and slow dancing with Frank in the living room. She filled her afternoons with neighborhood walks, decorated the nursery in a riot of pink, folded onesies and footie pajamas, and painted saltwater blessing sigils on the doorways. Occasionally, she would grab Alice's or Bronwyn's hands, press them to the tight drum of her belly, whisper, "Feel. Baby Leda is kicking."

It occurs to Alice now that Gisele had thought she'd won. That she'd manipulated the cards into a singular thread of perfect joy, and the promise of that happy life had reshaped her.

Of course, it didn't last. Miracles so rarely do. They most often are a flash in the pan, a glint of gold turned into the disappointment of pyrite. A leaf in the fall, hung suspended in the breeze before the wind whips it away.

The night Killian was born, their mother howled so long and so loud from her hospital room that Alice thought the baby was dead. She was inconsolable for days, wouldn't touch him, screamed again and again, "A boy. A boy." She wept through the night, tore her hair out in clumps, dug scratches into her face while Frank grappled her hands away.

THREE

ALICE SPENDS THE BETTER PART of an hour circling her neighborhood. Each time she nears her house, the panic rises again, fast and tight and knotted in her throat, so she keeps driving. These actions don't fit Alice's definition of a sane, logical woman, but telling herself that isn't the same as fixing the problem. Alice drives until the pear blossom trees lining the street become pointing fingers, until she pictures the red ribbon of Killian's grave marker tied to the bare tips of every branch, until her gas gauge droops toward empty, until fear corrodes her will to run.

Alice parks down the street from Eli's house under a copse of evergreens, thick-branched and sap-sticky with needles that scrape the roof of her car. Bronwyn has watched her from here. Alice knows it. She can see every other part of the street from her bedroom window. How many times has Alice scolded herself for her unreasonable paranoia about this exact spot, her heart-pounding terror that someone might be parked and waiting?

She used to think of Eli's house as safe, in the physical sense. A sturdy home, its foundation dug deep. Three weeks ago, Eli had suggested they install an alarm system and Alice laughed him off. How flimsy her arguments seemed now—it's an unneeded expense, Eli; it's only the illusion of protection, Eli; and besides, Eli, we live in a gated community, do you know how safe that is, do you know how ridiculous it is to think someone would skirt that fence on foot?—as if agreeing to an alarm would admit some weakness equivalent to a moral failing. As if to guard against something would be as good as inviting it in. But she'd been right to be paranoid, hadn't she? And now, because of her stubbornness, they'll catch her, they'll trap her, they'll chain her up again.

She has to breathe. *Alice, breathe*, she thinks. *Alice, you must breathe. Control yourself.* She can't afford to spiral. Not with Eli's mother on her way, not with her plane landing any minute. Alice needs to ready herself, ready the dinner she promised—except she didn't buy groceries. She abandoned her cart in the canned goods aisle, and now there's nothing to make, and Susan can't see her like this tonight, all blotchy with panic and horror.

Alice feels like she's choking. She unlatches her seat belt and shoves the seat back so she can put her head between her knees. She presses the crown of her head against the steering wheel. *Listen, Alice*, she orders herself. Outside the wind hushes against the car window and blows up crystals of powdery snow. She pushes her chin into the collar of her turtleneck and, beneath it, the plate of bone over her heart. Blood gathers in her forehead and she can count each heartbeat pulsing in her temples.

"I am sitting in my car," she whispers. "It's cold. My joints feel stiff. I can hear the wind outside. I feel the seat under my legs. I am present. I am here. I am safe." When her panic ebbs,

Alice's skin is cold and sweat slick. She restarts the engine and cranks the heat.

Inside the house, through the window, Eli is setting the dining room table. From this distance, he is little more than a silhouette. The chandelier flutes the light across his broad shoulders, haloes his hair. She imagines his satisfaction as he distributes each plate, adjusts the angle of a fork tilted off-center.

She's told him she had abusive parents, that she cut them out years ago, that she didn't want to talk about it. Of course, she hasn't been able to hide everything: She doesn't like small spaces, insists the bedroom door be left a crack open, can't abide certain air fresheners that remind her of incense, the keloid scars patterned on her thighs and hips from a box cutter blade. Her nightmares are lurid and graphic, if rare, and Alice wakes from them struggling to scream. He's a smart man—she's sure he has put one or two things together—and he means well, the way he asks every so often, as if speaking to some easily startled fawn, some cautious animal thing, would Alice ever tell him about her family? Each time, Alice answers, "It's nothing worth reliving," and he lets her change the subject. She warms with gratitude.

She thinks of what it would mean to tell him now. To say, *Eli, once I had a brother, and because I come from a line of witches—because my family is cursed—he died.* She imagines the knots forming on Eli's forehead, imagines him squeezing her hands and kissing the wrist of each saying, *Witches, Alice? Witches aren't real.* She imagines telling him about the pregnancy, what the curse means for a son born of her womb. She thinks of Gisele after Killian's birth, that wounded husk of her in the hospital bed, and Alice wonders if she would be the same, if she can bear the knowledge that her blood would sentence a son to an early death. If she, too, would weep and scream and tear, and slash scratches into her skin while Eli, like Frank, stood over her watching. How can she tell him about this? Not the magic and ghosts and blood oaths of it, not the gifts and the boys of it—essentially, none of it at all.

Alice lifts her cell phone, dials, and watches Eli answer. "Don't worry," he says, "text received. Bougie plates locked, loaded, and ready to serve. Long line at the store?"

"I can't do this tonight, Eli."

"Were they out of sirloin?" There's a lick of laughter in his voice. He thinks she's joking. Of course he does, because when has Alice ever failed him this spectacularly? The ridge of the phone digs into her fingers.

"Maybe the two of you should go out for dinner—she'd probably like that better anyway." Alice clutches the door handle when she thinks of being alone in that house where Bronwyn can find her. Still, it would be worse to endanger Eli—Alice knows all too well what violence Gisele is capable of and Bronwyn might have brought her mother straight to her door. *Breathe, Alice.* She must keep her tone casual if this has even the smallest chance of working.

"I can't tell if you're being serious." She hears a thud as Eli tosses down the long-necked lighter he's been using to light candles and disappears from view. She pictures him walking to the living room to speak with her, as if the dishes might overhear and worry. "Did something happen? Are you okay?"

"No." Alice kneads her left hand with her right, pushes the thumb hard into her left palm. "Definitely not."

"O-kay. What happened?" He won't let her out of this gracefully. Alice can hear it in his voice. Some men—many men—are fixers. They find a structurally unsound woman and want to build a scaffold around her, align her spine, open her up, play

Operation on her organs. Men like that do not love a woman—they love a problem, they love themselves for solving it. It would be so easy to manage that kind of man. Tell him, *There's been a trauma* and let him do all the saving. Alice has had too much practice submitting to men with tender scalpels. But not Eli. Eli has never been interested in fitting the knobs of her bones back together. Eli only asks her for honesty, which requires all the more finesse when she can't give it.

She mumbles, "Why can't you just take her out for dinner?"

Eli's voice slows into an over-enunciated calm. "Because she'll make us miserable all week if we don't make the goddamn cranberry beef, and honestly, I can't change dinner plans again." Eli never yells when she's hurt him—he rarely needs to. He makes a certain expression—the locked set of his jaw where he tightens on his back-most molars, the downward curl of his mouth, his civility fastened in place like the carefully clipped receipts in her car cup holder. "Maybe if you'd called me sooner, maybe if you hadn't already told her, 'Yes, Susan, I'll make beef and cranberry sauce,' of all things, but her plane lands in ten minutes, Alice. Where have you been for the last hour?"

There's no excuse that will make him understand, but when she thinks of what it would demand from her, to sit in front of his mother, with this thing in her womb and Bronwyn lurking nearby, Alice shudders. "Please don't make me do this."

Eli briefly reappears in the window. He's pacing, which he usually does when solving a difficult design problem. "Okay, new plan. I'll grab the groceries on the way back from the airport."

"Eli, you aren't hearing me."

"We'll tell her we lost track of time, and that dinner will be late."

"Eli, please. Stop."

"You can start on the potatoes while I pick her up," he says. "The sauce takes, what? Half an hour?"

"I'm not doing this tonight." Alice hits the steering wheel, hard enough to send shock waves through her elbow.

"No, you always do this. You always go off half-cocked and then regret it. It isn't fair to throw me into the cross fire. We're supposed to be a team." Eli's voice hitches on the last sentence. He isn't wrong—but she needs to insulate him from this more than he needs her as backup.

"I threw up in the grocery store. I barely made it to the bathroom before I puked." The lie sheens on her lips, slick as oil.

"You threw up in the grocery store." His voice flattens and he stops pacing. If she gave it any thought before she called, she might have opened with that.

"Yeah. I should probably go to Quick Care."

"You were fine when you left."

"Well, I'm not now." She's only making this worse for herself. He doesn't believe her, but she can't think of any other way to mitigate the damage. "Take her out for dinner tonight. Please. She won't even miss me. Tell her how sorry I am." Not as sorry as Susan will make her, though. Susan will add it to the long list of things wrong with Alice. She'll write *weak immune system* right under the line item *splurges on name-brand groceries.*

Eli stands in the window, bracing his forehead against the glass, the phone tight to his ear. "I know when you're lying to me," he says, voice soft with hurt. "And I do not appreciate it."

"Eli—"

"You're a terrible liar." He pushes himself off the window and retreats to the hallway, back out of view. "I need to leave for the airport. We can talk about this later. Please, just come home and deal with the potatoes." The line dies in her hands.

Alice throws her phone into the passenger side of the car, where it bounces to the floor. Crying isn't an option nor is sitting here idling. She should go somewhere else until Eli leaves, but the idea of sitting in a coffee shop or navigating a crowd of people, struggling to keep herself calm and controlled, feels like more than she can handle. She'll stay in the car, then.

The wait isn't long. The garage door rumbles open, and then Eli disappears down the road. She counts to twenty, then pulls into the driveway.

Inside, Alice navigates Eli's house by the light of her phone. It feels safer. In the daylight, Eli's house expands like a villa. He designed the cathedral ceilings, the walnut wood floors, the slab of black pearl granite that became the kitchen island. But by the gloomy light of her phone, the rooms become hollow and bare and the shadows form strange shapes in the corners as if to betray her to her fear. The light catches on the mirrors, and each time her heart flutters in dread. Each slow step to the kitchen feels like a miracle.

Alice ignores the pasta pot and the box of instant potatoes on the counter. Instead, she sets the phone down, flashlight up, and brews a pot of mugwort tea. She does it properly, with real mugwort she ordered online. She steeps it for three minutes and then cleans the infuser while it cools.

The first sip is always unpleasant, too musty, but it isn't like she drinks mugwort for the flavor. The second sip warms her down to her toes. Expectant mothers should not drink mugwort, as high doses can cause miscarriage, but Alice reasons that being pregnant is not the same as expecting to be a mother. If it pries the problem from her body before she must confront it, she'd welcome the intervention. Alice has already tried her hand at a kind of mothering and failed. She has no desire to try again. Regardless, right now, she doesn't have an alternative to safely put her in a trance, and she's no longer practiced enough to calm her panic without one. Gisele used to feed them mugwort before a big magical working. The irony of this is not lost on her.

Mug in hand, she retreats to the living room and angles the armchair toward the big bay window, pulls the knit blanket down around her knees. As she waits for the mugwort to take effect, the sky cracks into storm. The rain forms and reforms the shadows under the streetlight. Alice closes her eyes, and when she opens them, a car is driving out of view. Not Bronwyn. Not yet.

This house. This life. As a child, she'd known homes like this existed, with trim gardens and streets framed with pear trees and evergreens, neighborhoods with eager flower beds and brick walkways, and porch swings and heated garages, but she'd never dared dream of living in one. As a child, she'd thought the Little House, with its ramshackle crookedness, was the best she'd deserved.

Most of the time, Eli's living room décor bothers her—the coasters unaligned on the coffee table, the rumple of blankets over the back of the couch in imperfect folds, the bookcase wood darker than the end table. Adult Alice tends to images of houses she'd like to live in just as she'd torn pictures of women she wanted to look like out of magazines as a teenager. But with the light coming through the window—look how fine the carpet is, how deliciously spacious and delicate the living room. It is the kind of space that Isabeau couldn't even have imagined.

Alice rarely even thinks about Isabeau anymore, except on certain nights in the summer when it storms and the house shakes with both wind and thunder, and the air smells like lightning. That smell seeps into her nightmares, makes her shiver and search for ghosts. In every movie Alice has ever watched about spirits, they've looked strange—translucent or morphed in some inhuman way, but that wasn't how they'd appeared to her. Hers were not the all-knowing specters of Greek tragedy; they hadn't come bearing special knowledge or divine revelations. Her ghosts were exactly like the living and she could only tell them apart by a certain smell, that heat and smoke sweetness of ozone.

Why is Bronwyn here? Isn't Alice useless to the Family now? She cut her shadow out over a decade ago and her ability to see ghosts is long gone. She bled herself free, paid the price, has the bind runes on her heels to prove it. Tonight, though, she wishes she still had the witching to make herself completely safe. A protection spell to repel Bronwyn from her house, something to banish Gisele to the far ends of the earth so nothing can ever touch Alice again. In her living room, she tries to call her magic, to beckon the crackle of pins and needles in her fingertips, the copper burn at the back of her throat, the tingling at the seat of her spine. Nothing happens. Alice traces her bind runes, scouts her veins for her magic's absence, tonguing its hollow like a missing tooth. She reminds herself she chose this—that it is better to miss the limb than to suffer the trap.

FOUR

Age Eight

PERHAPS ANOTHER SET of sisters would've hated Killian for his fussiness and endless diapers and rash-raw skin. But from the moment Frank placed Killian in Bronwyn's arms and Alice warmed his squirming foot in her hand, he'd belonged to them. They'd exchanged a look over his tiny body, and a glance at the near catatonic Gisele in the hospital bed, rhythmically kneading a corner of her pillowcase.

Bronwyn had quirked an eyebrow, as if to say, he's a boy. Do we love him anyway?

And Alice had nodded once. A promise. Yes. They would love him so much that he'd never feel Gisele's lack.

Those months following Killian's birth held marvels.

The marvel, for instance, of Frank's mothering—as if he'd only been waiting for the opportunity to present itself. He burnt pancakes for breakfast, packed ham and mustard sandwiches for lunch, taught them to love gherkin pickles. He saved quarters for the gumball machine at the grocery store and bought the expensive brand of cartoon Band-Aids for their skinned knees. He brought home crayons and coloring books and Barbie dolls and signed them up for swimming lessons, for tutoring. Every evening after dinner, he guided Alice through her math homework and bribed Bronwyn with chocolate bars to memorize her vocabulary lists. On weekends, he strapped Killian to his chest as he taught them how to fish, how to identify milkweed, how to raise caterpillars into butterflies, how to pick a ripe melon at the grocery store the way his father had shown him. It was Frank who explained to them in a hushed whisper, Killian asleep on his chest, that sometimes a sonogram could be wrong about gender. "Especially with boys." Frank swallowed hard and his skin purpled. "Their—thingie. It can hide from the picture."

Another marvel was the relief of their mother's absence. Gisele slept most of the day—or pretended to. Each evening, Alice carried steaming cups of tea and bowls of canned soup to Gisele's bed. The untouched sustenance cooled on the nightstand until Gisele's cheekbones strained against her skin. Alice heard her stalking the halls at night, a soft cough or hard laugh from the other side of the door. A few weeks after Killian's birth, she started smoking again, and though Frank wasn't pleased, he still bought her a pack of menthols every day on his way home from work. Mostly, Gisele ignored his directive to smoke outside, preferring instead to smoke in the bedroom and leave her butts in coffee mugs or soda bottles filled partway with water. When she did leave her room during the day, she wandered around the house touching windowpanes, unresponsive and uncomprehending, caught in a grief that left room for no one else, not even her newborn. Alice and Bronwyn learned how to change diapers, mix and heat formula in the microwave, and burp a baby, scolding each other about the proper way to support his head. On the rare occasions they caught Gisele with Killian, Alice and Bronwyn hovered nearby, ready to leap at the first sign of harm.

That protectiveness never dissipated. Frank worked and Gisele withdrew, so Alice and Bronwyn filled the space. Their love for Killian was no bird-boned thing; it was dog loyal, so tender it chafed. When they returned from school, they waited anxiously for Frank to bring him home from day care so they could look him over. They needled blood from their thumbs for protection spells, put the shields of their bodies between him and their mother. Alice rubbed healing salves on his cuts, kissed away his bruises, packed his lunches, checked his homework. Bronwyn taught him to throw a punch, to catch salamanders in the creek, to bike as he shrieked and giggled their names. They fussed about his poor grades in math and attended every choir concert. Frank often cracked jokes that Alice and Bronwyn hogged the baby, even from him. They loved Killian without hesitation, in a complete and unequivocal way, which, given their differences, they could never love each other.

That love made it all so much harder in the end.

Gisele and Frank often argued late into the night, and Alice would creep along the wall to listen, peering through the slivered opening of the cracked door. Gisele stalked the room as

Frank sagged on the bed, fiddling his thumbs. "We can never tell him." Gisele pulled at her hair as she paced, coming away with metallic red strands. "That's the burden we bear for a son. He can't know that he can die on any corner, at any time. I saw how that played out with my brothers. It made them reckless, impulsive until they snapped their own lives in half."

"But if he doesn't know, he can't be careful." Frank spread his hands in front of him as if he were gentling an animal. "It's better if he knows young so he can take care of himself. It's like any other kind of illness."

"Because you have so much experience in curses?" Gisele whirled to face him, her face contorting with a snarl. "Because you read two magazine articles on chronic illness?"

"You're wearing yourself raw, El." Frank twisted his wedding band, the gold glinting in the lamplight. He'd been touching it more and more in the past few weeks. Reminding himself it was still there, Alice reckoned. "You're really telling me after all those impossible things I've watched you do that this is where you give up? Killian is the end of the line? Don't you love him?"

"It isn't *sane* to love him," Gisele snarled. "If I'd known he was a boy, I would never have given birth. I can't help him. My Sight can't change a curse—at best it will only delay the inevitable. He never lives past nineteen. Not in a single thread of any possible future."

"We can find a way—"

"To do what? Wither and die when the curse kills him? My mother had four boys. She thought she could fight it. Imagine that." Gisele threw her head back and laughed. "Every time, she thought she could save the next boy. Four deaths, Frances. I could See their deaths, and I tried to tell her, and she—what she did to me—" Gisele trembled. Frank rose, arms open but Gisele shoved him away. "Don't you dare ask me to become that woman."

"I'm not." Frank tugged her close, stroking her hair. "But I'm not giving up either. We'll find a way to save him. I believe that."

Gisele rested her forehead in the crook of his neck, shoulders shaking. "I'm begging you. I don't want hope, Frank. I can survive anything but that."

Alice must give credit where credit is due: Hope is a terrible and intoxicating medicine. She should have learned this lesson better.

In his first eight months of life, Killian developed cradle cap, then ear infections, then blocked tear ducts, then a kidney infection, then thrush, and then, as they finally began celebrating a month-long run of good health, he started teething. By the summer after his birth, everyone was unraveling.

Bronwyn and Alice had read, in their school library's edition of the *Children's Illustrated Encyclopedia*, that babies needed exposure to the outdoors, so every afternoon, for an hour before his lunchtime feeding, they bundled Killian into his carrier and toted him along with a blanket and a mound of pillows to the clearing near the creek. Bronwyn spread out on a stack of pillows, ankles crossed, fanning herself. "We need to do something," she was saying. "He needs Gisele."

"Why?" Alice huffed. "He has us."

Bronwyn fixed her with a look. "Because we are not his parents, Dumb-Beau."

"He's *our* baby, though." A honeybee bobbed lazily past Bronwyn's head, and Alice tracked its journey, almost reaching out toward it. She plucked a cattail from the grass instead, tearing its stem to shreds.

"Stop doing that," Bronwyn said.

"We don't need her help," Alice huffed. She peeled a chunk of cattail from its stalk, letting the seeds blow to dust in her hands.

"Beau, I'm serious."

"So am I."

Bronwyn hopped to her feet and trudged over, jerking the cattail out of Alice's grasp. "You're getting fluff all over the baby."

On cue, Killian stirred, sneezed, and started to fuss. Alice dropped to his carrier, gently rocking it with one hand, and soothing his cheek with the other. "Oh, Killy. I'm sorry," she murmured, dropping a kiss to his forehead. "I didn't mean to wake you." Killian's small hand patted her cheek, and she turned her head to catch it in her mouth, which always made him giggle. "We don't need her, do we? Tell your sissy."

Killian burbled.

Bronwyn studied them, putting her hands in her pocket. "Come on," she said quietly. "He needs to eat."

Almost every day, when it hit midafternoon, they rushed to the front steps of the Little House, impatiently monitoring the road for the curve of Frank's dusty truck. The moment he turned into the driveway, Alice and Bronwyn tumbled down the hill and ran across the dandelion-burst asphalt, until the Carriage House Ice Cream Shop materialized between the trees. The minty-gray clapboard building crested the top of a hill that lolled into a small clearing, bordered by a scattering of buckeyes. The gully beyond them smelled faintly of lilacs, and this was where, obscured from adult supervision, the nine- and ten-year-olds of the town played and bet their allowance money on games of tag and hide-and-seek.

Bronwyn would disappear down to the gully almost immediately, where she collected bets from the other children, using her tracking gift to cheat at hide-and-seek and con them out of their allowances. Alice, meanwhile, would wait above at the picnic tables, which speckled the top of the hill like squat blue birds' nests. Bronwyn tried to make this division hierarchal ("You're too *little* to play with us, Dumb-Beau, you have to stay with the rest of the littles."), but Alice preferred her own company anyway.

Alice still has an affinity for those amber evenings, the wind tugging at her hair—for sitting alone and imagining herself in a different life, a different family. Normal parents and their ordinary children, who rolled down the hill on their bellies, giggling, or who poked at anthills with sticks. A mother, softer than Gisele could ever be, who'd come to her holding a towering waffle cone of triple chocolate chip and wipe the ice cream melt from her chin. A Frank who'd take them home to a regular house and a regular life, where there were no curses and no gifts and where their brother would grow old.

It happened on one of those ungodly hot evenings toward the end of August, Alice's skin sweat-stuck to her metal chair. She was scanning the tree line for Bronwyn, bubbling with irritation.

Most nights Alice was indifferent to the ice cream itself, but she'd been craving orange sherbet all afternoon and her sister should have been back with the hide-and-seek winnings twenty minutes ago. Frank let them walk to the Carriage House but didn't like them to walk back alone so close to dusk. He would be there with Killian at any minute to pick them up, and while he always sent them out with money, it was only ever enough for the kiddy cones.

In her boredom Alice kicked up sand with one foot and watched it settle in a fine dust against the sweat of her legs. She didn't even notice the woman until she'd plopped down at the table. "What a pretty girl," she said. "My sister had red hair like that, but she wore it in braids."

In retrospect, it was almost infuriatingly obvious that the woman was a ghost. Her long-sleeved blouse was too warm for the afternoon, though Kirtland had experienced an odd blip of cold the day before. The woman also reeked of a chemical sweetness Alice didn't yet know to call ozone, didn't yet associate with the dead. "I'm not supposed to talk to strangers." Alice pulled her knees up to her chest, as if by making herself smaller she could make the woman leave, could will Bronwyn back. A shout came from near the tree line, and a flash of auburn hair darted between the trunks. Her hope rose, quick and tight, and then plummeted to panic when the shade was too dark to be Bronwyn's. "My sister's in the gully. She'll be right back."

The woman's mouth slipped open, as though in shock, closely followed by such a radiant, desperate joy that it made Alice nervous. "That's absolutely right, you smart girl. Strangers can be dangerous." The woman nodded, as if she herself were not one. Unsettled, Alice kicked again at the sand. "I have some good memories out here," the woman continued. "My grandchildren came here a lot—you know how children love ice cream. I wish I could hold them again."

"What happened to them?"

The woman looked surprised. "Why, nothing happened to them. They're likely snuggled up all tight watching TV. They moved to Columbus last month. I haven't been able to get away from the Carriage House since it happened." The woman sighed. "I did everything right. Didn't smoke. Didn't drink. Exercised. My mom lived into her nineties. I was only sixty-seven."

A strange darkness passed over the woman—a spiderweb rippling with the struggles of a caught fly. Dark veins, the muddy color of decay, rippled across her face. Alice decided that escape was worth risking Bronwyn's wrath. "I should go find my sister."

"Wait!" the woman shouted. Alice froze and the woman hesitated, suddenly sheepish. "It's only—you're the first person who's been able to see me all day." The woman leaned toward her, and despite the heat, Alice shivered.

Something is wrong with her, Alice remembers thinking, *there's something I'm missing here*. The smell made her queasy.

"It's only been a day." There was a desperation in the woman's voice, an aching loneliness. She patted the table. Her nails were caked in dirt. "Maybe it isn't too late. If you can see me—it means you're special. I've watched all kinds of TV shows about people like you. Maybe you can help." Her voice lowered to a soft whine. "My bones itch."

Alice's apprehension grew. The woman wasn't making sense. "Help with what?" she asked.

"Come. Let me show you. It's easier than explaining."

The urge to play with danger is a hunger born from the marrow. At the time, Alice couldn't say why exactly she went—why she followed the woman and slid halfway down the hill, skinning her knee. Why she pushed back brambles and branches and climbed into the gully. Alice spent the whole week after sick with shame. But then she would remember how her skin had burned and her heart had pounded in that moment, and underneath, something solid and cylindrical had whispered, *Help her.* Something had changed that day—Alice had sensed it, even then—different in a way she did not yet know how to understand.

"This way." The woman gestured. "I'm over here."

From between the long grass, a body. The gold green of her blouse. A crown of sunset gilding the dark hair that curtained her face. The movies Alice will watch later will show the dead peaceful, the body as if sleeping. Nothing like this: The woman curled into herself, nails craggy with her last earthen struggle. "Watch." The woman knelt beside herself and ghosted a palm over her own shoulder. "I can't slip back in. It *hurts*."

The air left Alice's lungs, and only this kept her from screaming. A retch whimpered up from inside her and she vomited down her shirt.

"Please don't do that." The woman stood and patted the air placatingly. Alice stumbled back. "If you scream, they'll find me and bury me, and then my body will be gone. But if you help me get back in, it'll be okay. I'll be alive again. I'm sure it'll work."

Several things happened all at once. Alice caught a lungful of air and tried to scream. As she did so, the woman lunged to cover Alice's mouth, but her hand passed right through. Cold burned Alice's gums. Like biting ice. Then the woman flickered. Disappeared. Alice's vision went static, then black. She crumpled. A marionette snipped from its strings.

Her temples pulsed, shatteringly loud—her heartbeat, she'd realize later. From somewhere up the hill, she heard Frank call her name. Her lungs burned, but she couldn't draw breath. She tried to claw at her throat. Her arms ignored her. This is how it would always be, with possessions. When splitting bodies. Alice would be suspended in stasis, unable to see, unable to hear, unable to move of her own volition, lost in time until the ghost slipped back out of her.

Then, the pressure lifted. The woman blinked into focus again. "I didn't mean to." The woman sank to the ground, clutching her own throat. "I'm so sorry."

Alice coughed out Frank's name, a rasping whisper.

"Please, don't scream. I didn't mean to! I didn't even know I could do that." The woman reached toward her again then flinched as Alice scrabbled away. As she did so, the woman's skin threaded with plum gray fissures, knotting over her veins, through her eyes. "I didn't want to die. I'm so sorry. Please."

Bronwyn appeared from between the trees, Frank a few steps behind her. Bronwyn pulled Alice close, vomit and all, as Frank stumbled back against a tree trunk, clutching Killian tight to his chest. Later, there'd be the flash of red and blue lights, and the silvery blanket that smelled of rubbing alcohol that the EMT wrapped around her. Her ice-chapped lips cracked and bloody as she told the officers again and again that the woman had shown her where her body was. "Poor bug," the EMT whispered when he didn't think Alice could hear. "Too much for her to handle."

They drove home wrapped in a silence thick as gauze. As Alice and Bronwyn kicked off their shoes, Frank leaned against the front door, shifting from foot to foot. Killian drowsed against his chest. Frank's hesitance reminded Alice of that first day he'd come to the camper and upended their lives. As if suddenly, they'd stopped being the children he'd spent the last year calling his own.

Alice made it halfway to the living room before Frank touched her shoulder. "You're sure it was her?" He swallowed. "The woman. She showed you her own body?"

Alice nodded. Her tulip-print socks were coming undone at the seams, and her big toe poked out of the right foot. She flexed the muscles and returned her toes to the ground one at a time. Pain pulsed at the base of her skull, an unfamiliar throbbing ache from how hard she'd cried.

"We need to tell your mom." Frank glanced down as Killian babbled. He cradled Killian closer, palming the back of his head. No one had taught Frank how to guard his face. He stood too stiffly, anxious and afraid. It was in the way he chewed on his tongue. The too-slow nod of his head.

Alice wrapped her arms around herself, shook her head. "I don't want to."

He pulled her into a sudden fierce hug, and she could smell smoke and sweat on his clothes, and the velveteen softness of Killian's skin. "It'll be okay," he whispered into her hair. "I'll fix it."

He loved you. You know he did. But did he love you as much as his son? He said he did. He pretended to. Would it be more forgivable if he'd left your mother? If he'd said, "I can't stand this anymore," and fled with Killian? Perhaps.

What kind of mother breaks the sparrow bone of a child's wrist? What mother makes a child stand barefoot on the ice-slick backstep in winter if she fails to fully recite the magical correspondence of northern monkshood? What monster hears a child singing and closes her hand around her throat, saying, "If you insist on squawking like a chicken, I'll show you what happens to one." Who watches and says nothing? Who says, "But don't you understand how much your mother loves you?" As if the loving really mattered amongst everything else.

If he could not be brave enough to save you, he could have at least had the decency to be a proper coward. To run, to hide, to be silent. He didn't have to buy you McDonald's after she hit you. Didn't have to drive you into Cleveland to the children's science museum. Didn't have to chaperone your fucking field trips.

Much later that night, Gisele padded into the living room. When the girls looked up from their bowls of mac and cheese, their mother stood in the doorframe, dressed in the same ratty t-shirt and plaid pajama bottoms she'd worn every day since Killian's birth. Alice flinched—she hadn't heard Gisele come downstairs. "Hello, little loves," she crooned. Then she waved Alice forward. "I heard you had a big day, Beau. Come tell me about it."

Alice shrank back into the couch cushions, using Bronwyn's body for cover. Beside her, Bronwyn tensed, ready to stand. Sometimes, Alice wonders if she remembers the intensity of her fear correctly, the way she shivered. Had she, at eight years old, really considered running from Gisele? Or has she painted over this memory with the terror that came after? Alice doesn't know.

"Leave her alone," Bronwyn snarled. "She doesn't want to talk to you."

Gisele crossed the room, her hand raised. Bronwyn flinched, but tilted up her chin in defiance. Then Frank scolded Bronwyn's name from the kitchen. Gisele dropped her hand a moment before he appeared in the doorway. A damp dish towel, printed with cartoon witches, was slung over his shoulder. Frank glanced between Bronwyn and Gisele, mouth stiffening.

"Don't mind her, El," Frank said softly, as if he were asking a favor. "It's been a long day. She doesn't mean it."

"Of course." Gisele's smile tightened as Bronwyn straightened. "But I do need to speak to Isabeau. Alone. Now."

Alice looked to Frank, and though he didn't seem pleased, he nodded her onward. Swallowing, Alice stood and followed her mother upstairs. Gisele guided Alice by the shoulder into her room, kicking the door closed behind them.

It had been weeks since Alice had gotten a proper look at Gisele, even longer since she'd been alone with her mother. Gisele drooped with exhaustion, her skin puffy and lilac with sleeplessness, hair escaping her braid in lank, greasy wisps, the hope hollowed out of her cheeks. When she sat on the bed, she motioned for Alice to sit on the tie rug in front of her. Alice plopped onto the floor, nervously crossing her legs.

"Am I in trouble?" Alice asked.

Gisele studied her through narrowed eyes, then, with visible effort, relaxed her limbs. "Of course not, little love. I just heard you had an adventure today and I wanted to have a chat about it." Her voice was too kind. She was speaking to Alice like she'd talk to one of her clients. The thread of fear in Alice's center tightened. Gisele smiled benevolently. "Will you tell me about the ghost you saw?"

As much as Alice feared her mother, she had always found it impossible to lie to her. Half of it, of course, was dread Gisele would bring out her cards. But she also had a way of making you want to tell the truth—of coaxing it from you, little by little, even the things you didn't want to share, with a well-placed head tilt or gently probing question. As if there was nothing in the world you required so much as her approval. Alice opened her mouth and obeyed.

When she'd finished, Gisele clasped her hands. She threw her head back, the lamplight catching the wildness in her eyes. "And you could see her solid as a regular person? She looked as real as me?" As Alice nodded, Gisele fiddled with the end of her braid. "And then she possessed you?"

Alice kneaded the stitches of the rug. Her mouth tasted chalky and dry. "She disappeared inside me and I couldn't move. I didn't like it."

"I didn't even know Mediums existed. Oh, Beau!" Gisele slid to the floor and knelt across from Alice, knee to knee. "You have no idea how lucky you are. What a blessing of a gift." Gisele cupped Alice's face, her fingers cold as they settled beneath Alice's ears. "Do you know why?"

Alice shook her head and Gisele's grip tightened. She pulled Alice forward and kissed the crown of her head. It was the first time in months Gisele had kissed her, and Alice knew it was dangerous to pull away even with the tension vibrating down her spine. Her mother's smell of stale cigarettes and animal sweat filled Alice's lungs, and Alice suppressed a gag. Gisele tilted her head, pressed their foreheads together.

Don't touch me, Alice thought. *Stop*. She felt like a rabbit in a trap.

"Because you can save Killian," Gisele whispered. "When he dies, you can keep him with us."

Alice went boneless in Gisele's arms. "How?"

"By channeling him. Like you did with the other ghost, the woman. You can share your body with him so he can have a life even after he dies. You could be a host for him. And that way, both of you can live." Gisele pulled Alice into a tight hug, crushing her. Alice could hear Gisele's heart racing. "We will have to work very hard, you and I—you must become the very best witch, my little love. There's so much we'll have to learn, so much research we'll have to do. Can you do that? Can you share your body with your brother?"

In her darkest and most secret heart, Alice cannot deny the way the idea of saving Killian thrilled her. The image of herself as a hero. Brave girl, favorite girl, and Killian kicking out his chubby limbs, the way he hummed and blew bubbles. She loved Killian ferociously. His small fists, waving in the lamplight. But life with Gisele had not given her the luxury of being a naive child. She knew better than to trust the anxiety in Gisele's shoulders. To buy herself time, she stammered, "I don't know."

"So, you want him to die?" Gisele's hand closed around Alice's scalp, nails digging in as she shook Alice by the hair. She wrenched Alice off her shoulder, bending to look her in the eyes. "You don't know? Did you really say that to me?"

"Stop, it hurts." Alice bit her lip. Things would get considerably worse if she cried or whimpered and she tried to hold steady.

"Oh, it hurts?" Gisele clicked her tongue and tugged harder, dragging Alice lower to the ground. "Good. Because it'll hurt a lot more than this when you let Killian die. When we lose him for good and it's your fault."

Then, Gisele wrenched her up and slammed Alice's head against the hardwood floor. Once, twice—until Alice's world narrowed, then dissolved. It wasn't the first time Gisele had hit her, but it was the first time Alice learned to slip outside her body. She looked at her hands and then quite suddenly, they belonged to someone else. The pain hadn't disappeared—her scalp seared—but it couldn't hurt her anymore, because she wasn't real. She didn't exist. She was several inches from her body. She stood by the foot of the bed, staring at the girl panting on the floor. Gisele grabbed that girl by the arm, twisting until the skin reddened in her grip. "How dare you, Isabeau."

"You didn't understand," Alice's body answered. "Of course, I'll save him. I only meant you need to teach me how."

Of the dead body Alice had found, Gisele said nothing. This would not strike Alice as cruel until years after she left the Little House.

Later that night, Killian lay in the crook of Alice's arm, tears beaded in his lashes. Her forefinger traced the softness of his cheek until his sobs hiccupped to a stop. Alice's tenderness swelled, and she moved beyond the fear she'd felt when Gisele had made her proposal, to an acceptance that was not about Gisele at all. In that moment, she agreed to do it for the marvel of his small toes and tinier fingernails. His dark wisps of hair and velvet skin.

"I'll always be here when you need me, Killy," she whispered. "I promise I'll never let you be scared or alone." How many ways did she fail him? Nothing she does will ever atone. As she smiled down at him, he reached up and latched onto her pinkie. With surprising strength, he pulled it into his mouth. It may have been the angle at which he grabbed her or the jagged sharpness of his baby teeth, but when Alice yanked away, her finger was bright with blood.

FIVE

AS ALICE STIRS low-fat sour cream and freeze-dried chives into the instant potatoes—the only way to prevent them from tasting like what they are—her phone vibrates in her pocket. A text from Eli saying only, *Around the corner.* Alice wipes her hands on her apron before hanging it on the hook beside the fridge. For the next three hours, she will not think of Bronwyn. She will not think about the pregnancy test either. She imagines a pair of scissors snipping those worries away.

On her way to the garage, she pauses in front of the hallway mirror. Normally when Susan visits, Alice carefully applies her whole cosmetic arsenal, but tonight the priority was speed over quality. The mirror reflects a woman too pale and a bit frightened, but passably ill. Her ears are already a sore and itching red from the chunky gold earrings Susan gifted her last summer. They are ugly and too heavy, but Susan will notice that Alice chose to wear them. She schools herself into a bright smile and flips on the hall light as Susan opens the garage door. A maroon

Coach purse dangles from the upturned crook of her forearm like the spoils of a hunt.

"There you are, Al." Susan proffers a cheek for an air-kiss. Her skin sticks, damp with moisturizer, and Alice stifles the urge to scrub her face with her sleeve. Susan's perfume, something subtle and floral and expensive, adheres to Alice's skin.

"Sorry I couldn't come to the airport with Eli," Alice says. "My stomach's been a mess today."

"Eli mentioned. Your poor tummy." Susan pulls back to consider Alice from top to bottom, then peers beyond her into the house. Some women can declare war with the flick of an eyebrow. "I'm impressed. You've been here a whole month and haven't redecorated."

"Mom." Eli appears behind her, lugging an oversized geranium-print suitcase in one hand and a paper grocery bag in the other. Perhaps to someone who didn't know him quite so well, Eli would seem positively cheerful, but his jaw keeps twitching.

"Only teasing, sugar cup." Susan swats Alice's arm and Alice presses her palms to her thighs so she won't swat Susan back. "I know you're not one of *those* girls, who moves in and stages a hostile takeover."

Alice judders as a sudden flash of violence rips through her. She did not survive the Family to be sneered at by a woman who still wears leopard print in her sixties—but if she snaps back, if she shows that kind of weakness, Susan will have an opportunity to bloody her. Eli didn't deserve that tonight. "Of course not." Alice forces her smile wider.

"Mom, enough," Eli repeats, but there's no bone in it. One car ride alone with her and he's already ragged. Alice twinges with shame—she should have been there. Eli extends the rain-damp paper bag, concentrating on the wall over her head. If he'd only look at her, she could show him she's on his side, but he doesn't. "Would you mind taking this?" he says to her, with more heat than Alice thinks is strictly necessary. As soon as the bag is in her arms, Eli bounds up the stairs with the suitcase. Susan trails Alice to the kitchen. She hangs her purse from one of the barstools at the island, then leans across the granite on her elbows. Alice flinches—she cleaned that countertop this morning.

Even with her back turned, Alice can tell that Susan is inspecting the kitchen. Judging the vegetables spilling over the cutting board, the pot of rotini on the stove, the Italian dressing. Alice removes the sirloin from the bag and kneels in front of the wine cupboard beside the sink, debating cabernet or merlot for the sauce.

"Pour me a glass of that, would you, sugar cup?" Susan says. Alice has forgotten that Susan sticks her neck out when she talks, her head tilted as if she can catch all the light in the room on her cheekbones; that she speaks with her lip quirked like everything she says is a secret. "There's a stunning vineyard right near me. They do such a lovely full-bodied red, great oak notes. I'll send you a case."

"We'd love that," Alice says, though she and Eli rarely drink and the bottles will just collect dust in the cabinet until Susan's next visit. Alice picks the cabernet and pours a glass before passing it over the island. Susan tilts the wineglass into the light and wipes a smudge with the sleeve of her jacket. Alice returns to the cutting board, chops the sirloin into smaller pieces than the recipe strictly requires. Susan drops her voice to a whisper, and the hair prickles on the back of Alice's neck. "Eli gave me the runaround in the car, and I want a second opinion. Is he looking slimmer to you?"

"No." She'd expected this conversation sooner or later, but she'd banked on later. "He's not counting macros anymore, he's even put on a couple of pounds. There are still hard days, but we're working through it. He's okay, Susan."

"Really?" Susan nods slowly, the type of nod that's less agreement than evaluation. A forgivably maternal fear. Eli's latest relapse was only four months ago.

"I promise. He hasn't had a bad day in a while. He's managing."

"Would you tell me? If he wasn't managing?" Susan lowers her wineglass and tries to pin Alice with a hard stare, which might have been sufficiently intimidating if Alice hadn't grown up on the receiving end of Gisele's glower.

Alice juts out her chin. "Only if he wanted me to."

"He's my son."

"Your adult son who's entitled to his privacy and can make informed decisions about his own health care."

For a moment, Susan stares at Alice like she'd love nothing more than to slap her. *Do it*, Alice thinks. Her skin strains toward the impact. Then Susan clucks her tongue. "Of course. How silly of me." She nods again and tucks a piece of hair behind her ear. "Did Eli tell you I redecorated our summer cabin? I think I have a few photos of the wood stain we did on the deck. Come look."

Eli returns to the kitchen as the oil begins to spit in the pan. Susan is rambling on about a shameless young woman in her yoga class: "Oh Al, can you imagine a flock of birds tattooed on your lower back, and if this atrocity weren't enough, this rude girl never tucks in her shirt. I end up staring at those birds half the class, totally lose focus. It's one thing to make your own poor decisions, but why subject everyone else to them?" If only Susan knew that in college, her son had had a pair of incandescent purple lips tattooed on his ass as a drunken dare. If Susan drones on one more minute, Alice will tell her all about it.

"You were upstairs awhile," she says to Eli as she pours the meat into the oil and lowers the heat. The smells of garlic and lemon pepper fill the room. She regrets that she didn't pour a glass of cabernet for herself, but wine goes to her head too quickly and she needs to keep her wits about her tonight. If Gisele were to—no. Alice will not think of that right now. And of course, she can't anyway, not with the—Alice shakes that thought away too. She imagines a metal crusher under her diaphragm, compressing the flare of panic into a flat disk.

"I saw a car idling in the driveway." Eli hovers beside the island next to his mother, arms crossed.

Alice steadies herself against the counter, her legs suddenly unstable. "Is it still there?"

"No," Eli says, which Alice would find more reassuring if he didn't look so troubled. Beside him, Susan studies her wineglass. "I stayed until it pulled away."

"Did you see who was driving?"

"It was dark, Alice." Eli clears his throat and adjusts his arms.

"What kind of car?"

"A hatchback, maybe? It was hard to see." Eli studies her face, and seems to soften. "Listen, it's not a big deal. It's hard to make out house numbers in the dark—they probably got turned around."

Something inside Alice cracks. Her mask, slipping like plastic film. "Oh," she says.

"Sugar cup." Susan gestures at the pan with her wineglass. "Is the sirloin supposed to be smoking like that?"

Susan and Eli both assure her that the beef and cranberry sauce cooked perfectly, Susan pausing with her fork midair over the plate to mumble a thank-you. Alice drags a fork through her mashed potatoes. They've congealed at the edges, glossy and unappetizing. She'd picked the seat nearest to the window. Every few minutes, she eyes the driveway.

Halfway through dinner, Susan wipes her mouth and places the napkin deliberately on her lap. "There's something I think we better discuss."

Alice, with some dread, lowers her fork. Eli leans forward onto his elbows. "What's up, Mom?"

"Aunt Lindy isn't well enough to host Easter this year—her sciatica's acting up—and no one's stepped up to host." Susan puts up a hand, though neither of them make a move to interrupt her, at least not yet. Beside her, Eli tenses. "I put out a couple feelers, and if we host, everyone would be able to come."

"To Scottsdale?" Most of Eli's family are Michigan natives. Susan only moved to Scottsdale full-time after her divorce.

"No, honey." Susan chuckles as if this is the most ridiculous idea she's ever heard. "In Saginaw. Here, actually."

"Here, as in our house?" Eli blinks and bites his lip. "And why exactly would you volunteer us to cook an entire Easter dinner?" His leg begins to jiggle, the tablecloth shifting with it. Alice places a hand on his knee to still it.

"No, I never volunteered you to cook—all you'd have to do is host. I'll fly down a day early and do most of the cooking. Alice can help if she wants." Susan eyes her, as if Alice cannot be trusted with the precious ambrosia salad recipe. "Everyone will bring dishes. We'd only be in charge of the lamb leg and the deviled eggs."

"That isn't the point, Mom. You can't volunteer us to host a holiday—an entire holiday—without clearing it with us first!"

Alice wrings her napkin in her lap. If she stares straight ahead, into the stylized painting on the wall behind Susan's head, she can curate the illusion of eye contact. She does her best to pretend she's listening and perks up again at the sound of her name. Eli is rubbing the back of his neck, saying, "Alice and I don't want to host. That's all there is to it. You can't sign people up to host holidays. It's invasive."

"And you, Alice?" Susan turns, daring Alice to disagree. "Do you agree with all this fuss?"

"No, I—"

Eli cuts her off. "I already told you we aren't hosting Easter."

"Why don't you let the poor girl talk? You keep insisting that she lives here now and gets a vote." Susan pauses, then cocks her head. "You're so pushy, Eli. God knows where you get it from—it isn't me."

As her gaze wanders, Alice catches movement in the driveway. An almost imperceptible metallic shine in the streetlight. A car? She peers out the window. She might be sick, truly sick this time, and she clutches the drape of the tablecloth so she can ball the frustration around something she cannot injure.

Alice hasn't thought about cutting herself in a long time, but the old hum now buzzes under her skin. She rubs her forearm, trying to soothe the urge by dispersing the bind rune patterns she imagines under her skin. As a teenager, Alice collected sharp things—pocketknives, X-Acto knives, box cutters, slices of broken glass. She cut for the sake of purging until her fifteenth birthday, when Gisele slipped her a handwritten notebook of carefully inscribed bind runes. On the front cover, written in Gisele's spidery cursive: *Runes work best when drawn in blood. Make each one count.*

Some witches cast best with herb satchels; others prefer candles or crystals. From that day on, Alice's medium was blood. She would sit on the shower floor under the hottest setting, and in the blistering water, slash herself open line by careful line. She'd knot jera and ansuz on her forearms to expand her retention of academic texts, dig vegvisir above her knee to navigate difficult magics. Never too deep—only enough to write the spell in, the way her mother showed her. Alice would test her magic after, by calling a witch ball—a dime-sized orb of light—to her fingertips. If the light shone brighter, the rune worked. If it looked the same, she'd have to cut deeper.

After she'd hidden the evidence of her spells—under floorboards, in shoeboxes, in a secret pouch sewn into a stuffed horse's neck—Alice would lie in bed exhausted, her skin tingling, her muscles twitching with new magic. What is the body but a tether? One that held her in place when all she wanted to do was slide out of it? When she only wanted to move out of the way?

Once Frank noticed what she was doing to her arms, scars peeking out from under her long-sleeved sweater, he tried to intervene. "Maybe you should take some time off. This isn't healthy," he said, touching her shoulder. "Tell her you need a break. She'll listen. I'll help you." Frank's help didn't carry much currency. Alice heard them through the wall later that night. "Our daughter is hurting herself. You don't see a problem with that?"

"She's not your daughter, Frances," Gisele said. "She's my daughter. And I will raise my daughter however I see fit."

There had been slammed doors and thrown lamps, and Frank had slept on the couch that night. When he went to work the next morning, Gisele had woken Alice in her bed and held her by the face, digging troughs into her cheeks. "If I'm hard on you, it's because I love you," her mother had said. "To be loved like this, you have to earn it. If it doesn't scar, then you're just wasting skin." Then, she paused in the doorway, one pale white hand on the frame. "And for god's sake, hide it better." After that, Alice only marked covered places. Hips, waist, the meat of her thighs.

"Alice?" Susan says. Alice jolts, returning to the dining room table. Both Eli and Susan are staring at her and a flush crawls its way up Alice's throat. It's clear she hasn't been listening, that this is perhaps not the first time that Susan has said her name. "How do you feel about this whole arrangement?" When Alice blinks, Susan's face tightens with annoyance. "Hosting Easter?" she prompts.

"Susan." Alice clears her throat. "I honestly don't care either way."

"Hm," Susan says. Eli kicks her ankle under the table, but Alice shifts out of reach. "If Alice can be flexible, why can't you?"

"Please excuse me." Alice stands and walks with deliberate slowness to the bathroom.

She turns the water as cold as it can go, pressing her cold palms to her temples. *Calm down*, she instructs herself. *You need to breathe*.

When the interminable dinner finally ends, Susan and Eli carry their plates to the sink, and Susan pours herself another glass of cabernet. Alice insists that Susan make herself at home while Alice finishes meal-prepping for the rest of the week. Susan makes a few half-hearted protests then wanders off toward the living room.

Eli hesitates near the sink, watching his mother until she walks out of earshot. "What was that?" Alice shakes her head and reaches toward the faucet, but he catches her arm, his hand light as a bracelet around her wrist. "What happened to having my back tonight?"

"You were handling it." She pauses, listening. The living room remains quiet. "You didn't want saving, remember?"

"Yeah, well, I wasn't expecting her to sign us up for Easter. Shit, Alice, you're fine either way? I can't host an entire holiday that revolves around food." He shoves his hands into his pockets and rocks back on his heels. "Do I really need to explain why it's unfair to put me in a trigger scenario?"

Alice pats his arm, and through the thin fabric of his dress shirt, she relishes the warmth of his skin. His color is high and bright. "We'll manage a work-around." She places a careful kiss at the base of his neck.

"If Mae and Stevie already bought tickets, it's too late to stop it." Eli picks at a shred of carrot stuck to the counter. "I can't do it, Alice. I can't handle this."

"I couldn't handle tonight either, but here we are. Thousands of people survive hosting Easter every year, Eli. It isn't that big of a deal." Then Alice shuts her mouth, her teeth clicking together. She hadn't meant it to come out so harshly—she'd meant it to be comforting, actually. No success on that front. Eli recoils as if she's struck him. "I only mean that we'll figure something out."

"Right. Okay. We'll figure it out," he says. He exhales hard through his mouth, then stares at her until she meets his eyes.

"What happened at the grocery store?" The sudden pivot startles her, and she blinks at him, taken aback. Eli drops his gaze, his bravery apparently spent.

"Nothing happened." Then she corrects herself. "I threw up."

"Clearly something else happened."

"I got sick." Alice stabilizes herself against the counter. "That's all."

The center of Eli's forehead knots—she can tell he is straining very hard to believe her. He tucks a strand of hair behind her ear, and then runs his thumb from the tip to lobe. Alice eases into his touch—it's such a relief to have the comfort of it after all this misery—but he pulls away. "Your ears turn red when you lie." Eli shakes his head again and brushes past her. Alice tries to catch his arm, but he slips her and darts into the living room.

The kitchen smells of cranberry and meat, and Alice swallows back a sob as she scrapes the plates into the trash can. Everything about today keeps tripping her. She and Eli never fight like this. Never. She used to be such a good liar as a teenager. How dare he know her so well. How dare he use that knowledge against her.

The knock on the porch door is so soft that Alice thinks she imagined it, until she turns and spots Bronwyn behind the glass. Alice drops the fork she's holding. It clatters to the ground, the sauce splattering on the floor. Alice balls her fists.

She wants nothing more than to run, but she can't risk Susan or Eli spotting her sister. Her mind flicks through half-sketched terrors—truths and traumas she'd rather not confront, pity softening Eli's eyes, disgust twisting Susan's mouth, Bronwyn's grating satisfaction at the chaos she's caused. Alice must keep these two parts of her life from colliding, and that makes confronting Bronwyn her only choice. Still, it takes great effort to convince herself to crack open the door. The only thing between them is an inch of open air, an icy lick of wind twining its way inside. Goose bumps prickle along her arms. "You need to leave," she whispers. "I have a guest."

"You think I enjoy showing up like this?" Bronwyn rests her forehead on the doorframe, the rain slicking her hair to her neck. "Are you going to ditch your own house now too?"

Alice squares her shoulders and folds her arms, eyeing the darkness behind Bronwyn. Her sister laughs quietly, a single exhale of air. "For fuck's sake, I came alone, Beau."

"I don't believe you."

"She isn't here." Bronwyn smears a bead of water on the glass door. "Yet. Will you let me in?"

Alice shakes her head, wets her lips. She won't allow Bronwyn near Eli, but her sister won't leave without some sort of concession. "Come back tomorrow morning. He's driving his mom to Detroit. We can talk then."

Bronwyn hesitates, her face unreadable. "You won't run out on me?"

"I swear." Alice shakes her head again, and tugs at the door. "Please. Before they see you."

Bronwyn nods. She turns and disappears through the evergreens in the backyard. Only her footprints in the slush indicate she's been there at all. Alice kneels and smears the footprints, hides the evidence. As she watches the tree line, Alice whispers her old name—once, twice, again. As she tastes the syllables on her lips, Alice tells herself that Isabeau cannot hurt her anymore.

SIX

Age Ten

IT WOULD BE EASY to call Alice's childhood unhappy. Whenever Alice thinks of it, a dull ache settles behind her molars, along with a sharp desire to swallow it down. What Gisele didn't know about ghosts, they had to learn, and Gisele didn't know much. Enter an unrelenting march of books: obscure folklore, spiritualist treatises, parapsychological studies. Alice had memorized Crowley's works on Thelema long before she learned decimals.

After theory came application. In the afternoons after school, she studied herb and crystal properties; her nights belonged to walks in cold graveyards and abandoned buildings and other places ghosts were expected and almost never were. Their spare money was spent on ghost-hunting equipment that hardly ever worked, except for, sometimes, the thermal camera.

With each passing year, the techniques they tried grew more radical, more urgent. They started first with a spirit box, an EMF radar (useless), before progressing to Ouija boards, which the ghosts couldn't touch. They attempted spiritualist invocations, which they would later incorporate into their séances, and once even a spirit trumpet that tasted of dust. This was all before, with desperate urgency, they turned to necromantic rites—attempting to invoke spirits into a cat's head, stripped of flesh by beetles, purchased from a curio store in Chardon, and to offer the ghosts a drink of the sheep's blood they bought from a butcher in Willoughby, which the spirits she encountered politely refused. The worst of it was the exorcisms they attended—in each case, the possessed person in the grips of nothing more paranormal than mental illness, which always left Alice with a solemn, unarticulated horror at the back of her throat.

Alice would lay awake reciting their hard-won knowledge: *To banish a ghost, bury selenite at the four corners of the property. To banish a ghost quicker, burn angelica. To lure a ghost from the far corners of a house, burn dandelion root. Trap them in place with mugwort and wormwood. Create a safe room pouring thick lines of salt along the perimeter of the desired space.*

When Alice was ten, Gisele placed a new ad in the local paper for *Glass Girls Psychic Services*. Ghosts were rare but they were found faster with séances, and Alice needed ghosts to practice on. Even so, Alice only stumbled on maybe five genuine hauntings a year. But the séances, even the ones they had to fake, made them $400 a week, so they conducted an endless parade of them. "At least you have a client list. That's more than my mother gave me." Then, tucking a strand of hair behind Alice's ear, Gisele would murmur, "This is how you let me take care of you, Isabeau."

As Alice aged out of a child's inherent credibility with the clients, Gisele tweaked Alice's training regimen to incorporate acting. This is how you roll back into the whites of your eyes. This is how you throw your voice. This is how you tense your muscles and seize in your seat so the clients believe you're possessed. Stop smiling, you stupid girl. To put on a séance is to put on a show. It is a rule of any market that the customer craves both authenticity and ambience. A séance cannot only be something you do but must be something you do beautifully. Your clients don't want to sit in their sunny living rooms and sip earl gray tea while they chat with the dead. They want to feel something, so make them *feel* something.

As Alice's lessons ramped up, Bronwyn's disappeared entirely and all of Bronwyn's spells became contraband that Alice snuck her, written on gum wrappers and the backs of leaves. Particularly since Bronwyn used magic most often to circumvent Gisele's specific prohibitions. Her punishments came later, when Frank was at work or out at the bars with his friends, like a twisted affection Gisele could only show in private. "You are a waste of a gift," Gisele said as she pressed a cigarette into the soft skin of Bronwyn's inner elbow, after the fourth time she'd been caught brewing love potions for her friends. "I told you that you couldn't go," she said as she striped Bronwyn's back with a belt after Bronwyn used a luck spell to win enough lottery tickets to pay for a theme park field trip. A room over, Alice would clap her hands tight over Killian's mouth so he wouldn't scream. If a part of her whispered, *You can't live like this*, Alice banished it. For Killian, Alice could manage anything.

"We're running out of time, Isabeau," was the refrain of her childhood. And still, Alice failed to hold the ghosts in her body for longer than a minute. "Every day that goes by, Killian is running out of time. You must learn to share your body at will."

When she pulled all-nighters practicing spells until her head swam and her temples throbbed and migraines were triggered by every light in the house, she tiptoed to Killian's doorway and watched him sleep. The way his body curled around his teddy bear, huffing his breath into its neck. Alice would cup his skull and Killian would smile, nestle into her palm. Yes, she loved Killian; that loving hounds her still.

But there *was* happiness, wasn't there? Few moments, far between, like marginalia—but they were there.

The last weekend of September every year, they attended a carnival in the elementary school parking lot, licking crystalized beads of cotton candy from their sticks and taking dizzying turns on the teacup ride. Alice's shoulders heavy with the comforting warmth of Killian's small body, his sticky hands tangling in her hair. Every year, Frank won them a goldfish, all of whom he named Barnum.

Alice won first place at the science fair in sixth grade, testing the heat retention of different thermos brands. Bronwyn took horseback riding lessons every Thursday with Frank's friend at the local stable until her favorite horse startled at a barn cat and sent her flying, ass over head. Killian did youth debate, and Alice did Model UN, and Bronwyn hung out and smoked cigarettes at the skate park. Twice a summer, they piled into Frank's truck and drove forty minutes to the beach, stuffing themselves on grilled hot dogs and collecting pretty pebbles and sea glass, which they painted with clear nail polish to preserve the bright colors.

It could be happy, Alice's childhood.

Alice had liked the séances, once. It's hard to remember, but she had—and perhaps that should be another tally for her fucked-up childhood. The magic singing in her blood when the ghosts spoke to her, the exhilarating slide of ice down her throat, the golden shine of the candlelight on her skin, her control over the living. It was the only time she held any power, the only authority in the room—even Gisele, captive to her mercy. Is she supposed to be ashamed of how the séances kept her safe? That they protected her from the split lips and black eyes that would have prevented her from performing?

When Alice sees ten-year-olds now, she's struck by their smallness, pictures adults sobbing their loss into those child palms. Such small bodies to be holding space for all that grief.

Still the ghosts were never any immediate threat to her, not when the biggest threat in any room was her brother's death, coming ever closer. The danger, not in the ghosts who begged to be let into her body, but in their inability to stay there. Their eyes, hungry. "Let me in." Their prodding cold touch, grasping tightly, but she couldn't hold them inside her for longer than a moment before they popped out, shuddering, their skin corded with fading black threads.

With every failure, she begged, "Please. Take it over. It's yours."

And the pale ghosts saying, "I want to, believe me, but no one can make a home inside you. Do you understand?"

There were other variations on this answer—Alice was slippery, Alice was uninhabitable, Alice's body was only a temporary respite, Alice's body failed. And so Killian would die and slip away from them and it would be her fault.

When there were bad séances, rough hauntings, she'd disassociate from her body and banish those sessions to her hollow place. The naked middle-aged man, skin pruned from the shower tub he slipped in; the teenager, frothing from the allergen she ingested; the old woman in the kitten-print nightgown, the back of her skull caved in like a peach from her tumble down two flights of stairs. They happened to a different child, not to her. Not to Beau, and definitely not to Alice.

They were worth it, for the other séances. For the first time she'd kept a ghost down longer than fifteen seconds, and how his eyes had glazed with relief. "Thank you," he'd whispered afterward. "I feel better now." By the summer she turned seventeen, she could hold them a minute and a half. This was the service she had to offer. This is the way she'd keep Killian safe.

The session that night had been scheduled on short notice. The couple had only lived in the house for a few months and after a series of strange occurrences, their research had unearthed that in the early 1920s, a little boy had died from typhoid in the upstairs bedroom. His mother had been a spiritualist who'd fled the state amidst rumors of black magic.

"Keep your head tonight," Gisele said. Alice closed her eyes as her mother misted a setting spray over her thick eyeliner. The afternoon sun pressed in heavy as a hand around her throat, and Alice was already sweating through her velvet dress. In all of Alice's memories of the Little House, it is always summer. Summer never-ending; summer-stifling; summer, the season no one would notice her missing. "This haunting seems especially promising."

"I wish I could talk to him." Killian sat on the stairs, fiddling with a balding spot on the carpet, dark hair slipping over one eye. By the time he reached age ten, he'd grown from a sickly toddler to a healthy child with Frank's hawkish nose, a scattering of Gisele's freckles, and a barbed wire smirk that was all his own. "Being a ghost sounds so cool."

Alice and Gisele flinched as one. Gisele had won the argument with Frank, and Killian had never known about the curse, but he had a longing to be different that alarmed Alice. An ache for magic and the spells on his fingertips. An exaltation of ghosts. Any slip of the tongue posed a danger to him, a threat that the knowledge of the curse, and their subsequent plans, might spur him to hurry the process along. It was an impulse Alice wouldn't understand until much later, that the desire to be special came less from excitement than guilt and longing. That in the absence of any coherent explanation, he assumed it was their gifts that drew Gisele's attention and spared him from her anger—and also, perhaps, the full extent of her love.

When they didn't answer, Killian pressed on. "Was his mother a witch too? A Medium like Beau?"

Alice bit her tongue, pretended to focus on her makeup. The singular time Alice had asked Gisele about other witches, she'd slapped Alice across the face so hard her last baby tooth had fallen out. She'd told Alice that she'd Seen that if Alice went looking for other witches it would set off a chain of events that would result in Killian's contracting cat scratch disease from a neighborhood stray and dying of sepsis before the end of the month. Did Alice want her brother to suffer? Even though Alice had long since learned the taste of Gisele's lies, her mother raised the stakes so high, Alice never dared to disobey on the off chance she was telling the truth.

"Don't be an idiot," Gisele said to Killian. "Of course not. There are no other witches outside this family." She pulled back to assess her handiwork, then carefully adjusted the clasp of Alice's necklace. Alice stiffened at her touch. "Stop distracting your sister. Tonight's séance is a big one." Gisele always had a little more patience for Killian than the rest of them, so she continued, "It'll take all your sister's focus. Tonight's ghost is different."

Each time Alice thought of it, her stomach did somersaults. Excitement mostly, she told herself, trying to ignore the undercurrent of fear. Gisele had been making ominous declarations like this since they scheduled the clients, but had refused to elaborate, no matter how many times Alice had asked.

Killian's eyes instantly brightened. "I want to come!"

"No."

"But, Mom—"

Gisele arched an eyebrow, and Killian leaned against the banister. "It isn't a magic show, little love. Leave the ghosts to your sister."

Killian rolled his eyes.

"How about I take you to the library tomorrow?" Alice offered. He wasn't allowed to go to sleepovers or ride roller coasters or attend field trips, but Alice could give him this: skateboarding lessons in their driveway, video game marathons, and a stack of historical fiction and gory thrillers that he wouldn't be able to check out otherwise.

Killian considered this for a moment. "Satisfactory," he said, though his mouth twinged briefly with disappointment. It was one of his vocab words this week at school and he'd been using it at every opportunity he could.

Alice picked an asteria stem from a bouquet on the side table and wove it into her braid. She angled toward the mirror, inspecting her makeup. As she leaned forward, the fresh scabs on her hips cracked and stretched. She'd etched twin runes for opening herself to the spiritual world there to smooth the possession. Alice hissed.

Killian peered at her through the railing. "Are you okay?" Too observant by half, her brother.

The question drew Gisele's attention. "What now?" She met Alice's eyes in the mirror, tapping her foot.

Alice fiddled with the cap of the foundation bottle to cover her wince. "Are you sure we're out of the waterproof stuff? I'll be dripping mascara by the time we get to the car."

"We'll be under candlelight," Gisele said. She moved deftly through Alice's hair, securing a circlet to the top of her head with bobby pins. Alice stifled the urge to scratch her scalp. "Besides, tonight will be too spectacular for them to notice."

"They'll be especially shocked that they hired a psychic raccoon," Killian quipped. Alice flashed him the finger as Gisele made an impatient noise. Alice was halfway through putting away her makeup, when Killian cleared his throat. A small sound, hesitant, as he asked, "This ghost won't be dangerous, will it?"

"No, little love." Gisele patted Alice's cheek, a flash of warmth. "As long as Beau doesn't lose her head." Then, to Alice, she said, "I'd never let anything hurt you."

"It's only—" Alice darned her courage. "I've never met a ghost that old."

Gisele scooped up the bag of Alice's Medium supplies and the glass votive holders clinked together. "Why do I waste all this time teaching you, Isabeau, if you can't handle one little ghost?"

Always one little ghost. But the dead who remained did not rest comfortably. Most people passed immediately after they died, to what Alice could only assume was a peaceful afterlife. Those who remained did so because something was holding them back: firm attachments to the living, improper burial rites, unfinished business, violent deaths. Loitering in the world of the living brought on what Alice called the death itch—a need to pass on so fervent it caused chronic episodes of excruciating pain and reenactments of their deaths. And to stay longer than a year brought serious consequences. A ghost started lucid, but the longer it fought the death itch, the less it could be reasoned with, the more degraded its sense of self. It couldn't leave the radius of its death. Alice had never seen a ghost who'd stayed longer than four years.

Most ghosts required Alice's help to pass on. Some could pass on without assistance, but it was often trickier and usually involved effort on the part of the ghost and their loved ones—resolving their attachments to the living, performing their own rites, scraping up some justice for their violent deaths. She'd seen a total of six manage it on their own, including the old woman outside the Carriage House all those years ago. The rest needed her services, which the living clients paid dearly for, and which sent Alice off on quests like digging up a buried box of letters or acting as a mouthpiece between a father and his dead son. Shepherding the ghosts into passing required a steady hand and a mediating touch, which often made Alice feel less mystic and more school guidance counselor. But the end—the gradual dissolving of the ghosts into shreds of silvery light—never ceased to take her breath away with its beauty.

Alice had learned to recognize her clients—to understand what made different kinds tick. There was the client who kissed her hands after Alice pretended her mother had a message of love and light for her, and asked for forgiveness when the old woman had failed to manifest. On the other end of the spectrum was the client who cursed her out, called her a charlatan and a whore's daughter because his father's ghost refused to disclose the location of a prized candlestick heirloom. Alice tailored herself to each like slipping on a dress—now the naïf, now the mystic, now the sunny little girl. She practiced her facial expressions in the mirror until she knew exactly how to comfort with the tilt of a head or frighten with the wobble of her lip, until she could manipulate her face exactly the way her mother could.

The woman that night couldn't maintain eye contact, and the man made far too much. They stood together in their entryway, the woman readjusting the hem of her polo shirt, the man waiting a beat too long before extending a damp handshake to introduce himself. This should have been the first warning.

The woman ushered them into a claustrophobic dining room. An oversized table swallowed a lion's share of space, followed closely by a massive bowfront curio cabinet. Otherwise, the room was undecorated. Nothing on the shelves, not even a salt and pepper shaker on the table. These domestic contradictions should have been the second warning.

As Gisele spread the black velvet tablecloth, Alice wandered the room. The house didn't smell like ozone—wherever the ghost was, it wasn't down here just yet. She hesitated near the far wall, in front of a shattered mirror, missing whole chunks of glass. Alice's reflection returned to her in fractures, doubled across the cracks. She touched a jagged edge—though not hard enough to draw blood—her veins humming with longing. Then she turned around and chose a seat at the table that put her back to the mirror.

Alice first smelled the sulfur after Gisele finished the initial circle of incense, but it disappeared quickly. While Gisele walked the room, the man glared at the chandelier, and the woman studied her chipped acrylic nails. Then she bent over the votive candle, the fire hesitating at the mouth of her long-necked lighter. Gisele stared Alice in the eyes as the wick submitted to the flame.

When Gisele instructed them to hold hands, the man ignored her. The candlelight threw dancing shadows across his face. His skin shone with a film of grease Alice hadn't noticed earlier. "I don't think I want to do this," he said to his wife. "It won't help."

The woman squeezed her eyes shut as if holding in a scream. "Do we have another choice?"

"Something wrong?" Gisele's hand clamped down on Alice's shoulder, digging uncomfortably into the plate of Alice's bones in an unnecessary warning.

"Give us a moment," the man said at the same time as the woman said, "Nothing's wrong." The woman pulled her husband's hand from his lap and plopped it, with a thump, onto the table. He scowled but didn't move.

"We're ready," the woman affirmed, and she stared into the candle in front of her, unblinking. Steeling herself, Alice thought. Unease prickled at the base of her skull, and Alice willed Gisele to intercede. But Gisele only squeezed her shoulder again. Alice reluctantly took the woman's clammy hand across the table, trying and failing to smother her shiver. She willed herself to stay focused. Accomplishing the possession was the most important thing. Anything else was jitters to be dismissed.

She slowed her breaths, first in through her nose then out through the mouth. Deeper on the in, hissing through her teeth on the out. She inhaled deeper and deeper, audibly now. *Put on a show*, she thought. The inhale a pull, the exhale a sigh. Louder now. Faster. *Make them feel something.* "Spirits, I call to you through the veil of shadow. We would hear your message and beg your wisdom. Appear to us. I incite you, appear to us. I demand you appear to us. Come, spirits, I call you through the veil of shadow. Let us hear your message. Appear to us." Alice tensed her back, rocked in her seat, rolled her eyes into their whites. All theater of course, but the clients ate it up. The woman's hand tightened on hers. Gisele pressed her thumbnail into Alice's knuckle—time for the finale. Alice gasped aloud and strained to a tight whisper. "He's here." Her throat burned from the rasp of her performance, as she opened her eyes.

And there, unexpectedly, he was. Alice choked on a shriek. He knelt between the votive candles, a boy a little younger than eight-year-old Killian, though it was hard to place his age exactly. All the parts of him that should have been pink, like his nail beds and lips, were ichor black instead. His eyes, set deep into his mottled gray skin, contained no iris, no sclera. He looked like he was in the process of decomposing—his shape, twisted, wrong and decaying. What had happened to this ghost?

Alice froze. The prey instinct of a mouse trapped in the gaze of a cat. If she didn't move, if she didn't acknowledge him, maybe he wouldn't hurt her.

Then the boy screamed. Alice screamed with him. He picked up the chain of the censer and threw it, with all his strength, at the curio cabinet. The glass exploded. Gisele pulled Alice to her, protecting Alice's face as the poltergeist began throwing the candles, one by one. The smell of burning tablecloth, the singe of velvet, the man yelling somewhere behind them. The hot rush of pain when they stood and tried to escape, tripping over broken glass as they ran. The pop as Alice's ankle twisted. The woman's cheek crowning in an ugly purple bruise. Someone chanting, "We aren't here to hurt you." Her surprise when she realized it was her.

"Let me out! I want out!" the poltergeist screamed. "Tell Mommy I don't want to be here anymore. Tell her it's time to let me out." Later, Alice would recall other things—the wobble of his mouth, the shaggy hair grazing his eyelashes, the rounded contour of his cheeks. He was scared. Whatever else he was now, he had once been a child.

When he rushed at her, the cold froze Alice's bones. Her limbs cramping as the pain shot through her bones, body buckling over as her lungs strained for breath. Her limbs numbing as the poltergeist failed to move her legs mid-run. The sides of her vision went a sticky viscous black—not an absence of light, but a smother of it. A black that had never been acquainted with it. The poltergeist filled the space inside her body like tar, pushing her selfhood down, where she couldn't get free. Then, as suddenly as the pain had come, it disappeared and blackness consumed her.

The world roared back to color around her in fresh shades of pain. Her ankle throbbing in mechanical sharp bursts. Her skin pincushioned with glass up her left arm, bruises surely setting in on her right. Something itchy and damp pressed into her body, and she realized she was laying in the damp grass, her forehead in the dirt. A dull roar of panic surrounded her, a woman shouting at Gisele in a high register that Alice couldn't focus long enough to parse. A man standing over Alice, and when he noticed her awake, shouting to her mother. Alice tried to ask what had happened, but the words stuck in her throat, which was painfully raw. The world burned. The summer night pressed in around them like a fever and yet Alice was so unspeakably cold.

Across the lawn, at the foot of the entryway, the poltergeist mirrored her position, half-sprawled across the concrete steps, and she recalled where she was: the client's house. The poltergeist. "Come back," he begged, hand outstretched. "It didn't hurt inside you." Alice began to whimper.

Then Gisele cut in between them, dropping to her knees. "Hush, hush, hush," she murmured, her hand heavy on Alice's head. "You'll do better next time."

When you were seven, she braided you flower crowns, slipped her gold rings onto your chubby fingers, and declared you queen of the fairies. She tickled you with dandelions until your chin yellowed with pollen. Her perfume smelled like lilies of the valley, and you loved to put your face in her hair.

She threw you onto the driveway in a rage five weeks after you moved into the Little House. You were fresh from the bath, and she handed you a hot dog from the grill, and the ketchup dripped into your hair. You couldn't catch your fall, landed on your chin, split your lip. "Stupid, clumsy pig, why can't you be more delicate, why can't you act like a fucking person, stupid, idiot bitch."

When Frank came running, you parroted the lie, "I fell, I'm so clumsy, it was stupid, I have to learn to be more delicate."

She came to your room later with iodine. Petting your hair, patting your cheek. She kissed your bloody chin, licked the blood off her lips. You mustn't make her angry again, because she loved you so, so much. She hated hurting you, but how else would you learn?

Frank was reading a Dan Brown novel in the living room when Alice stormed in. "Jesus," he whistled. "What the hell happened?" Alice touched her swollen cheekbone.

"Ghost threw a candlestick at her." Gisele trailed in after her, Alice's duffel bag of séance supplies slung over her shoulder. "It shook her up."

"A *ghost* gave her that black eye?" Frank studied Alice, then patted the spot on the couch beside him. "I thought that ghosts couldn't touch things?" Alice hesitated. That urge to cut was unfolding in her center. She could almost feel the rune already, the bright burn of the galdrastafir on her upper thigh, to amplify her courage. But Frank patted the spot again, and Alice never did know how to disappoint him.

"Not a ghost. A poltergeist." The word itself sounded right: a malevolent spirit driven to cause harm by the extreme social deprivation and constant pain of the death itch sustained for too long. These things, this isolation, couldn't occur naturally. Alice knew that instinctively—someone had made that boy what he was. As the horror of that realization crested over her, Alice curled herself around one of the throw pillows and winced. Every time she moved her swollen ankle, it flared with pain. "And apparently, a poltergeist can." Even as she said it, it made intuitive sense to Alice that the potential energy created between the itch to pass and the inability to go would manifest like this.

"So much drama, little love." Gisele dropped the duffel bag by the door and eased against the wall, arms crossed.

"He was different than a regular ghost. I think the boy's mother did a spell to keep him here," Alice said. It was a dangerous subject to broach, given Gisele's denial of the existence of other witches. She waited for her mother to react, to scream, but Gisele only watched her. Alice picked at a loose thread on the throw pillow. "I think she was a witch, and he could only possess me because she did something to force him to stay. Before he possessed me, he kept saying it was time for Mommy to let him out because he didn't want to be here anymore. And now a hundred years have gone by, and he's still stuck."

"Perhaps." Gisele stared over Alice's head, out the window, gnawing a corner of her lip. "If so, it might be something we can replicate. We'll go back and try again, see if we can get the boy to interact with us. Determine what he knows about whatever ritual was done. The Novaks won't mind—I doubt they'll be stepping foot in that house again anytime soon."

Frank scratched the back of his neck. "I don't know about all that, El. Give her time to heal that ankle, at least."

Gisele picked at a loose chip of paint on the wall. "Beau's strong enough to power through. She needs more training on possession, and the Novaks will toss that house on the market faster than a hot potato."

"More training like this?" Frank gestured to Alice, who flinched. She wondered if she could get away with sneaking up the stairs, but unless she wanted to skirt the whole room, she'd have to pass between them.

Gisele didn't move, but the air around her crackled with a sudden electricity. "I won't allow my daughter to act like some naive gift-less girl who trembles at her own shadow. We don't cower, Frances. My girls aren't built that way."

Frank leapt to his feet, the novel falling from his lap. "Damn you, woman! You want to talk about cowering? Our daughter is seventeen, and you brought her home looking like the aftermath of a bar fight."

Gisele snorted. "You're content with Killian dying then? Disappearing off into the ether because you can't handle seeing a few bruises?"

"Quiet," Frank snapped. "You'll wake him."

"I cannot bring myself to be quiet about this, Frances. You're not hearing me!" Gisele's voice reached a near-hysteric octave. "He's going to die if we don't do something."

"Maybe—" *we should let him go*, Alice thought. *Maybe keeping him here will turn him into that rotting little boy with all his pain and all his suffering.* But when Gisele's face smoothed into porcelain, Alice thought about the topography of scars on Bronwyn's back and stopped. "Please don't fight."

"We aren't fighting, sweetheart," Frank said.

Gisele rolled her eyes. "What else would you call this, Frances? Pillow talk?"

"I'll be okay tomorrow. I'm fine. Really," Alice added, as Frank tilted his head skeptically. "An ice pack tonight, and I'll be right as rain."

"That's my girl." Gisele plucked a strand of hair from her blouse, then squared her shoulders. "She's a fighter. I knew my girl would come out of this stronger. I told the Novaks, no matter how vicious their ghost, I knew my girl could handle it."

And maybe they could have escaped the evening intact. But Frank slumped, mouth tight. "You knew, El? What exactly did the clients tell you?"

Gisele reddened as if slapped. "Nothing," she said. "Only that the ghost could touch them."

Frank half-sat, half-fell onto the couch. "They told you the ghost was hurting them, didn't they? Did they tell you the ghost had attacked them?"

"Gisele didn't know. My focus slipped tonight," Alice said. She felt herself begin to shake her head, even as the truth settled in.

Frank bowed his head. "Tell me something, El. Do you even love your daughters?"

Gisele rounded on Frank, sneering. "I do this because I love her. Because she needs to be strong enough to bear this. Do you want to know exactly how many futures Isabeau ends up failing in? Shall I tell you?"

Gisele crossed the room and knelt in front of Alice. "Should I list it for you? Should I tell you how many fatal spider bites Killian avoided tonight? How many car accidents? Killian has died a hundred times over, and he'll die a hundred more. Don't you understand the nature of a curse? He's always dying, and I pull card after card, and all I can do is twist the how. I delay it an hour, a day, a month—all in the prayer we'll find a way to keep him before it's too late. And yes, there was some pain for you tonight but this haunting was essential—my god, a ghost who can attack people? Cause injuries? We've been waiting for something exactly like this for years. And you're fine, little love. You're fine." She patted Alice's hand.

"So you did know?" Alice pushed herself off the couch, her ankle flaring with pain. And wasn't that just like Gisele—to use her as a tool instead of preparing her for the pain. As if Alice didn't know what was at stake, as if she wouldn't have gone in anyway, even knowing the danger. "You knew the poltergeist could hurt me and you sent me in there anyway."

"Sit down. We aren't finished." Gisele stood, shaking with rage, and there would be hell to pay, but Alice brushed past her.

"Let her go," she heard Frank say.

Halfway up the stairs, she spotted a silhouette in the hall, the shape of a boy. Her chest seized before she realized it was Killian.

"What happened to your face?" He reached up to touch her, but Alice jerked away. "Should I grab the healing salve?"

"Don't touch me." Alice tried to push past, but Killian grabbed her wrist.

"I only heard, like, half of that." It was untenable, his need. "Beau, please. What happened?" Alice should have been kinder that night—pulled him to her like she did when he was a baby. "What is a poltergeist? Why did it hurt you?"

She thought of the way Gisele stared at him sometimes when she didn't realize anyone else was watching. Her face contorted, half agony and half tenderness, a certain tightening in her jaw, as if she had to pry herself away or else she'd stare and stare until she'd memorized the constellation of his freckles. "Beau, I heard my name. I heard her say I'm dying. You have to tell me what's going on."

Love me, Alice would think. *Love me like you love him*. Resentment festers. It can't help itself. Her knives sang to her from their hiding places, and she didn't fight their song.

"Family Council in the morning," she said. "Tell Bronwyn."

"Isabeau." His face twisted when she pulled away, near tears, but she had nothing left to offer. "Isabeau, please." And she should have stayed. But she didn't. She abandoned him at the lip of the stairs with his terror ringing in her ears.

Of course, it wasn't all bad with her mother, but it's the good memories that will sear Alice later. The tender readjustment of a necklace before they walked into a client's house; the year Gisele hand-stitched her dress for prom because they couldn't afford the one she wanted; the autumn neither she nor Gisele could sleep and watched reruns of comedy shows into the early hours of morning, bathed in blue light.

On her best days, Alice can believe her mother loved her as an appendage, as a tool. That those moments of gentleness were Gisele's way of using a carrot instead of a stick. Another manipulation tactic in her quest to save her son. It is easier to think of her mother this way, as someone too damaged to love at all.

SEVEN

ALICE WAKES TO Eli's alarm but pretends to sleep through it while he stretches to consciousness beside her. Over the past few months, the new therapist has worked wonders. He's acquired a new solidity, abandoned some of that gossamer litheness. When Eli sits up, she continues to feign sleep, but he brushes her cheek, and she twitches into an involuntary smile.

"I thought you were awake." He flicks on the lamp.

Alice groans and rolls toward him, blocking the light with one elbow. "Nope. Too early."

"You kicked like a rabbit all night." Eli tugs a strand of hair near her neck, and Alice peers at the sleep-mussed mess of him from below her forearm. "Bad dreams?"

"Something like that."

"You know what we should do once my mom leaves?" Eli curls toward her, lowering his voice. "Take an extra day off work and marathon *Hannibal*."

"We've already seen *Hannibal*," Alice protests. Crime shows are their guilty pleasure. They've never had a bad day they couldn't weather with a procedural. "Twice. I want *Criminal Minds*."

"You and your crime boys. We've watched *Criminal Minds* triple the times we've watched *Hannibal*."

She presses her nose against his ribs, draping her arm around the comforting warmth of his waist. He smells like sleep and the oak moss and sandalwood of his bodywash and his own clean scent, and Alice can't resist nipping the strawberry birthmark high up on his rib.

"Hey, Dr. Lecter!" Eli flicks her shoulder. "My mom's right down the hall."

"So be quiet." She places another bite on him for good measure, before turning the bite into a kiss.

He murmurs her name and curves toward her but accidentally brushes against a rune scar on her thigh in the process and Alice tenses. Eli pulls back. "You okay?" When she doesn't answer, he nudges her. "What's wrong?"

Because she cannot be honest, she says, "Are you still mad at me?"

His touch whispers through her hair, the line of her neck, and he grabs her chin, tilting it until she meets his gaze. "Yes." He thumbs her lower lip. Alice's breath catches. He traces a line along her jaw until his thumb presses gently against her pulse point. "I'm mad. Furious, actually. But it's morning, and if you're sorry, and if you tell me the truth, it's fine, okay?" Even in this abysmal morning light, his gaze is awake and desperately vulnerable. He did nothing to deserve the mess she has made of this week. "It'll be fine, I promise. Whatever it is."

"Do you really want to know?" Alice's heart trills against his touch, betraying her. "I mean, really?"

A shadow of doubt passes over his face. "Is it—about us?"

Alice shakes her head. "Gods, no." And there's a moment, where it's in her mouth before she can help herself: *Once I had a brother, Eli, and sixteen years ago, he died, and after he died, I betrayed him*, and she is shaping the first word, she is closing around them, she is saying his name, she is safe in his arms, and he is looking at her with so much love that she thinks maybe it'll be okay, maybe she is brave enough for this, she is saying, "Once I—"

But then, down the hall, a hair dryer roars to life and Alice chokes on the words. Eli lets out a long stream of curses.

"Guess she's up early." He grimaces and rolls onto his back. Eli waits for her to continue, but when Alice doesn't, he sighs. "Are you coming with us to Somerset?"

Despite her promise to Bronwyn, Alice is tempted. A trip to Somerset Mall would buy her another day—as if a day mattered now that Bronwyn has an energy lock on her again, could track Alice to the ends of the goddamn earth. But she can picture herself in the blue light of the mall, nibbling a chocolate-covered biscotti from the coffee shop next to the Nordstrom, loitering with Eli in the flush crowd outside the Banana Republic while Susan shops, the snarky comments they'd text to each other like sulky teenagers, so Susan wouldn't overhear them. Later, they'd mock the outrageous things Susan said, collapsing in helpless laughter against each other's shoulders. All Alice had to do was say yes.

"Eli." His name comes out as one long sigh. "My stomach is churning."

"All right, then." Eli pushes himself off the bed and out of reach. She will not cry. Not where he can see.

He dresses with his back to her, but she catches his expression in flashes, the patchwork of reddening skin. He hesitates in the closet, lingering on his favorite button-down flannel, soft and pilled under the arms and the fabric thinning at the elbows, then removes a charcoal sweater instead, pulls it on over a white dress shirt. During Susan's visits, he dresses like a J.Crew model. He's so beautiful in this light, it hurts, but he also looks nothing like himself.

When he's dressed, he walks to her side of the bed, waiting, Alice thinks, for her to glance up. She doesn't—focuses instead on the wall clock. Eli smooths her hair, plants a kiss against her temple. "I love you," he whispers. He lingers above her, but when she doesn't say it back, he sighs and turns away.

She waits until the bedroom door clicks shut before she punches the pillow. Again, then again. "Fuck," she whispers, and then because she is so fucking fucked, she repeats it until her fury gives way to exhaustion, and exhaustion yields to a clutched pillowcase and the prickle of tears. When she's certain Susan and Eli have left, she rises alone.

Over the course of the morning, Alice's fear hardens to anger. Bronwyn will be here soon—the only thing left to do is wait. Well, that's something she can do well. Alice knows the alchemy of waiting—the slippery length of it, tracing shapes in the dust and sand to still the skipping in her brain. She nurses a mug of chamomile tea and recites the alphabet in reverse to ward away the memories of metal clinking around her wrists, the rust of Killian's off-key voice as he sang to comfort her. Everything reminds her of him today. The chamomile that she brewed for him on the nights he couldn't sleep. The blanket on her lap like the weight of him nestled against her as they watched *Dragon Ball Z*, later acting out scenes, jumping from couch to couch while Bronwyn, fourteen and too cool, stared them down.

Alice retrieves the book of Sudoku Eli gave her as a stocking stuffer for their first Christmas and which has lived in her bedside table ever since. She prefers to play Sudoku on her phone, where the numbers erase without residue and where she can strive to beat her best time, but she appreciates the challenge of pen and paper. The certainty of a binding decision. Alice steeps another cup of tea and passes the time whispering numbers and pretending she doesn't see Killian's face every time she blinks. The doorbell finally rings two hours later.

When Alice opens the door, Bronwyn is standing on the stoop wearing the same clothes she had on yesterday. Her hair sticks up at odd angles, as if she forgot to brush it, and the mess adds an inch to her height. The daylight reveals the fracture of blood vessels on her cheeks.

She thinks of all the parties where Bronwyn never let her tag along, all the skirts Alice wasn't allowed to borrow, the untouchable tubes of lipstick on Bronwyn's dresser. They are the same height, almost the same build, but her sister has aged ungracefully. She doesn't want the neighbors to mistake Bronwyn for her. Alice pulls her sister inside by the matted fur of her collar. Bronwyn stumbles over the doorsill but catches herself and slinks into the foyer like an indignant cat. It's anachronistic, Bronwyn shifting from foot to foot below the sculpted metal fish Eli purchased last month from a local art show. Two eras of

Alice's life layered atop each other like sediment. Alice closes the door. "You're tracking mud."

She points to a wire and wood shoe rack. Bronwyn bares her teeth and tilts her head. Alice recognizes the expression, it's the one Bronwyn used to give to teachers who told her to stop passing notes in class, the one she used to give their mother when told to eat her greens, the one that always preceded some show of casual cruelty. Alice had forgotten that about her, her insistence on defiance when defiance seemed unnecessary. Bronwyn walks the few steps to the staircase, shoes still on, and sits, grinding one heel, then the other, into the beige carpet. Alice eyes the trail of slushy footprints and tightens her lips.

"Nice place. Very tasteful." Bronwyn nods at the crystal chandelier.

"Does Gisele know I'm here?" Even if Gisele isn't with her now, she could be coming, and Alice must mitigate the damage.

"It depends."

"Depends on what?"

"If you're as big a bitch as you were yesterday." Bronwyn plants her elbows on her knees, and her chin on the interlocked weave of her fingers. Their mother used to adopt this same gesture when negotiating pay with difficult clients. On their mother, it had been an act of softening, of making her expression guileless and simple, the practiced chew of the lip. How absolutely helpless, this mother of three children who needed their bellies filled. It's cheap of Bronwyn to give her this look, as if Alice herself didn't spend hours learning to mirror it.

"You scared me." Alice forces out a smile, and she presses her hands against her thighs so Bronwyn will not see the hate balling inside her.

"I could've scared you a lot worse. I could've pushed my way in here last night and introduced myself to your replacement family."

"You said you want to talk. About what?"

"And I told you it was important, so what'd you do? You bolt right out of the goddamn grocery store."

Alice sweeps her arms out wide and turns in a semicircle. It is a way of making herself bigger, filling the space, like a bird spreading its wings to threaten with the bulk of its plumage. "You got my fucking attention. Talk."

"What, you're not going to feed me like a proper guest?" Alice no longer knows her sister well enough to tell if Bronwyn is making a peace offering or being sarcastic.

"Sure. Do you want some tea, a slice of cobbler? How about a cucumber sandwich?"

"How about some liquor?" Bronwyn half-rises from the stairs. She moves slowly, a wild animal easing into a crouch to pounce. "Any whiskey?"

"I see you still have the same excellent habits you did in high school."

Bronwyn's back snaps straight. "Don't start being a bitch again, Beau, or so help me, I'll call Gisele right now and you can mouth off to her in the Little House instead."

They were so close as teenagers, two halves of a whole. But there is a decade and a half sprawled between them now. This woman is a stranger. The Bronwyn that Alice knew would never have come looking for her. The fact that Bronwyn came to her house is an unspeakable betrayal of who they were, and this means Alice must tread carefully. "All right," Alice says. "Fine. But take off your shoes."

Bronwyn chucks the shoes, one a time, toward the door. One lands with a soft clop on the pink tie rug. The other smacks the rack and a shoehorn, which, balanced precariously on the wire, clatters to the floor. Alice deliberately turns her back to the jumble. "Kitchen's through here."

Alice's mug and book of Sudoku lie in her usual spot at the kitchen table, but Bronwyn puts out an arm, cutting Alice off, and drops into Alice's chair. Another gesture her sister has stolen from their mother. "I wasn't kidding about the booze."

"It's eleven in the morning."

Bronwyn squints, then raises an eyebrow. She stands, waggles her forefinger, and spins on one heel, the sweat of her socks leaving a wet crescent on the hardwood until she comes to a stop in front of the cupboard beside the fridge. Bronwyn moues in mock surprise over her shoulder, lips curling into an *O*. Then, she throws open the door. Triumphant, she raises the bottle of good bourbon Eli saves for special occasions. "Want a glass?"

"Please. Make yourself at home." Alice almost forgets herself, almost chuckles. She thinks of her sister, age twelve, wearing their mother's clip-on earrings. Plastic tigers and stick-on rhinestones, hair wrapped in a pink scarf, blue craft glitter freckling her cheekbones. Bronwyn's arms sweeping wide as she declared, "I am Madame La Luna. You will fart on the man you love tomorrow."

Now, Alice says, "They're over the sink."

Bronwyn returns to the table with two rocks glasses and pours a slug into each. She throws hers back in one long gulp. "This'll go down easier with a drink." Bronwyn nudges the other glass toward Alice, but Alice shakes her head. "What, you pregnant or something?"

This surprises Alice. She opens her mouth and then snaps it shut. Her ears flush with shame.

"Shit." Bronwyn whistles. "Congrats. How many weeks?"

Alice can't help the strangled sound at the back of her throat. It's the memory of course, of her mother screaming, "A boy, a boy."

"Ah. Not congrats yet." Bronwyn nods slowly and traces the lip of the glass. "Did you tell your husband about the curse and all that? Is he ready for the gift?"

"He's not my husband."

"Okay. Well, did you tell your *boyfriend* about us?"

"You came here to talk to me. So very important, you said."

Bronwyn glances out the sliding glass door where the rain has thickened to snow, settling now like white blossoms on the evergreens. "You've done real nice for yourself, Beau. Very healthy." She reaches toward Alice's face, but Alice jerks away.

"Stop calling me that."

"Calling you what?"

"That's not my name anymore."

"What, you want me to call you—Alice? That ugly name? You think you're in wonderland or some shit?" Bronwyn drinks straight from the bottle this time. "Changed your name so I couldn't find you? That it? To Haserot, of all things? I'm not stupid, Beau."

Very slowly, Alice says, "Why are you here?"

"It isn't easy to say this, okay? It's—gods—" Bronwyn shoves the bourbon into the center of the table, as if suddenly disgusted by it. Then, abruptly, she rocks forward and shakes out her hands. The burst of movement sets Alice's teeth on edge. "I had a daughter." Alice's lips part, and her hand drops to the tablecloth, coarse with crumbs. The past tense catches her, the *had*.

"Oh," Alice says faintly.

"She was sixteen. Her name was—Willow." Bronwyn's voice cracks, and then she laughs, raspy and crow-like. "Willow's gift wasn't a good one. She could sense emotions. The good, the bad, the joy, the pain. All of it."

"Empath."

"Yeah. Empath. Strong one. The gift came real late for her." Bronwyn angles her body toward the patio and shakes her head. A clump of hair curtains her face. "She died. Did it to herself."

"When?" There are other words Alice wants to say, but they wilt on her tongue. Alice tries to picture Bronwyn's daughter. A colt-legged girl, hanging from a clothesline, perhaps. A pale freckled child, smelling of milk, lying in a bath of blood in a cascade of pills. It morphs into Killian's death face, the sickly white of his skin, the bluish hue of his lips—the only other child that she has seen die. Alice doesn't trust herself to speak.

"Three months ago." Bronwyn shivers and her hand disappears beneath the veil of her hair. Crying, Alice realizes. She's crying. Alice should touch her, offer a pat on the back, some comfort, but Alice doesn't want to, doesn't want to feel sorry for her, doesn't want to think of another child limp with death. Bronwyn presses her fist to her mouth before continuing. "The thing is, something's wrong. She's not passing on."

Not all the dead turn into ghosts, but there are certain factors that make it more probable. "It's been too soon. It can take up to a year with violent deaths. You know that." Alice is taken aback by the speed with which she remembers. Gisele would be proud of how deep that knowledge stuck. The thought is bitter.

Bronwyn's laugh strangles into a cough. "The entire house smells like rotten eggs. The bathtub keeps overflowing even when no one is home. Last week, our trash can caught fire. You ever met a ghost who could even touch shit, let alone fuck with faucets and lighters?"

Alice knows of only one type of ghost who can do something like that. She knows it wasn't like that, but in her memories, Killian's eyes blackened from one heartbeat to another. "You didn't try to bind her, did you?"

"Of course I fucking didn't." Bronwyn swallows hard, knocks her knuckles against the dining room table. "But something is happening to her. She's turning into a poltergeist. I'm sure of it."

"If you didn't bind her, she isn't a poltergeist, Bronwyn." No matter what Bronwyn believes, a poltergeist can only be made deliberately by magic. There is nothing incidental or natural about the process. "It's a rough passing, but that's it. I'm so sorry." This time Alice does reach out, locking her fingers around her sister's. Then, after a moment, she flattens her palms on the table, beside the bottle of bourbon. The sun coming through the windows lights up the gold in Bronwyn's lashes. "I'm sorry," Alice says again. "I can't imagine what you're going through."

"You hold on to that 'sorry.'" Bronwyn says it like a threat, but her eyes shine too brightly for there to be any real force in them. "I need you feeling sorry."

"I don't understand," Alice says, though she does. She tastes metal and sawdust, and her arms jolt at the memory of pain.

"Help me. Come to Cleveland and talk her into passing."

"Absolutely not." Alice leans back in her chair and tightens the grip on her wrist. "Not happening."

"I'm asking nicely. Not sure you'll like it if I stop being nice." Bronwyn's been hinting at the *or else* since she stepped through the front door. And what can Alice possibly say? There is no arguing with a mother's grief. The white hands of a clammy woman, begging, bruising her forearm. The clink of the chains.

The bluff that is no bluff—bring her to me, or I will hurt you. Bring her to me, or I'll destroy you. Bring me my little one, willing, or bring me my little one, broken. Gods, but she is sick to death of a mother's grief, a mother's parasitic all-consuming love.

"You don't understand." Alice grinds her heels back against the chair leg. "I bound my shadow as soon as I could. I haven't seen a ghost in years. I couldn't talk to her even if I wanted to."

Bronwyn slouches as if all the tension in her body has snapped loose. Her skin pales at the forehead, the neck. "I'm not stupid, Beau. I figured you did." She half-shrugs, waving a hand. "I'm disappointed, sure, but not surprised."

"I won't cut off the bind runes. Not for you, not for anyone. You can tell Eli, you can drag me back to Gisele—I won't do it." Once those runes came off, there would be no redoing the binding spell—the skin would be too damaged to hold further scarring.

Bronwyn's eyes harden. No, not harden. It's a determination—an authority. She's calculating something, and Alice crosses her legs, hiding her heels under the seat.

"Pretty speech, but unnecessary." Bronwyn wrinkles her nose at the bourbon bottle in the middle of the table. It sprays a watery dapple of sunlight across the tablecloth. "Like I said, I expected that. Keep your binding. I need that encyclopedia of ghost shit in your head. I need the Isabeau Glass who could cast spells in her sleep." Bronwyn's smile tightens, a touch feral. Alice doesn't want to test her temper. She thinks of tea light candles; of the itch of tulle against the underside of her arms and the thick smoke of myrrh that made her cough as a child; of the destruction on her body when the ghosts came. She thinks of the twin lines of the pregnancy test; of the decisions she must make;

of how to best keep Eli out of this debacle. But then she thinks of metal carving into the skin of her heels, of blood and wounds and the smell of ozone. Of what she did to her brother, of the lie she told, and how he might retaliate should she remove the bind runes and be able to see the dead again. He would kill her this time. She is sure of it.

And because she cannot be found by Gisele, cannot think about what might happen with the return of her magic, she says, "All right. I'll go."

EIGHT

Age Seventeen

THE MORNING AFTER the poltergeist séance, Bronwyn woke Alice with a finger pressed to her lips. A witch ball hung in the air over Alice's head, casting the room in a silvery-white glow, so bright it made Alice's eyes water. "Let's go, asshole. Family Council time."

Alice squirmed and squinted at her alarm—6 a.m. She rolled her head back into her arms, groaning. "Why's it so goddamn early?"

"I brought coffee, didn't I?" Bronwyn wafted a thermos near Alice's nose, the smell of maple and cream making Alice's mouth water. "Hurry the fuck up. Killian's already in the car."

Bronwyn was nineteen that summer, and hardly home. When she wasn't pulling shifts at Yankee Candle, she was out with friends and came back late in the night with the smell of cigarettes and hard liquor in her hair. Alice caught her presence in artifacts around the house—an uncapped tube of red lipstick by the house phone, a gold wrapper from her Marlboro 27s stuck with static to the carpet, a spiked bangle hung from a doorknob.

The times Alice actually set eyes on her sister were an omen. Bronwyn only showed up when trouble was brewing.

"How's Killian?" she asked as she pulled a sweatshirt over her head.

"How the fuck do you think?" Bronwyn handed her the thermos and Alice took a blistering sip that scalded the roof of her mouth. "Are you fully insane? Talking about this shit where he could hear you?"

"I wasn't the one screaming about the curse in the middle of the living room." He'd looked so small on the stairs last night.

Bronwyn snorted. "No, but you clearly did something to piss him off. He wanted to leave without you. Get a good look at him when we get to the car."

When they came downstairs, the kid in question was already tucked into the back seat of the car, his eyes red-rimmed and dark with exhaustion. He didn't acknowledge his sisters as they approached, but the line of his jaw told Alice how hurt he was. Killian never sulked. "Shit," she said.

"'Shit' about covers it," Bronwyn agreed.

They always went to the cemetery for Family Councils. Alice had never especially disliked cemeteries, particularly historical ones. Fewer accidental Medium encounters there—people rarely died in or near graveyards. Bronwyn parked in their usual place, near the angel statue. Technically, her name was the Angel of Death Victorious, but mostly, people called her the Haserot Angel, for the family she minded. She was enormous, oxidized bronze, her wings thrown back as she planted a sword deep into the earth.

Through some chemical foresight on the part of the sculptor, the angel wept black tears down her cheeks and throat. She'd always unsettled Alice, but Killian adored her, and Bronwyn had smugly decided that the Angel of Death Victorious was the perfect hangout spot for a Medium.

"Are you really going to make me start?" Bronwyn rolled down her window and the humid air infiltrated the crispness of the air-conditioning. Alice and Killian exchanged glances. "I wasn't even there, kittens. One of you better start jabbering." Killian glared, lips pressed into a thin line, clearly waiting for Alice to take an initiative she had no interest in either. "Fucking fine." Bronwyn kicked her legs over the center console, her sneakers landing on the passenger side in Alice's lap. She stuck her toe into Alice's rib cage as she reached into her satchel and shook out her pack of cigarettes. Alice tried to grab the pack, but Bronwyn held it out of reach. "What was our lovely mother screaming about this time?"

"Something happened at the séance." Killian scooted forward in his seat. "And then by the end of it, there was something about Beau getting hurt, and poltergeists, and curses, and dying. I'd love to get some details on that, if you can spare them." With this, he sent an eye full of daggers toward Alice.

Bronwyn also pivoted to Alice, and Alice buried her nose into her sweater, wishing it offered better protection. "What the fuck happened at the séance?"

"A poltergeist happened, I guess." There was no more delaying it—it was time. It shouldn't have fallen to Alice to tell him. The job belonged to their parents. But when had they ever stepped up to do the hard thing when it came to Killian? Perhaps it was better that he be told by the sisters who loved him most.

In her memory, Alice calls that time the Lost Days, the Dark Times, the Poltergeist Summer. To name something is to distance its power, and these names can't hurt her the way it hurt to watch Killian in the cemetery that morning. As the words tumbled out of her—her fight with the spirit and Gisele and the curse—a light went out in Killian's eyes. She doesn't remember the order of her words, or what questions Killian asked, or precisely where Bronwyn made comforting noises. She can't recall how long they sat together in that graveyard. She does not want to. But what she does remember from that morning is the moment Killian leaned back into the car door, his expression still, as if Alice had finally arranged his world in its proper configuration. Her brother had always seemed so much older than his age, but that day in the graveyard, he could have been as small as the infant she used to cradle—and she wished he still was. That she could soothe him by rocking the bad things away.

When Alice finished, Bronwyn sucked down a shaky breath. "You're sure?" she said, her voice cracking. "That the spell that kept him here hurt him? The boy?"

"He begged me to come back and tell his mommy he needs to go." Alice swallowed. "It's the first ghost I've ever managed to hold down that long, I think because a poltergeist is something different. The poltergeist changes things."

"Which is important because I'm dying," Killian whispered. His face had gone green, his hands fidgeting in his lap.

"Yes." Alice tried to steady her voice.

"And I have—I only have nine years left? At most? That's it?" Killian's dark hair slipped into his eyes, and he shoved it back angrily. Killian had the palest eyes of all of them. A gray that was almost white. "Fuck."

"Watch your gods-damned language," Bronwyn barked, "or I'll scrub your fucking tongue out with wet wipes."

"Yeah, right. *My* gods-damned language. Were you ever going to tell me?"

Neither Bronwyn nor Alice answered, skirting his glare.

"Beau." Killian leaned toward her, his hands resting on the center console, their cuticles bitten near to raw. "Were you ever going to tell me?"

Alice tucked her chin down, pressing it against the hard plate of her shoulder. "No," she admitted. "I wasn't."

"You've known for years, and—" He turned his head abruptly, hair hiding his face again.

"Gisele said—" Bronwyn began, but Killian cut her off.

"I don't care what Gisele said," he snapped. Bronwyn stuffed her fist against her mouth, breathing quickly. "You're my sisters. You should have told me."

"Look, it'll be okay," Alice murmured, reaching across the center console to clutch his knee. "Gisele and I will figure it out. You won't be alone. And you won't really be dead either, if everything goes right. I promise."

Killian sucked his teeth and put his hand on Alice's. His palm was sweaty, and he wore a leather cord on his wrist, a hagstone woven into the center. She had made it for his birthday last year. "What kind of life is that anyway?" Killian shook his head. "To stay in Kirtland, taking turns in one body until you die?"

"You get odd days, I'll get even ones. How about that?" But Alice's joke fell flat.

"Work on the logistics later." Bronwyn's leg jerked, her heel digging uncomfortably into Alice's kidney. Alice flinched. "You've got a whole life to figure it out. But that's the point, Killy. You'll actually get to have one."

“There’s time, Killy,” Alice whispered. “We’ll manage it together.”

And Killian met her eyes in the rearview mirror. A beat later, he nodded.

Bronwyn suggested swinging by Coventry Village on the way home, perhaps as an apology for losing her temper in the car. It was a strip of stores in a neighborhood adjacent to the cemetery—not the safest part of town, but Alice and Bronwyn had visited plenty of times to thrift or restock at the only New Age store in the area. Killian trailed behind them, complaining that he would have brought his MP3 player if he’d known they’d be shopping. They bought a pair of fluffy iced coffees and a matcha frappe for Killian, selected for its color. At the New Age store, Killian made a beeline for the display on tarot cards. He flipped through the decks carefully, occasionally pulling out a card, studying it, setting it back.

“What are the cards telling you, oh mighty Oracle?” Alice asked as she came up behind him. She put her hands on his bony shoulders. He held up the Eight of Wands: in this case, a woman arcing a scythe toward the tall grass while a child, clutching a scroll, bolted through the field behind her.

“It’s telling me that you need to stop sneaking knives up to your room.”

Her throat stuck as she tried to swallow. “How did you—”

He shrugged, then shuffled the card back into the deck. He returned it to the display. “Beau, it’s eighty degrees out, and you’re wearing a hoodie.”

"It was cold this morning." Alice dropped her gaze to the coffee cup, rubbing at the damp sticker. It rolled off into grayish flecks.

Killian lightly kicked her ankle. "Don't lie to me. I know about the cutting." Then quietly he added, "We share a bathroom, Beau."

Alice gathered herself enough to force a smile. "Come on, Killian. How do you even know what that is? You're a baby."

Killian glowered at her from under his bangs. "I read things. Which is how I also know you're trying to change the subject."

"Did you tell Bronwyn?" Across the store, Bronwyn knelt to the herbal display, inspecting the monstrous jars, a baggie of witch hazel already tucked under her arm.

"Nah. I figured that's your business. I will, though, if you don't stop."

"It isn't what you think." And as Killian waited for her to continue, eyebrow raised, Alice shrunk into her sweatshirt. "They're spells. Bind runes to make my magic stronger." Killian continued to stare at her and Alice flushed. "I'm being careful."

"No, you aren't." He rounded on her, hands planted on his hips. "If you think you're doing this for a good reason, you're being stupid."

On any other day, Alice might have been offended, might have asked him what the hell he knew about magic and told him how much she was sacrificing for him to survive. Not today though. Today, she sighed. "It makes things easier. It feels good, after. The magic is better. I can channel longer."

"I repeat—stupid. Stupid, stupid, stupid."

"The runes make it easier to cope. I'd fall apart without them." Alice studied the patterns in the worn carpet, toeing a clump of dust with her toe. "Sometimes I'm afraid I'm going to die in that house."

"Then leave. It's that easy."

"I won't leave you or Bronwyn. We're in this together." She tried, meagerly, to smile. "Speaking of deflecting—you okay?"

Killian held up a deck decorated in thick reds and blacks, the images within blurred. It reminded Alice of an Impressionist painting, if the Impressionists had fetishized skulls. "This is so metal," he said. "I wish Mom would teach me tarot."

"You don't have to do that for me, you know. Pretend it isn't bothering you. I can see your hands shaking."

Killian tossed the deck back onto the shelf and smoothed his palms against his jeans. "I'm not pretending for you." Killian nodded over Alice's shoulder, to where Bronwyn knelt in front of a clay bowl of raw tourmaline. "Something has been going on with her lately. I haven't been able to figure out what, but I don't know if she can handle this right now."

Alice filed this information away for later and returned her focus to her brother. "We'll understand if you're upset. This is crazy—you can say it's crazy."

Killian swirled his frappe. The force in his eyes made him look startlingly like Gisele. "I don't know what to feel about it, Beau. My two choices are dying soon or sharing a body with my sister as a fucked-up ghost."

Alice gently took his hands in hers. "I won't let you suffer. You know that, right? We'll find a way to share the body without pain." Gisele, she was sure, would find a way. And if not—Alice considers what it would mean to give up her body entirely—to be less sister than organ donor, to undo the bonds that tether her to her life, but she doesn't offer, even though she feels like a coward, even though it stands in opposition to her entire upbringing.

"It's still your life—we're talking about sharing *your* life." He turned from her, eyes wet. "I want my own. And that's not something any of you can give me."

Alice opened her mouth to respond, but Bronwyn walked up behind them, balancing five crystals in each hand, and announced it was time to go. They left the store in silence, but as they approached the car, Bronwyn suddenly said, "I'm thinking about asking Gisele to put me up on the Glass Girls ads."

Alice sipped her coffee to buy herself time to answer, but couldn't come up with anything other than, "Why?"

"Money, mostly." Bronwyn shrugged and switched the record bag to her other hand. "I want to get my own place. I mean, I'm almost twenty. It's ridiculous that I still live at home."

"What about us?" Alice's voice came out thin. "You'd leave us all alone?" The Little House without her sister would be too large, too quiet, too empty—too unsafe.

Bronwyn studied the tips of her shoes, her shoulders set at a jagged angle. Killian and Alice exchanged glances. "It's okay," he said, stepping up to slip his hand into Bronwyn's. She smiled down at him. "We'll be okay."

"It's just you're both still in school," Bronwyn muttered. "And I don't have legal custody. It wouldn't work. Not right now."

"What about after I graduate?" Alice asked. "I only have a year left."

"It'll take me a while to save enough." The corners of Bronwyn's eyes were taut with tension. "But all right, after you graduate, you can move in and be my roomie, and Killy can come stay with us on the weekends."

"It's a plan, then," Killian said, bumping his arm into Bronwyn's and making her smile widely. Alice let out the breath she'd been holding. Her promise didn't fix everything, but on that golden day, with her sister and her brother at her side, for just a moment, everything felt in perfect alignment. The world, at least for today, was safe. Enough to ignore the curl of unease, the knowledge that it would not last.

When Alice thinks back on her living, breathing brother, it upsets her that she remembers less of who Killian was than what he would become. But that's the way of trauma. It eats the good that came before it.

Killian loved berries and devoured entire containers in a sitting. Alice used to sneak them up to his room, and they would sit on his bed eating them handful by handful. He hogged the TV to play *Spyro*, and for a short time he played Little League, though she couldn't remember whether he'd actually enjoyed baseball or been humoring Frank. He loved wandering the woods, even though he was begged not to. Bronwyn and Alice were often enlisted to track him down and shepherd him home.

In the year after the Poltergeist Summer, Killian changed. He withdrew. He stopped being careful, started sneaking out to the creek at night, stealing Bronwyn's weed and Gisele's cigarettes. He went rollerblading with his friends near the ravines, where one wrong move would send him tumbling into a chasm that ended in a dry riverbed littered with sharp rocks. He picked fights with the biggest and meanest bullies in school and came home fat lipped and bloody nosed. Some days he didn't come home at all. The harder Frank and Gisele tried to keep him safe, the harder he chafed against them. "I'm going to die one way or another," he said. "In the meantime, I'm going to make the most of living."

One evening at the start of the school year, Killian took a nasty tumble while rollerblading and split his chin. As he sat holed up on the armchair, sulking and playing Xbox, Gisele took the controller from his hands, knelt at his feet, and held his hands in her own. "Please," she said. "Don't do this to me. I can't bear it, Killian." The sob caught in her throat, her face flushed. "I can't bear to watch you die."

Alice, around the corner, stepped back and out of view into the hallway. The soup tray she'd brought Killian felt laden with bricks.

Killian shook his head. "I need you to promise me that you won't make me suffer." He patted her hand. "I don't want that, Mom. I don't want to become a poltergeist."

"I can fix this, Killian. I can make it so that you survive, I can improve the spell—"

"I don't want to," Killian insisted. He pulled his hand from hers and shifted to move back to his game. He stilled halfway through the motion. "I want your promise. If you don't, I'll run away. I'll go somewhere you'll never find me, and I'll kill myself there. I won't be a ghost. I won't let you do that to me. So if you want me to stay alive, you better promise."

The words suspended between them. Alice waited for the reaction she expected from Gisele—fury, rage, lashing out to deliver pain. Instead, Gisele bowed her head. "Okay." Gisele wept. "I promise."

Killian seemed to watch her for a moment, then he touched her hair. "Mom," he said quietly. "Do you want me to show you my game?"

A fragile smile broke across Gisele's face, and she wiped her tears away. "Yes, my love. I'd love to see your game. Show me."

It wasn't fair, Alice thought, that after all she and Bronwyn suffered at Gisele's hands, only Killian received her tenderness. That Gisele could grant him the mercy of making his own decisions while she beat Bronwyn bloody and tossed her aside, while she strangled Alice with the strands of her own power. She was happy for Killian, that he had Gisele's love, but it didn't lessen the sting of not having it herself.

Later that same night, Killian knocked on her half-cracked door. His face was wan and determined.

"What's up?" Alice asked.

Killian closed the door behind him, then crossed the room to sit on Alice's bed, his legs pretzeled. The mattress depressed with his weight, her calculus textbook sliding toward him. "I need to know. He was in pain? A lot of it?"

"The poltergeist?"

"Yeah."

Alice swallowed thickly. "Yes," she said. "He was in a lot of pain."

"For years?" He was avoiding her eyes, rolling his hagstone bracelet around his wrist. "And he didn't know what was going on anymore? He didn't know himself at all?"

"That won't be you, Killy." Alice reached out to still his fidgeting. "I won't let it be."

"How?" He barked out a humorless laugh. "Because you offered so much help to that boy? What's the chance you'll find another poltergeist to practice on before I die, Beau?"

Alice flinched. "You have to trust me." Alice forced a smile. "I've been preparing for this my entire life. You know I'm an overachiever—I'm hardly planning to drop the ball when the stakes are this high."

Killian skirted her gaze. "I've made a decision. I've already told Mom."

"Oh?" Alice closed her calculus textbook, leaving her pencil inside as a bookmark.

"I want to die for real." Killian leveled his chin. "I have to be able to say no if I don't want it. And I don't want it, Beau."

Alice's hands clapped around her mouth, her breath moving fast through her fingers. It had never occurred to Alice that "no" could be an option where her mother was concerned. Even though she knew it was coming, she was freshly stunned, not only by the force of Killian's "no," but by his ability to say it at all. His self-proclaimed agency in saying, "I will not follow Gisele's plan, I do not want this, you cannot make me." And in doing so, his saying, too, that Gisele did not know him as well as he knew himself. Alice's mouth parted, and she wet her lips, trying to scrounge up the words to tell him how brave he was, but they slipped away at the looming and terrifying presence of a future without him, even as the smallest, faintest trickle of relief settled near the bottom of her spine. *What will it mean*, it whispered, *to be free of that yoke?* She shook the thought away.

Alice reached across the bed, took his hand, and squeezed it tight. "We can still do this, Killy. I'm willing to find a way to make this work. I can save you—you just have to let me. Give me a chance."

"It's your life, Beau, and I don't want it." He swallowed thickly. "I need you to promise you won't let me become like that little boy."

After Killian went to bed, Gisele and Alice sat in the sickly yellow light of the kitchen. Gisele had brewed a pot of chamomile tea, and the only sound in the room was the clink of her spoon against the china as she stirred in her honey. An abandoned cigarette smoked in the ashtray by her elbow.

"He doesn't know what he wants," Alice said. "He's only a child. He could change his mind when he gets older."

"Yes," Gisele agreed.

"But if not, we have to do what he says. Don't we?"

Gisele said nothing. She tilted her face toward the light, looking suddenly old. "We'll make a contingency plan."

"Contingency for what?"

"For if he changes his mind, of course." Gisele gnawed on her lower lip, a moment of uncharacteristic weakness. "It's better to be prepared."

"And if he doesn't?"

"Then, we promised," Gisele said quietly. "We'll let him go."

And so every day that summer, Gisele dragged Alice back to that haunted house until Alice could channel the poltergeist at will, for as long as he wanted. He would watch her approach from the window with hungry eyes, grabbing at her frantically as he slipped inside her body. That first roar of pain as her selfhood was shoved out of the way, her gums burning, veins searing. Gisele interrogated the poltergeist for hours on the ritual his mother had conducted to trap him there. The one mercy was that possession always blacked out her memories beyond the first few moments. She almost came to look forward to those sessions, if only to have a few hours of respite from inhabiting her own body. The blackouts offered solace, even if she paid a price for these long sessions of channeling—her muscles cramping and aching as they chattered with cold; the devastating brain fog that clung to her waking hours; a continuous exhaustion that saw her sleeping thirteen hours a night. When Gisele finally learned how to perform the ritual to her satisfaction in August, it took Alice weeks to readapt to the daily task of inhabiting her own body.

She could have asked Gisele about those sessions. Her mother almost seemed to be waiting for it, her lies prepared. But Alice didn't care to look behind the curtain. She was afraid of what she might find there, in the smooth cool darkness of what her body chose to forget.

NINE

ALICE PACKS SPARSELY: t-shirts, jeans, thick socks, toothbrush. She changes her mind about makeup twice. Eyeliner might grant her confidence, but where does she expect to wear it? A tube of lipstick, then. A canister of dry shampoo. Now, her comfort sweater.

It isn't real—that she's packing to leave, that she doesn't know when she'll return—until she spots Eli's glass of water still on the bathroom counter, and then, very suddenly, it hits her all at once. He doesn't know she'll be gone by the time he returns tonight, and she can't tell him because she can't tell him why. Alice careens over the sink. She digs her nails into the meat of her cheeks, breathing hard and fast. Even in the moment, she's ashamed by the drama of it, the loudness of her breath, as if there's a protocol to breaking down correctly.

Not now, of course, but during other, more quotidian nightmares, Alice prides herself on her cool head. During Eli's relapse, she was the one who packed his bags for the in-treatment facility; she'd called Susan, made all the arrangements within an afternoon with brutal efficiency. Alice's "scary calm," Eli called it. She imagines it comes from conducting the séances—from swallowing her own panic and fear to prioritize managing others' overwhelming emotions. It's a lesson she applies to all parts of her life—with Eli, with her clients, now, at the salon—letting her persona bob her along outwardly while she situates her true self at a distance, untouched.

In all her imaginings of this moment, she'd thought Bronwyn's finding her would prove the exception to her calm. She'd thought there would be more screaming. She's expected, at the very least, to cry. But she's holding relatively steady. *Reach for that calm, Alice. A deep breath, and another. Grab your towel and keep going.* She considers, in a feeble way, if she could get away with running now that Bronwyn has found her. It wouldn't be as easy this time, with her scent so fresh, though a border might do it since Alice doubts Bronwyn owns a passport. Another new life, a new name, a new self. But this, too, would require leaving Eli, and that banishes the air from Alice's lungs.

She thinks of the last time Eli's recovery slipped, and she covered all the mirrors in his house with spare bedsheets. The times he's kissed her cutting scars as if he could read the trauma from her skin. How he sits knee to knee with her after a nightmare, whispering, "You are here, you are sitting on the bed, the comforter is bunched around your knees, you are safe," with unending patience until the sun eases through their blinds. How he makes her French toast waterlogged with syrup every Saturday morning, shuffling around solemn and attentive, refilling her coffee. How their first date lasted two weeks—bouncing between each other's houses with brief intermissions for work. How, the first time they had sex, Alice planned to leave as soon as he fell asleep, but he kept her awake—talking about favorite films, worst manager stories, strangest dreams—until Alice lost her desire to escape. How on the second night, he talked about his eating disorder and Alice, her cuts. That she'd known from that second night that this was someone she wanted to build a life with because he, too, had survived an unspeakable thing, and understood everything she could never say. The way he felt, if not like safety precisely, like coming home. No. There will be no more running.

She lugs the duffel to the bedroom door, then she thinks of Bronwyn, in her rumpled and sweat-stained clothes, and Alice returns to the closet. She picks out a sea foam green sweater and another pair of jeans. Soft black socks. A pair of clean underwear that may be too big for her sister. Sets them all on the bed alongside a fresh towel. This is above and beyond her blackmail-conscripted duties. No one can say that Alice doesn't care.

Bronwyn is waiting at the foot of the stairs, her hip against the banister and one foot a step above the other. The gesture is probably meant to look casual but it comes off as uncomfortable, uncertain. "You shouldn't be lugging that duffel." Bronwyn reaches for it but stops when Alice waves her off.

"You need a shower," she says. As Bronwyn's face twists into a snarl, Alice hastens to add, "Genuine offer. Use my bathroom. I left some clothes on the bed if you want them. Last door on the right." After a moment, Bronwyn nods, a semblance of—dare Alice say it—gratitude, and squeezes by. Bronwyn doesn't thank her, but then again, Alice isn't sure why she'd expected her to.

In the kitchen, Alice rinses their glasses and sets them in the dishwasher. She still hasn't eaten yet today, but she feels nauseous, and in all likelihood, if she puts anything in her mouth, it'll likely come right back up. Not morning sickness, though. She can rarely stomach anything most days but cold water and coffee until midafternoon. Still, she should give herself the option to eat later. She scans the pantry and shoves a fistful of protein bars into the middle pocket of her purse. Then she spends a few minutes scrubbing the stain of Bronwyn's heel prints from the stairs.

When she finishes, Alice tries to sit at the kitchen table, to wait like a reasonable person, but there's too much nervous energy in her body, and soon, she's up and pacing the first floor. She finds herself in the living room and touches the cool panel of the bay window. It leaves her fingerprints on the glass. The truth is that Alice loves this life. Maybe not the neighborhood, but the garden out back and the landscaping service that mows their lawn every Tuesday morning in good weather and plows the driveway when it snows. She loves the photo of her and Eli on the wall, the one where his kiss is pressed to her temple and she's cackling because at the moment the picture was snapped, Eli whispered, "A mosquito definitely bit me in the ass." She loves that in this life, her most complicated problem is that Susan disapproves of her, that the worst Susan can do is impose on them for Easter and criticize what brands Alice cooks with.

She doesn't think about what she'll say to Eli when she pulls her phone from her pocket and dials his number. She doesn't think up acceptable excuses, doesn't consider last night's fight or its resumption that morning, or what it'll mean if he actually answers. In that moment, the only thing she wants to hear is his voice. It overpowers all of her better instincts.

"One second." There's the faintest whisper of mall music in the background, the soft murmur of many voices. "Hey. Are you still planning to meet us for dinner? Because my mom decided on J. Alexander's, and she pitched a Susan-grade fit when she found out they moved to West Bloomfield." Alice steadies herself against a wall. He sounds cautious but gentle, as if their fight never happened. This is the hardest part of loving Eli—he will let her hurt him over and over and forgive and forgive, even when he shouldn't.

She blinks back the sudden sting. "Eli, listen. I have to leave for a few days." In the silence that follows, Alice tries to imagine his face. Likely frowning. She'd love to smooth the knots between his eyebrows away with her thumb. She knows she's acting unforgivably.

"So you weren't sick in the grocery store yesterday," he says. She shouldn't resent his being right, but she does. She resents herself more for expecting him to believe her.

"I wasn't," she confirms. "You're right. I lied." There's nothing she can say that will satisfy him and still be true.

"Where are you going?"

"It's an emergency."

"What kind of emergency? What's going on, Alice?"

"It's a family emergency." This is a mistake because it raises more questions than Alice has time to answer. She can taste the truth in her mouth and how bitter it will be.

"*My* family?" It's an understandable confusion.

"No. Mine."

"I'm coming home." It's the matter-of-fact way he says it that frightens her. The calm in his voice, the decisive force. It's unexpected. She hasn't told him enough to warrant it. What is he imagining for this to be his first response? What would his response be if he knew the truth? Alice wants him here, wants him here until her skin twinges, but if he comes, the door on her past will swing open so wide that she'll never be able to close it again. "No," she says. "Don't."

"Alice."

"Don't come home."

"Is this what happened yesterday? Why you lied?"

Alice hesitates, then decides she might as well be honest since everything is already going to shit. "Yeah."

"Mom and I can be back in two hours, tops."

"I don't want you here." Another lie, of course, but she hasn't done all this running to expose him to the Family now. She can't allow her fear to outweigh his safety. She's not that selfish.

"You don't mean that." His voice sounds husky and he stops to clear his throat. "Your family can't even come up in conversation without you shaking like a leaf. You don't have to handle this alone."

Alice can't help herself—she buries her mouth against her sweater and sobs. "Promise me you won't come."

"Can you at least tell me what's going on?"

"I can't. Please don't ask me to."

"Haven't I earned your trust by now? After everything we've shared, how can you still think I'll hurt you?" The first time she'd let him properly see her scars, they were two months into their relationship. She'd found excuse after excuse to avoid undressing in front of him, once even desperate enough to wear a dress during a late September snowstorm so she could wear her clothes during sex. It had been one thing for him to know they existed, to feel them on her skin. It had been another thing entirely to lay them bare. A vulnerability she wasn't ready for. She couldn't meet his eyes until he reached out to trace the vegvisir on her hip. "I didn't realize they were patterns," he said quietly. He pressed her palm to his own scarred chest. "We've survived so much to find each other." Then, with a mischievous smile, he added, "Between the two of us, we have enough scars to impress even Papa Roach, don't you think?" Their bodies, nothing to be ashamed of, toughened with survival.

She wants to tell him. It's right there, at the top of her throat. Alice swallows, then says, "You've never asked me about them before."

"You didn't want to talk about it. I didn't need to. I don't know." He sighs. "You told me you weren't in contact with them?"

She hears the question in his voice, so she redirects. "It isn't about trust."

"Then why won't you tell me what's going on?"

"You wouldn't believe me." Her tears leak between her phone and her skin, and she wipes the screen with her sleeve. It makes her feel scaldingly like a teenager. "You wouldn't believe me even if I told you."

"Of course, I would—"

"No, Eli." Her laugh is bitter. "No one would. It sounds crazy. It *is* crazy."

"Try me."

"Beau." Bronwyn's voice echoes from the end of the corridor, bouncing off the high ceilings of the foyer. "Do you have a belt somewhere I can borrow? These jeans are falling off me."

"Give me a minute," Alice shouts back. Into the phone, she whispers, "I have to go."

"Is someone there?" In Eli's voice she hears a curl of fear. She shouldn't have called him. "Alice, are you safe?"

"I have to go."

"Are you safe? Do you want me to call the cops?"

"No, don't do that. I'm safe, I swear. Don't call them and don't come home early."

"Alice—"

"I have to go."

"Isabeau!"

"Don't do this, Alice."

"I love you." Alice hangs up the phone and wipes her face before she walks into the foyer.

"Some help, please?" Bronwyn stands at the top of the stairs, leaning over the railing.

"Is that my bathrobe?"

"Well, the pants are too big, and I didn't want to put my dirty clothes on again."

Alice pinches the bridge of her nose. "In the closet, second shelf from the bottom."

"Cool, thanks." Bronwyn straightens as if she's about to turn, then she hesitates. "You all right? Your face is red."

Alice touches her cheek. "I'm fine."

When Bronwyn meets her in the foyer, she smells like Alice's perfume. She's successfully found a belt for the jeans, but the sweater slips at her shoulder, showing the concerning jut of her collarbones. Alice is sure that if she went upstairs, she'd find the bathroom counter a mess of creams and lotions, clothes hanging like pulled intestines from the slit of the dresser.

Bronwyn looks scrubbed and raw but clean. Better than before. She doesn't thank Alice for the clothes. "Were you talking to someone?"

"Just Eli. I told him I'd be gone for a few days."

"What'd he say?"

"Doesn't matter."

"Sure it does." The way Bronwyn controls all the space in a room has always astounded Alice. Even in the Little House, the air gasped after her. Even now, Bronwyn's presence encompasses the whole of Alice's house. "Is he going to be cool about it?"

"As a cucumber," Alice deadpans. "Nothing more peaceful than being abandoned with your batty mom by your partner with zero context. He's positively serene."

"Will he try to pull some hero bullshit?"

"No. He wanted to call the cops, but I told him not to. So, unless you want me to change my mind, let's get a move on."

"All right, all right, I get it." They head into the kitchen, where Alice left her luggage. Bronwyn slings Alice's duffel across her shoulder, then staggers before catching her balance on the pantry door. Alice can't help herself—she laughs. Bronwyn grins, a touch wolfish. "What the hell did you pack?"

Alice waves her through the garage door but hesitates at the threshold. Her book of Sudoku still sits on the kitchen table amongst crumbs of whole wheat bread and Eli's favorite seeded crackers. The brush of late winter light patches across the table and the carpet. She promises herself this won't be the last time she sees it. She'll be home soon.

TEN

Age Eighteen

In Alice's first apartment, one of her neighbors had a loose mushroom vent they refused to fix. They were older, couldn't hear the sound it made, which bore a disconcerting resemblance to tinnitus. It went on for months, with no escape, worse on the windy days, piercing through Alice's dreams until eventually, she stopped hearing it at all. When the health department accrued enough complaints to issue the neighbors a fine, and they reluctantly fixed the vent, Alice noticed more acutely than anything else, the absence of it. Killian's impending death was a thing like that. It draped their lives like a blanket. Fear, yes, always; terror, yes; risks and adrenaline and too much cortisol, yes—until eventually they forgot to be afraid.

In late July, Frank talked Gisele into an overnight trip. With tight lips, Gisele explained that Frank wanted some time away as a couple to try to reconnect. They left Bronwyn in charge. When

Gisele tried to check the cards for Killian's safety, Frank confiscated her deck, slipping it into his front pocket. "No excuses, no future-watching, no magic," he said firmly. "We're going on this goddamn trip, woman." And though Gisele picked up her overnight bag, her eyes were trained on the tip of the black velvet pouch, it's dark contrast against the red of Frank's shirt. Alice suspects the only reason Gisele went at all was because he had them.

The minute Frank and Gisele pulled out of the driveway, Bronwyn dragged Alice to the living room, where Killian had already set himself up in front of the Xbox. She had to shake his shoulder to get his attention. "What do you want?"

Bronwyn patted his shoulder. "How would you like to be a big boy today?"

"You don't have to talk to me like that. I'm ten, not two." Killian rolled his eyes, but he paused his game.

"We're going to a party tonight," Bronwyn said.

Killian frowned. "No, you aren't. Gisele said you had to watch me."

The party was Bronwyn's idea, to celebrate Alice's graduation. "He's been fine ten years. We can take one night off," she'd said. Alice wasn't convinced, but when she tried to argue, Bronwyn had scoffed. "Come on, you're always a good girl. Do something bad for once." There'd been something feral in Bronwyn's eyes as she said it. Her sister was not taking no for an answer. "I'll even be DD."

At Killian's protest, Alice glanced at Bronwyn and swallowed before reciting her scripted lines. "We think you're old enough to behave. I used to stay home alone when I was your age." He'd been better that summer about keeping out of trouble. Alice told herself that their leaving him alone was a reward, proof that he could be trusted. She swallowed the unease at the back of her throat.

"It'll be our little secret, okay?" Bronwyn gave him a big smile and ruffled his hair.

Killian tussled it back into place. "What's in it for me?"

"Weren't you listening? You get to stay here by yourself."

"You're going to have to sweeten the deal."

"Seriously?" Alice said. "What do you want?"

Killian thought about it for a long moment, putting his hand on his chin in a mock thinking face. "I want you to get me *Grand Theft Auto V*."

Alice blinked. She'd expected something bigger. "Why don't you just ask Gisele?"

"Dad already said no. He said it's too old for me."

"Don't you think they'll notice?"

"Mom won't care." He shrugged. "And I won't play it around Dad."

Bronwyn glanced down to check her cell phone. "All right, all right. *Grand Theft Auto V*, it is. Make sure you stay in the house, though, okay? And don't get into trouble."

"Sure." Killian shrugged, already pulling the game up again. "I'll stay right here."

After Alice dressed, she went to Bronwyn's room. Bronwyn was leaning into the mirror above her dresser, applying a brick-red lipstick with the focus of a chemist mixing precarious chemicals. On the bed, she'd laid out a black dress, a few long necklaces to be layered on top of one other, and a pair of fishnet tights.

Bronwyn's eyes found hers in the mirror, and she set the tube of lipstick down on the dresser. As the tube hit the wood, her glamour spell kicked in. Her skin took on a sun-kissed bronze cast, and her eyelashes lengthened. "Fuck." Bronwyn inspected herself in the mirror, wrinkling her nose. "I fucked up the glamour again—my eyelashes look like feathers." She reached for her makeup remover and began to scrub her mouth. As the lipstick came off, the glamour faded.

Alice stepped up beside her to inspect the sigil carved on the lipstick. "Give me your tweezers. The line on this part of the sigil isn't long enough, see?" Alice used the tweezers to carefully correct the spell and handed the tube back to Bronwyn. "Try it now."

Bronwyn nodded her thanks, then paused, blinking. "Why are you dressed up like Hippie Sandy the Psychic?"

Alice looked down at her own dress, the long length of it—one of her Medium outfits, the rhinestone belt cinched around her violet waist—and the back of her neck prickled with embarrassment. "I don't have anything else."

"You're not wearing that to the party." Bronwyn leaned back into the mirror, reapplying the glamoured lipstick. This time, she smiled at what she saw, and picked up her mascara. "Borrow something from my closet."

"It has to be long-sleeved."

"Why?" Bronwyn's face was tight as she met Alice's eyes in the mirror. "The runes again?"

"I don't want to show them off. That's all." Alice hugged her arms and glanced back at the dress on Bronwyn's bed. "And I don't think anything in your closet is going to fit me. Are you wearing that tonight?"

"Do you want to wear it instead?"

Alice imagined wearing the dress and Bronwyn's many necklaces while flirting with a boy over a beer keg and swaying to a pop ballad she'd heard on the radio and hated. How incredibly normal it seemed, how simple. When she pictured herself there, she lurched with an excited, awkward dread. "Maybe I should stay here with Killian."

Bronwyn strolled over and pulled the dress over her head. For a moment, Alice could see the curve of her stomach. Bronwyn had always been colt-thin, but now there was a heaviness to her, a heft to her where there had been none before. It looked good on her, this filling out. She looked healthy. "Stop worrying, Dumb-Beau." Bronwyn flashed Alice a grin. "What's the worst thing he can do? Eat all the chips in the house?" When Alice said nothing, Bronwyn continued. "Isabeau Glass, you are not backing out of this party. The kid will be fine."

"Okay, okay." Alice plopped on the bed as Bronwyn flipped through the other dresses in her closet. After a few minutes of hemming and hawing, she pulled out a green velvet dress with long sleeves, and threw it at Alice with barked orders to put it on. "I've got some extra fishnets, too, that'll cover your thigh scars."

As Alice looked at the dress, her cheeks heated. "I can't wear this. It's so—"

"Hot?" Bronwyn tilted her head and raised an eyebrow. "Normal?"

"Short," Alice finished. "It's so short."

Bronwyn rolled her eyes. "That is the point, Isabeau. Now hurry up and put it on."

The party, according to Bronwyn, was a dud. Too much beer and not enough liquor, too many sweaty boys playing beer pong. Bronwyn's boyfriend was supposed to meet them there but never showed. They called it an hour in and Bronwyn drove them home. She was in a sour mood, scowling as she stared out the window. Perhaps this fall, Alice thought, she could apply to colleges. If she left home, she could do this all the time—go to concerts and stay out late with her friends. Every day could be like this one. Every day could be filled with normal things.

Later, Alice would revisit that drive home a million times. What if they'd left half an hour sooner? What if they hadn't gone to the party at all?

Mostly Alice knows they couldn't have done anything differently. That it wasn't fair, what she and Bronwyn were asked to do for their brother, that they deserved any and all shreds of happiness they could find. Mostly. But some days, Alice knows in her heart that it's her fault, what happened next.

When Alice opened the front door to the scent of cooking, she knew they were fucked. The clock over the mantel said eight thirty, too late for dinner, but Gisele always cooked off her sadness. Bronwyn paled. "Wasn't she supposed to be gone all night?" Alice whispered.

Bronwyn nodded, her eyes wide, and she peeked around the corner. Alice took a step behind her. "You're home early," Bronwyn said, with feigned casualness.

"So are you." Gisele glanced up from the pot, and grimaced. "Didn't enjoy your party?" Seeing the expressions on their faces, Gisele's lip curled. "You should know by now what a bad liar your brother is."

"Where's Frank?" Bronwyn pulled out a chair from the kitchen table and plopped down. Alice followed, awkwardly hovering near the head of the table, trying to stifle her panic. Bronwyn went out all the time, so what did it matter if Alice had too?

"Frank's staying elsewhere tonight." Gisele looked Alice up and down with a raised eyebrow that made Alice want to disappear. Then Gisele turned back to the stove. "I expected better of you."

Bronwyn and Alice exchanged a look. "Did you guys get into a fight?" Bronwyn asked.

Gisele slammed the wooden spoon down on the counter. "Why, no, of course not, little love. It was a beautiful evening."

Bronwyn tilted her head, her expression blank. Alice sucked in a breath as Bronwyn quipped, "Peachy! Sure is swell to hear your date night went so well. A-plus day for the Glass family. We're thriving."

Gisele crossed the kitchen so quickly that Alice barely had time to jump away before Gisele whacked the wooden spoon across Bronwyn's face. The crack left a silence in its wake, barely broken by Bronwyn's gasp. Her eyes watered and her cheek turned a streaky red. She blinked slowly before her face morphed into manufactured boredom. "You're losing your touch. That barely even hurt."

Gisele raised her hand again, but Bronwyn's arm shot out and ripped the spoon away. There was a moment where the room seemed to still at the arc of Bronwyn's arm rising, all of them watching it, the impossible parabola of it, until Bronwyn brought down the spoon with cold fury against Gisele's jaw. Alice threw herself between them. She tried to grab Bronwyn's arm, but at the same moment, Gisele lunged, bodychecking Alice, who fell back against the wall. Alice's arm rang with pain as she instinctively threw her hands up, protecting her head, while Gisele pivoted toward her, shoulders heaving. But before she could attack, Bronwyn brought the spoon down again between Gisele's shoulder blades. Gisele's knees buckled but she caught herself against the kitchen counter, toppling against it. She closed her eyes briefly and when she opened them again, her face had relaxed. As if none of it had ever happened. "Go fetch your brother from the yard. The pot roast will be ready in a few minutes."

Alice scrambled up and tugged Bronwyn by the arm until her sister tossed the spoon onto the kitchen table and followed her. Outside, the dusk was settling into the mocking cruelty of a perfect sunset, in layers of orange and purple, the blue lingering at the crown of the sky like a fog. The light darkened the tops of the trees. "What the fuck?" Alice was chanting under her breath. "What the fucking fuck did you do?"

As soon as they slid the door closed, Bronwyn hissed a stream of expletives.

"What the hell were you thinking, hitting her like that?" Alice grabbed Bronwyn's shoulder. "What the fuck is wrong with you?"

Bronwyn ripped her shoulder out of Alice's grasp. "Like she didn't deserve it. Maybe next time, she'll think twice before she hits me."

"She's going to kill you in your fucking sleep, is what she's going to do. And probably me, too, for just happening to be in the same room."

"Please," Bronwyn snarled. Her cheek was already beginning to puff, the welt darkening to maroon at the edges. "You're too precious to die, you spooky bitch."

"Bronwyn." Alice tried to reach for her arm, but Bronwyn jerked it out of reach, stomping a few feet away to stare down the spirea bushes. Lightning bugs flickered in the distance, their dark bodies strangely naked and vulnerable in the receding light.

"I'll sleep at my boyfriend's tonight," Bronwyn said finally. The wind lifted strands of her hair into her face, the sunset coaxing gold highlights across her head. "You should find somewhere else to sleep too."

"I don't have anywhere to go." Alice swallowed hard, tightening her fists around the fabric of her dress. Her sister shrugged. "Bronwyn—"

"Not my problem." Bronwyn folded her arms, glaring off toward the tree line. "Let's just find Killian, okay?"

Alice scanned the backyard, though she knew if he'd heard their voices, he'd have already come running. "I don't see him."

"I'm going to strangle that weasel when I get my hands on him," Bronwyn whispered, baring her teeth. Then she shouted, "Fuckhead! Get over here!"

"You think he's in the clearing?"

"He's always in the damn clearing, the little—"

Alice spotted Killian's hoodie draped across one of the swings on the playset and handed it to Bronwyn.

Bronwyn huffed and stalked down the path toward the clearing, Alice half-jogging to keep up. The long grass whispered along their ankles, tickling through their fishnets, and the softness of the evening reminded Alice of that first day when they'd moved into the Little House. The sweet hot smell of summer, the sticky sap of dandelions on their shins.

When they stood in the middle of the clearing, Bronwyn stopped. "Shut up a sec."

"I wasn't saying anything—"

"Then why are you still talking?"

"Bronwyn, this isn't my fault!"

"Fuck, just shut the fuck up, Beau, and let me find him."

From the outside, Bronwyn's gift didn't look impressive. She stood entirely still, eyes closed, spinning in a slow circle, one hand held out in front of her. But as Alice looked toward the creek, Killian emerged from behind a faraway tree. He looked a little frightened. "You ass," Alice shouted, running toward him.

Behind her, she heard Bronwyn whimper, "I can't feel him, oh gods. Beau. Fuck. He's not there."

They found him caught between two boulders, face down, blue lipped, water bloated. Later, Killian would tell Alice that he'd climbed a tree to read and had fallen asleep on a branch. He'd rolled off and hit his head on the rocks below.

A million times, Alice had imagined what it would be like when Killian died. She'd pictured his room, lit by candles, him lying in bed pale but peaceful, his hands crossed over his chest. But not this violent grief. Not Killian perfectly whole and dazed, standing beside his own ruined body as Bronwyn and Alice wept.

ELEVEN

ALICE TRIES TO INSIST they drive her car, which is new with good mileage and has had an oil change sometime in the last decade, but Bronwyn points out that she can't abandon hers in Saginaw.

Bronwyn's hatchback doesn't look up to the journey. None of the panels match, and the interior of the driver's side door has been stripped of all its civilizing plastic, leaving only the wire and thin brown metal frame. The only thing that comforts Alice is the wooden disk hanging from the rearview mirror—a sigil warding away harm, promising safe travel, and rendering them invisible to speed traps. The back seat is cluttered with fast food wrappers, empty soda bottles, balled-up receipts, and a fiberfill pillow placed neatly atop a folded fleece blanket.

"Have you been sleeping in here?"

Bronwyn shrugs. "You have any idea how long I looked for you? Working with an energy lock isn't an exact science." The dashboard knobs are missing, so Bronwyn turns on the heat with pliers. "Some of us can't afford three weeks of hotels."

"You couldn't have tried a location spell?"

Bronwyn pulls out of the driveway before she responds. "I would've, but I couldn't get the damn thing to work. I couldn't remember what oil Gisele used on the cord."

"Jasmine," Alice offers.

Bronwyn gives her a sidelong glance. "I'll keep that in mind next time I have to track you down."

The whole car reeks of smoke. Bronwyn has been disposing of her cigarettes in the remains of a Big Gulp Slurpee, and the stubs and ash clump together in the blue raspberry syrup. Alice rolls down her window, and sucks in the cold clean air. "Pull over at the gas station up the street."

"Why?"

"The cup."

Bronwyn snorts. "A couple inches left at least." She shakes it at Alice, the cigarettes sloshing. The pre-bile sours Alice's mouth and she gags. Barely manages to hold her stomach down.

"Seriously?"

"We should buy some air fresheners."

"Behold—how far she's risen. Your ash trays scented or something?"

"I can't drive all the way to Ohio with that thing in the goddamn car."

"Gods save me." But mercifully, Bronwyn stops at the nearest gas station. Alice throws her door open so hard it bounces on its hinges, Bronwyn's cackle chasing her inside. When Alice returns with a handful of scented trees, Bronwyn is lounging against the hatchback. A quick glance reveals other minimal tidying, the back seat now mostly wrapper-free and the Slurpee gone.

"Happy?"

"Better."

Bronwyn works open one of the packets and hangs the tree on the rearview mirror. It works, at first, but after a few minutes of the cardboard trees clacking softly together, Alice begs Bronwyn to smoke with the windows down. Bronwyn snaps, "For the love of fuck!" but agrees to crack the windows.

It's near 4 p.m., and the sun is already setting by the time they pull onto the highway. Bronwyn holds the cigarette pack out toward Alice. In their teenage years, they stole their mother's menthols from her purse, and traded drag for drag on the roof of the camper. The space behind Alice's back-most molars aches with the memory of nicotine. She shakes her head.

"Right." Bronwyn bumps her palm against her skull. "I keep forgetting. You aren't showing."

"I'm barely anything yet. Maybe five weeks." Alice debates telling Bronwyn she quit smoking thirteen months ago, but most likely, Bronwyn would view that as a low-blow brag. Alice forages through her purse and finds a piece of pineapple-flavored gum, which will busy her mouth and ward off the nicotine cravings. "I found out yesterday. Before all this."

Bronwyn whistles. "Rough day, then."

"Oh no, super stress-free."

"Your boyfriend must be thrilled."

"He has no idea." Alice flinches. Eli and Susan are likely at dinner by now, Susan insisting Eli eat. Alice imagines the plump black and red leather booth, the red and silver glints in Eli's golden hair under the glass chandeliers, anxiety stifling his appetite as he picks over his wedge salad and shoves off the dressing with the side of his fork. Susan, with her vermillion nails, trying and failing to gracefully inhale an onion ring the size of her cell phone. "We don't want kids."

"You plan on telling him?"

Alice shakes her head and pulls her phone from her pocket. She means to scroll through her email, but there's a missed call from Eli. She drops the phone onto her lap.

"Hard to hide it around week twelve. Especially with our build."

"It's none of your business."

"Hey, we don't need to talk about it if you don't want to." When Alice doesn't respond, Bronwyn clears her throat. "You panicking yet? About being a mom?"

"I don't know that I will be."

"Assuming it's a girl, I mean."

"I don't know if I'll be a mother either way."

Bronwyn turns her attention to the road, worrying the corner of her mouth. "Fair enough. It's not like raising girls is all rainbows and unicorns either."

Eli will be devastated that she told someone else first. She's ashamed, will add this to the tally of domestic treasons she's committing. But right now, the second line of that pregnancy test is an argument limited to her and her body. Once she tells Eli, they'll be in it together, with all the deciding and weighing and factors and compromises involved, and her body will become at once *the problem* and *the baby*. For now, the pregnancy is fermenting, is still as hypothetical as the consequences of not telling him yet.

It's uncomfortable, being alone with her sister. It could be the years apart, or it could be that they don't know how to speak to each other without their brother perched between them. Her eyes keeping flicking to the back middle seat where Killian should be sitting.

When Alice doesn't respond, Bronwyn sighs. "I'm not trying to upset you, Isabeau." Then she should not have come to Alice's house with her mouth full of threats. But she says nothing, balls the paper wrapper of her gum, slips it into her purse. The low sounds of a saccharine pop ballad float from the radio.

"Do you ever think about Gisele's people?" Alice asks. It's a desperate attempt to change the subject, one that Bronwyn clearly doesn't appreciate.

Bronwyn makes an impatient noise in the back of her throat and flips the visor to block the setting sun. "Why?" The bitterness in Bronwyn's voice startles her.

Alice finds a loose thread on the sleeve of her turtleneck, and pulls it between her nails, considering the way it strains the fabric. "If we could find our family," she says finally, "we could ask them—"

"How they handled the curse? I've tried to find them, but I've found jack shit. Gisele did a great fucking job of isolating us." Bronwyn glances at Alice's waist and nods to herself, as if deciding something. The hairs on Alice's arm prickle. "Glass probably isn't her real name."

"I figured."

"And I'm pretty sure Gisele isn't her first name either."

"Oh?"

"Ann-Gisel Glass, a French actress from the eighties. That's what pops up if you search Gisele's name online. And if there are other Glass families out there, no one's plugged them into Ancestry.com yet. I've tried every variation of her and her brothers' names."

Alice has heard this story before: A daughter escapes her mother and creates a new life for herself. She starts fresh, down to her name. The past can't hurt her now. Not after how deep she buries it, how many nails she hammers into its coffin. Denial like hers? It rewrites history. Repeat a lie enough times and it tastes like the truth. It's so damn tidy until the threat of resurrection.

"She had to have come from somewhere." Alice can't help but imagine what they could've learned, what their lives could've been like, if they'd had other family. Others with the gifts. She imagines how much less clumsy their adolescent experiments would've been, how much less dependent they might've been on Gisele. Alice's fingers spasm with the muscle memory of magic, and she must remind herself that the feeling no longer means anything to her, not practically. Not with her shadow bound.

"We could always try 23andMe." Bronwyn chuckles. "Find some info on our bio dad too—wouldn't that be wild?"

"Right, because that's the only thing we've been lacking on the family trauma front." Alice means it as a joke, but Bronwyn doesn't laugh.

For a time, the road hums between them, the cold whipping its way through the car. Bronwyn drums the steering wheel in time to a song on the radio. Each fingernail has been painted a different color, now thoroughly chipped. There's a type of sympathetic magic that corresponds to fingers, but Alice can't remember how it works. These kinds of glamour charms, which integrate outward appearance as a spellcasting ingredient, were always Bronwyn's specialty. Neither Alice nor Gisele had the patience to experiment with them, so Bronwyn made all their makeup. Alice had forgotten how each year, Bronwyn had filled their stockings with beetroot blush or arrowroot foundation.

Bronwyn finishes another cigarette and lets the wind drag the butt down the highway. She reaches into the cup holder for her pack, which surprises Alice. Teenage Bronwyn only smoked socially. Once Bronwyn has the cherry lit, their eyes meet. Alice drops her head and pretends to adjust the hem of her shirt, but Bronwyn's gaze lingers uncomfortably.

"Tell me how it's going to go, when we get to the house," Bronwyn says finally. It's an obvious attempt at placation, and it sets Alice's teeth on edge. "We can stop for supplies if there's a Michaels en route. Want to check Google Maps?"

Alice shakes her head. "You'll already have everything I need."

"What, no velvet tablecloth? No Ouija boards and pendulums?" Bronwyn's mouth curls into a smile.

"That's all set decoration. You know that." For a moment, the scent of dandelion root incense burns at the back of her throat, but Alice shakes it away. "We're not going to sit around and hold hands and chant at her."

"What's it going to look like then? Now that you don't have your gift."

Alice considers. "You said she's been touching things?"

Bronwyn swallows thickly. "Yeah."

"Then maybe a Ouija board isn't such a bad idea. It's not like I can talk to her." Alice shifts, clenches and unclenches her fingers. "But I also haven't had the best luck with that in the past."

"Guess we'll wing it then," Bronwyn murmurs. "That's reassuring."

Alice bristles—*then why did you drag me out here?*—but decides it's in her best interest to leave it alone.

After that, they drive mostly in silence with the radio playing a gentle lull, flattening the sounds of the road. An hour in, Alice offers to drive. She means it genuinely—she's made the choice to follow this through, after all—but Bronwyn only laughs. "Yeah. Sure. Good one."

The farther south they drive, the broader the highway, the sharper the trees angle in toward them. Soon, the sun will sink, and Alice wonders if, with the coming night, the trees will braid leaves overtop the road, forming a dark portal to an uncertain future.

TWELVE

Age Eighteen

THE CREMATORIUM RETURNED Killian in a small ceramic pot that was green as new spring shoots. They buried his ashes before dusk in the clearing out back beyond the shed. A two-minute walk from the creek where he'd died. Gisele insisted they dig a hole big enough for a body, refused to explain when Bronwyn asked her why. Their mother stood at the head of the hole, her hair dirty and matted, unbrushed since they'd found Killian's body. Alice braced for Gisele's screams, but she didn't make a sound.

It's hard to grieve someone watching you from a boxelder maple. Alice's mind couldn't process it. Killian in the tree and Killian in the urn. Tree Killian was in a good mood, sitting on a branch, kicking his legs back and forth as if about to launch himself skyward. "This is a good place." He tipped his head back as if he could feel the breeze. "Tell Gisele that I'll like being buried here."

Bronwyn choked when Alice relayed the message but Gisele nodded, her mouth tight. "Good."

Frank didn't come to the funeral. He'd barely spoken since they'd found the body. If he came home, he came late, the air around him hazy with liquor. He slept in Killian's room, the door locked. "He cries," Killian told her, kneading his hands into his thighs. "He thinks it's his fault, because he took Gisele's cards the night I died. He's the only one who doesn't talk to me, but Beau, he has to know I'm right there."

Alice didn't mention the way Frank spat at her, "Damn witches. He was my boy, and you killed him." Everyone grieves differently, and he was drunk and he did not mean it.

When the hole was dug, Gisele upended the urn. She spread Killian's ashes in the dark earth in a chalky line.

Alice's skin chafed against the shovel, a blister forming at the base of her thumb, and she focused on the pain as they filled the hole. Bronwyn gave the earth a final pat, then pulled a long length of crimson ribbon from her pocket. She fastened the knot on a low-hanging branch above. Not a tombstone, but a grave marker all the same. He'd be safe there, where nothing could hurt him again. Soon, it would be Alice's turn to ensure the same for herself.

At the prelude of every séance, her mother would tell those gathered to speak to their dearly departed. "The gifts in our family go to the daughters because power and mourning are always women's work." But in the clearing where Killian lay buried, mother and sisters held hands and didn't speak at all.

In the hours after Killian's funeral, with the evening still wearing dusk at its hemline, a shiny red Grand Am pulled into their driveway at the Little House. Alice's room overlooked the front yard, and the sheen of its headlights caught her attention, flaring across the wall over her bed. She went to the window, watched as Bronwyn slipped from the house, stealing glances over her shoulder. She lugged a small suitcase behind her, an overstuffed backpack slung over one shoulder. As she opened the car door, she paused, noticed Alice framed in the window. By the time Alice raised a hand, she'd already closed the door. Bronwyn hadn't even waited to make sure Alice made it out too. It will eat at Alice later, that vision of the closing door, the headlights pulling out of the driveway, disappearing down the road, leaving Alice behind.

Beside her, Killian said, "I didn't think she would leave without you. I mean, even I waited for you to get out, and I'm dead." He shot her a teasing glance.

Alice couldn't return it. Some pains are so sharp they can't be acknowledged. Instead, she said, "We can still do this, Killy. We can split my body, and we can live together. We can switch week by week, or day by day, or whatever you want. Just don't—" *leave me*.

Killian shook his head. When he spoke again, there was a pleading note in his voice. "It hurts, Beau. Being a ghost. Like my skin is full of bees and I can't do anything about them. I can't live like this."

"Only if you're sure," she said even as she thought, *Please gods, let me go. I'm so close to getting out, to having a life, please hold me to my promise, please let me free.* "Because once I leave, you can't change your mind."

Killian stared out the window, his head tilted up toward the sky. "I'm sure."

The air released, bit by bit, from Alice's lungs.

As the night thickened to miasma and the Little House fell silent, Alice stuffed a duffel bag with clothing, jewelry, and a toothbrush. She pried up the loose floorboard in her room where she'd hidden her savings. The wad of bills was thick, straining the rubber band, but in the scheme of things, insubstantial. It was a combination of her cut of the séance money, and the occasional bills slipped to her by Frank. As soon as she arrived in Columbus, she would need to find a job to support herself, then she could apply to Ohio State in the fall. Of course there was every possibility Gisele would come after her, but what precisely could her mother do? Drag her back to Kirtland by the ear? By then, Killian would have passed on and they'd all be safe. She crept through the house to Gisele's office, breath caught like a binding spell in her chest. If Gisele caught Beau in the filing cabinet, she was dead. She kept waiting for her to appear, eyes darting around the room, plants mimicking the shape of her mother. But she never materialized as Alice retrieved her important documents. Birth certificate, social security card, high school diploma. Then she snuck back to her room and tucked them into the duffel bag.

When she turned, Killian was waiting for her, sitting cross-legged on her bed, like he'd done so many times before. The differences were subtle. The way the weight of him, for instance, didn't distort the mattress. She sat beside him. "There's so much I want to say."

"Me too." Killian passed a hand over his face, a Frank-like gesture, which despite everything twitched a smile out of her. "But it's time to let me go. You promised me." Killian tried to pat her hand, but he passed through her. Her hand, briefly, felt like ice. "I keep forgetting about that." He shook his head.

"I'll miss you more than anything." Alice wished she could hug him, hold his hand, anything to make this final act of leaving feel something like closure.

"I'll miss you too," he said, his smile soft. Even as Alice felt her heart breaking, she rose from the bed and lifted her duffel bag from the ground, slinging it over her shoulder. Killian raised his hand once more and Alice echoed the gesture. She pushed the door open, turning to leave, then staggered back as it swung wide. Gisele was standing there, just outside her room, holding a rag. Before Alice could move, her mother lunged, the rag smothering her face, burning her lungs, her vision blurring to black. The last thing she heard was Killian's wail.

You come to in the shed, slumped against a table. Your throat stinging, nostrils burning from the ether, head pounding the thoughts from your brain.

Your mother paces wall to wall in front of you, pausing now and then to rock on her heels. "It's time, Isabeau. The spell is ready." Her eyes sparkle as she pulls a thick cloth braid from her pajama pants. It's a foot long, two black ribbons woven around a strip of pastel pink cloth, six knots tied down the center like beads, streaked with dried blood. Killian's baby blanket. His blood. Binding magic. Knots can be used to hold intentions, and though you don't know what precisely your mother has knotted into it, you can guess.

"I got the spell to work, just like we imagined," Gisele says. "Except it isn't one spell. It's two: one to make him a poltergeist, the other to tie him to the body instead of the Little House." *The body. Not yours.* Gisele sticks the braid back into her pocket. Killian, hovering nearby, blanches. "Beau, we need to get out of here."

"But before we talk about that, I want to check something." And then your mother holds out her open palm. In the end, she didn't even have to try very hard, did she? You can say you were groggy from the ether. Likely concussed, confused. But the truth is that there's no world in which you would have ever disobeyed her. She'd done such a good job of training you out of questions. Of making sure you knew better than to say—or think—no.

You set your hand in your mother's, your mother gripping tight enough to bruise. You don't move when she reaches into her pocket. *Her tarot cards*, you think. *Where will she put them? The table's in the corner, we're too far away.*

You can't face the intensity in your mother's face, so you glance away. You're looking up at a ruined spiderweb in a corner of the ceiling, the dust and detritus caught in it, when your mother slashes the knife across your palm. You don't flinch till it's already done. And as you curl in on yourself and try to yank your hand back, your mother's grip repositions around your wrist. Blood pools in your palm, and she drops the braid into it, crushes your fingers around the cloth. Killian flies at her, through her, shouting himself raw. *No*, you are thinking. *Even she wouldn't do this to me. It's too far.*

Your mother digs her nails into your wrist until you shriek. "You have to say the words, Isabeau. 'I swear to share this body and share this blood with my brother.' Say it!" You stay silent, her nails squeezing harder and harder. Finally, "It didn't have to be like this. All you had to do was say the words." She twists your hands behind you into cuffs, shackles you to a support pole.

Your molars grind, your palm burning. The faint smell of ghost is masked by the choking ammonia of your urine. If you throw up, you'll suffocate. You don't want to die there. *Please. Not like this.*

The blood on the braid predated Killian's death. Did she plan this from the day he died? Or from the day she promised to let him go?

In 1874, Blanche Monnier fell in love. She begged her mother to let her marry him, but her mother didn't approve. And so her mother did what she reasoned any good mother would do—she locked Blanche in the attic. "I'll let you out," the mother said, "when you agree to break off this foolish engagement."

For twenty-five years, she kept Blanche prisoner in that attic. Naked, shivering, chained to a bed amidst food waste and excrement. Alive but barely, while outside that house, her mother pretended she was dead. She never gave in, not even after her lover passed away—all the articles agree on this. But Alice used to wonder—even if she had relented, would her mother have kept her trapped there anyway?

When they finally found Blanche, chained to her bed, she weighed fifty-five pounds. She had not seen sunlight for two and a half decades. A police officer opened the shutters to her window, and she laughed, breathy and lucid, "Oh, how lovely it is."

In the early years, before Alice became Alice, she used to google pictures of Blanche. Would stare at her skeletal hands and scratchy face and Alice would say to herself, *You see? It could have been worse. You were only locked away for ten days. In the span of a life, it's so little. A mere breath.*

Killian slipped through the doorway of the shed, and Alice strained forward with the instinct to comfort him. If ghosts could cry, his face would have been swollen and red. He clutched his head as if tapping his skull would stimulate his mind. "Ghosts can move things, right? I'll find the key. I'll figure it out. Can't be too hard. We'll get through this, Beau. I'll figure it out."

But she couldn't respond. Couldn't tell him that only a poltergeist could move objects like that. Not with the gag in her mouth.

Alice will only think of Killian before the shed. She will think of him as her sweet, bratty younger brother. She will think of him as a baby cuddled in the crook of her arms, as the feverish six-year-old she fed saltines and barley soup, sour with lemon. The boy who hated chickpeas and lasagna, who plastered his room with Tony Hawk posters, who trusted her.

Before he became that poltergeist, Killian was her brother. And he wanted so very much to be allowed to die.

You can't have this story. This story belongs to me. You can't make me tell it.

But things slip through, don't they, Alice? Beau? The copper blood overflowing in her palm. The ash like broken stars in the earth. The first night, Gisele forgot a bucket and Beau peed herself. Gisele brought a bucket then, set it right beside her, but not a change of clothes. "This is punishment," Gisele said. "You aren't supposed to enjoy it."

Killian sat on the floor on the other side of the shed, his arms draped over his knees, stayed with her the whole night. Probably, he meant to be comforting. He was ten years old. He never wanted this. How can she blame him?

Gisele returned midmorning, carrying a plate of rosemary biscuits slathered in honey. There was a spell baked into the bread—rosemary added for remembrance. Gisele knelt in front of Alice, set the food out of reach on the floor. "You had to know I'd find out about your little escape plan. As if I don't know what kind of weakling I raised." Gisele flicked out a hand, inspected her nails. "If you take the oath, you can eat."

Killian, who stood behind Gisele's shoulder, shook his head. Oh, they were so brave that first day, so strong. They refused to look at Gisele.

"I didn't want to do this to you, but you left me no choice." Gisele's voice was quiet. Threatening. "And you know what I can't comprehend, Isabeau? Is why you're fighting me. If I'd had a chance to do this for my brothers, I would have done it. I wouldn't have needed a chance to think. Don't you love Killian?"

"You're hurting him," Alice said. "You're going to hurt both of us. You promised him this wouldn't happen."

"I didn't have a choice. Why can't you see that, Isabeau?" Gisele glanced up at the ceiling, tears welling in her eyes. "He hasn't even had a life yet. Seventeen, I could accept. Eighteen, I could accept it. But not *ten*."

"He doesn't want this," Alice said, trying to lace her voice with gentleness.

Gisele scoffed. "He doesn't know what he wants. He's a child."

Alice shook her head.

"Swear the damn oath, and everything will be okay. I can fix the rest, later, so he won't feel pain, but first, Isabeau, we have to keep him here. I can't turn him into a poltergeist without knowing he can leave the Little House. He didn't want to be trapped—this is the only way to keep him and keep some of my promise too. You need to be brave now, little love. You need to say the words."

Alice stayed silent.

"Well, little love, I can also tell you that I've drawn more than fifty cards for your future, and in all of them, I win. My love for him wins. I can afford to wait." Gisele picked up the biscuits and left.

In August 1984, Elisabeth Fritzl went missing. Her parents filed a missing person report. Her father passed a thick palm over his mouth as he spoke to the police. "She left us a letter. She's joining a cult." A thing, her father insisted, that Elisabeth had been threatening to do for a while now. It was believable. There was evidence. Planted, of course, because twenty feet below, Elisabeth was trapped in the basement, in an apartment her father built. Like Gisele, Elisabeth's father subdued her with an ether-soaked towel. That basement would be Elisabeth's prison for twenty-four years, and the birthing room of her seven children.

Elisabeth's mother would claim she never suspected anything awry, not once.

If a tree falls in the woods, and a mother locks her daughter in a shed for ten days, and no one bothers to check on her—who is to blame? Whom can you bring yourself to forgive?

If not your sister, then certainly not Frank. Where does he think you went? If he suspected what your mother had done, what part of him won? The monster or the coward?

There is a Frank who drove you to get your ears pierced at thirteen despite your mother forbidding it and a Frank who came alone to every student-teacher conference, and then there is a Frank who saw blood in your mother's eyes and still closed the door and left you alone with her. There is a Frank who loved you and a Frank who didn't love you enough.

On the fifth day, Gisele stopped acknowledging Alice altogether. Her eyes roved the walls, lingering on the chairs and the corners of the room. "Killian, my little love. I miss you," she crooned. "We miss you. Your father cried himself to sleep again last night. Did you see him? He dreams of you. He says your name again and again, like a prayer."

Alice wanted to scream at her, to howl, *You don't love him half as much as we do. We raised him, I bled for his protection spells, what have you ever sacrificed? Even your desire to keep him is selfish.*

Killian knelt in front of her. "Don't look at her. Look at me. We're going to get you out of here. I swear."

You try. You try to hold on. He is so brave for you. He is so young.

You are in your body. Your nails dig into the heel of your palm to the point of pain. Your feet are cold. The car is cold. Bronwyn's car. You are sitting in Bronwyn's car. Your purse is on your foot. Your butt is in the car seat. You are in your body. You are safe. Well, you are safer than you were. Hold on to that: You are not in the shed anymore. No one is hurting you. And you aren't hurting anyone else either.

Yes. Alice blames him. She blames all of them. She blames herself most of all.

If Alice ever retells this story, she will lie. She'll say Beau was strong. She'll say, "I spat at Gisele. That monster. That bitch. I fought, tooth and nail. I told her to go fuck herself. I told her to die. I told her, you'll have to kill me because I won't do it."

Who needs to know she wept in humiliation? That she called Gisele *Mommy*? Begged her, "Mommy, please. Stop. I'll do it, he can have my body, let me go." That in the moment she needed to protect him most, she chose to save herself?

"I swear to share this body and share this blood with my brother. I swear that so long as I have this gift, we will be twined together, soul to soul." The two spells kick in at once—one to turn him into a poltergeist, which sends Killian crashing to his knees. And the other, to bind you together, which you feel as a wrenching tear in your chest.

"Now was that really so hard?" your mother asks. She tilts her face up like she's searching for sunlight. "I want to speak to my son."

Killian looks between you and Gisele, trembling with shock. "You promised me," he whispers, staring directly at you. There's something wrong with his eyes, the sclera threaded with fine black veins, the irises darker than they should be. Blood is both a promise and a tether, a connection and a warning. And a binding like this—braiding one person's soul to another's—there are consequences to this kind of magic. Gisele has turned him into a poltergeist, has tied him to your body, had known he would suffer.

You anticipate Killian's lunge a moment before he leaps for Gisele. He scrabbles at her wrist, leaving scratches on her skin, and she gasps, stumbles back. The braid drops to the floor. Killian grabs it. And though he can hold the knot in his hands, you see the panic on his face as he tries to undo the knots and can't. You don't know exactly what Gisele has done but it's clear the spell is structured so that he cannot damage it. But perhaps you can. You struggle against your ties, trying to reach him, trying to help. The horror mounts in his face as he tears at it. Gisele rises slowly, watching until at last, Killian gives up, drops the braid, falls to all fours, panting. Gisele strolls to the center of the room. She stuffs the braid into her pocket. Then she leaves without another word.

It's day six. Did you really think she would let you out? That it would be that easy?

On day ten, Killian stole the keys to her handcuffs. A simple oversight on Gisele's part really—it never occurred to her that she would not be able to See the actions of the dead. The dead have no futures to speak of, no energy for the tarot to read.

The shock of her free hands froze her. She held her wrists up in front of her, studying the dark bruises ringing them. "Hurry up," Killian said roughly. "She's asleep, but you don't have long."

Alice barely remembers the escape. How Killian escorted her through the house, as she staggered under the weight of her duffel bag. How Killian tossed her Gisele's car keys, saying, "Don't argue." How when she tried to thank him, he stepped away. "I'll never forgive you. You could have left sooner. You could have stayed strong, could have let me find a way to save you. We would have made it through, Beau, together, if you trusted me to take care of you. You're worse than her because you've always acted like you were better," he said, walking through the passenger side door and settling into the seat beside her. "But you still don't deserve this."

"Killy—"

"You don't get to call me that anymore," he snapped. "That name belonged to the sister who wouldn't have done this to me."

If only this suffering could belong to Beau and Beau alone.

He's able to follow you anywhere, after the blood oath. It doesn't matter if you go past his death radius, the spell makes your body part of his radius. It wraps you up like one person. He isn't tethered to his body or his ashes—he's tethered to your gift.

Months from now, you'll watch Killian scream, his nails gouging and failing to find purchase on his skin. Scratching the walls, the floorboards, choking out prayers for it to stop. The broken-doll angle of his limbs as he seizes, endless brackish water leaking from his eyes as he drowns again on dry land. Him begging you to let him into your body, his only sanctuary from pain, for just a little longer, just another day, another week to give him mercy. Mercy, please, Beau, he can't bear it. Each of his limbs snapping in half, every finger cracking backward, until he's a pretzel of decayed meat convulsing on the ground. You can almost feel each crack in your own bones. How could you refuse to let him in? That horrible trade-off—his pain for yours. The cramping muscles, that suspended eternity of blackness, and the consequences of your kindness. Brain fog, chronic fatigue, ongoing pain. For months the two of you will negotiate and manage the balance of pain, even as you get a front row seat as the spell, the pain, twists up all the good in him, unmoors his sense of reality, until the only thing he remembers is exactly how much he hates you. Until one day, he stops asking permission to take you over.

It takes you over a year to concede to the intrusive thought that if you just bind yourself, you'll no longer have the gift—no longer be bound to your brother. That it will send him back to the Little House, trap him in his radius like any other normal ghost. In the moment in your mind, you promise you'll find a way to free him—but then you parcel those memories away where they can't touch you, can't interfere with your survival.

Alice has always believed that, if faced with the same choice, she would never bind her daughter to her son, would not braid a gift to a curse, would not force them into it. What Gisele did was unthinkable. Alice would make the moral choice.

But perhaps the best argument for why Alice shouldn't keep the baby is the way she keeps finding her hand at her belly. It takes so little time to recognize Gisele in herself, in her desperation to keep the thing inside her alive. This, Alice offers herself as proof: She will not make a good mother.

THIRTEEN

THEY STOP AT a Rally's near Toledo and order their combo meals at the drive-through window, but Bronwyn still pulls into the parking lot to eat. She reaches into the middle console and holds up a few crumpled packets of McDonald's sweet and sour sauce for her fries. "Willow used to call this Car Food," she says.

The mix of pine and ash and deep fryer kills her appetite, but Alice pops a few fries into her mouth to excuse her silence. Then she asks, "What was Willow like?"

"Strong." Bronwyn dips a fry into her sauce. "Too old for her age, even more so than us. She moved like an old woman. All those feelings, how deep the gift went, it wore her out. I tried to talk her into homeschooling, but she wouldn't have it. She wanted to be as normal as she could."

Alice tries to imagine Gisele offering similar leniency and fails. "Was it harder on her, being in school with the gift?"

"What do you think?" Bronwyn snaps. Then, after a moment, she sighs. "She liked art. Clay sculptures, some metalwork, but mostly painting. She painted every wall in her room, even the ceiling. I was hopping mad the first time she did it, but how do you argue with an Empath? She'd stomp her foot at me, and say, 'You're only mad because you didn't think of it first.' Real snippy when you got her riled. She was all alive, all color. It's hard to swallow, her turning poltergeist."

Alice unwraps her burger and takes a bite, tart with ketchup. There's no point in reiterating to Bronwyn that her daughter is not a poltergeist. "Why didn't she cut her shadow out?"

"She tried." Bronwyn sets her burger on her lap, and she inhales hard, as if she'd forgotten to breathe. "I talked her into it. She didn't want to, said she couldn't handle the cutting. But I didn't listen. I thought, how could the ritual possibly be worse than what she was going through?"

"What happened?"

"We didn't pack enough angelica and dill into the cuts. The scars didn't rise right."

Alice shivers, feels the screaming burn of packing her own troughs with ash, angelica, and dill, prying blood-dried socks from her skin each night.

"What happened after you left?" Bronwyn asks. "How'd you end up in Michigan?"

Alice hates revisiting that claustrophobic two years after she escaped, the years she spent running from city to city, bus to bus, zigzagging her way across the country because she mistook running for safety. Another inheritance from her mother. She ran when summer lurked at the edges of spring's thaw, ran through the whole of June, July, and August. And each time she started to settle, she'd spot someone with red hair in a crowd or a missing person's poster with her face. She ran when she heard someone mention Ohio in reference to football or Ohio in reference to awful or Ohio in passing. She ran at the drop of the word *mother*.

"I changed my name," Alice says. "If Gisele came around, I didn't want to make it easy."

"Then you shouldn't have picked Haserot." Bronwyn rolls her eyes. "I mean, you named yourself after the Angel of Death Victorious. The only thing less subtle would have been posting your court documents on Facebook—*Isabeau Glass, Former Medium, Changes Name*."

"I was eighteen." Alice rounds her shoulders. "At the time, it sounded clever."

Bronwyn huffs but skirts her gaze. "You ever make it to Ohio State?"

"No, I went to hair school near Midland. I figured she'd check Ohio State first." Alice folds her fingers in her lap. "And your gift gets unreliable at a certain distance."

Bronwyn hums. "Isn't Michigan a little close?"

"I bounced around a lot at first. By the time I ended up in Midland, I figured enough time had passed that none of you would still be looking." Her gaze is direct and sharp. Bronwyn is the first to look away. "Because you did look, didn't you?"

"I didn't want to help her, Beau."

Alice raises an eyebrow. "No?"

Bronwyn ignores the accusation. "She told Frank you ran away." She stares down at her burger. "Frank never bought it though—thought maybe someone kidnapped you. He bothered the cops for months, but you were eighteen and they pegged you as a runaway."

Alice presses her wrists against her jeans. A physical reminder to stifle the memory, but it rises anyway. "Why the fuck did you ever go back to the Little House?"

Bronwyn doesn't answer for a long time. Eventually, she says, "It was complicated."

"You got out. You were free. Why would you go back?"

"Two years in, my boyfriend started to drink. And then he hit me," Bronwyn says finally. "More than once." She shakes her head, reaches for a new cigarette, rips it free of the pack. "I didn't have anywhere else to go. And I was older. I thought that made me—I don't know. Not safe. But safer. I thought it'd be different this time." Something shreds in Bronwyn's face. Very softly, she adds, "For a little while, it was."

"I'm sorry." Alice hesitates, then reaches out, touches her shoulder. Bronwyn leans into her hand.

"Yeah, well. It took some time, but I have my own place now," Bronwyn says after a moment, shrugging. She hesitates, glancing at Alice as if to determine something. "He showed back up in the Little House, a couple years after you left." Bronwyn doesn't have to specify who. There is only one "he" between them. "In case you were wondering."

"I wasn't."

"Well, you should know anyway." Bronwyn always said this as a child, in those times when they lay in the top bunk of the camper with their heads touching, moments after Bronwyn had told Alice something she was too young for but needed to know to survive. Bronwyn would pick at the gray mottles of the glow-in-the-dark planets their mother had hot-glued to the metal frame of the ceiling, a few feet from their faces. In that alien green glow, Bronwyn told her about the necessary cannibalism of the Donner Party, how someday the sun would grow big and swallow the earth, and later, when their mother swelled with Killian, how babies were made.

"I didn't ask because I already knew."

"How?" Bronwyn stares out the driver's side window to the dumpster where a teenager lugs a garbage bag, her arms splotched white and pink below the sleeve of her t-shirt. It's too cold to be outside without a coat. Alice wonders if Bronwyn is thinking of Willow, if her daughter might have looked a little like this from afar. Alice pictures a girl who resembles Bronwyn, small and neat and redheaded and beautiful, who steals her mother's glamoured eyeliner and lipstick, who sneaks cigarettes from her purse.

"Where do you think he was before that? The spell Gisele did made my body his death radius. The only thing that could protect me was to cut out my shadow." The anger flares up as hot and sudden as the guilt. Speaking of Killian has always felt like it will summon him. "You know what else I can't stop thinking about?" Alice continues. "When we were running, Killian went through a fairy-tale phase. Andrew Lang—not the Grimm ones. When the death itch got bad, reading calmed him down. We read maybe twelve of the twenty-five books. And those things are as chunky as dictionaries." How many nights had they curled on the thin mattress in a hostel for comfort, Killian's arms only close enough for Alice's skin to prickle slightly at the proximity to the cold. Killian's soft murmur as he asked her to do the voices. "After a while, he started empathizing with the monsters, asking me why it was so bad for them to follow their nature."

"Don't." Bronwyn clears her throat. "Just don't." She takes another bite, letting the car fall silent. When she swallows, she says to her lap, "Those first years, you have no idea how many times I thought—is she happy? Is she safe? Is my sister warm tonight?" Bronwyn busies herself cleaning crumbs off her lap. "I did miss you."

Alice drops her last few bites into the wrapper then slowly cleans her hand on the napkin.

"I always thought she was batshit for what she did to you," Bronwyn says, "but now—yeah. I'd do a lot of things to save Willow. Tempting shit, that possession trick of yours. Being able to speak to your dead kid."

"Fuck you." Alice enunciates it, gives the *fuck* two hard *k*'s and draws the *you* long.

Bronwyn eases the car into reverse, and steers back toward the highway. The road chugs under them, the wheels on the ramp skitter. Bronwyn sighs. "I didn't mean it like that." After a pause, she adds, "I'd never do what they did. I'd never do that to Ryann." Bronwyn flinches, as if she's sharing something she doesn't want to—the information, an offering. It occurs to Alice that Bronwyn means this as an apology.

"Ryann?"

Bronwyn's mouth softens. "My other daughter. She's real bright. Wants to study computers. Maybe she'll even live as fancy as you someday."

"How old is she?"

"Sixteen. She and Willow were twins."

She thinks back on Bronwyn's roundness that summer, of the way she stopped drinking, offered to be the DD to that ill-fated party. "You were pregnant when you left?"

Bronwyn shrugs, as if this is self-evident, then readjusts her seat belt, the rearview mirror. So many years later, Alice can still make out her Bronwyn. She never could simply sit still.

"You didn't tell me."

"I figured you were too busy to worry about it, being a big bad Medium and all." This time, Alice can tell Bronwyn is joking. "I thought about trying to find you myself after you left, but I figured I'd only slow you down, and there was the father, right? I thought he—" She clears her throat. "Well. Like I told you, I bailed two years after you left. You'll be luckier that way."

Alice tightens. Eli had said, "It'll be fine. I promise. Whatever it is." But that clemency surely expired when she left this morning. That drowsy love in Eli's arms, and the warmth of his thumb against her throat, all gone now.

They'll be in Cleveland in an hour or two. She considers this in an abstract way, which is the only way she can. The Cleveland of her memories evokes brown brick and smoke and sweat. She wonders if they'll approach Kirtland Hills through the highway still studded with bare-armed trees and chunky cliffside, if her body will hum as they draw near, calling her home.

"Did Ryann end up with a good gift?" she asks.

"Well, I'm not worried about Ryann bleeding out in the bathtub, if that's what you mean."

"For gods' sake, Bronwyn. I didn't mean it that way."

Bronwyn turns the radio up. Well, if that's how she wants to play it. Alice angles her body away from Bronwyn's, though the seat belt buckle digs into her hip, and rests her temple against the window. Outside, the light fades from pink and orange to a lavender gray that blurs the snow alongside the highway. Backyards, enclosed by chain-link fences, flash by in smears of yellow slides and blue swing sets and dark wood porches. She wonders if the people in these houses live differently with their homes visible from the highway, if their movements are deliberate because at any given moment, they could be under observation.

She knows the feeling. She became Alice out of fear, remade after Beau's death with an eye planted over her shoulder, a breath always caught in her throat. How unfair that even after she's been found, she still has to remain that way, careful to suit Bronwyn's needs lest her sister's mercy slip, lest their mother be summoned.

FOURTEEN

ALICE DOESN'T REMEMBER falling asleep, but she wakes cold. She's been dreaming of the way the shed would drop in temperature at night, until her joints ached, of how her mother would refuse to bring her a blanket no matter how much she begged.

She opens her eyes on a cement wall, scabby with beige paint. A thick band of neon green circles the top of the building, above a narrower band of lemon yellow. She can't place the logo until she notices the gas pumps nearby. A moment later, Bronwyn rolls the windows down and Alice shivers. "Good evening, sweetheart." Bronwyn has dropped the driver's seat almost flat, reclining against the car door. Her boots are wedged between the gearshift and the center console, knees pulled to her chest. She lights a cigarette and absently taps the ash into the wind. "Enjoy your nap?"

"Where are we?" Alice shakes the sleepy thickness from her brain. Her contacts stick like sand against her lids.

"Mentor. We're almost to my place."

Alice's phone vibrates in her coat pocket, and she fishes it out. The lock screen announces two missed calls and six unread texts from Eli. The latest reads, *Please call me back, need to know you're ok*. Beneath it, and more worryingly, two texts from Susan, one beginning with, *You are endangering his recovery*. Her first instinct is denial. But that evaporates fast—Susan's right. Nothing she's done makes any sense at all. Eli must be in shambles. Alice places her thumb over the words, but she doesn't dare open the texts. She can't remember if she switched off her read receipts. Instead, she sets the phone screen-side down in her lap—if she hides the evidence, she can at least pretend to herself that she hasn't seen it. When she glances up, Bronwyn is frowning at her. "What?" she asks.

"The damn thing's been vibrating for the last twenty minutes straight. I'm surprised it didn't wake you. The boyfriend?"

"He's worried."

"You should tell him not to be."

"Great idea. I'll phone him and tell him, 'Don't fret darling, my sister just tracked me down like a runaway rabbit. Now I'm off for a few days to talk to her daughter's ghost! Also, you know how we didn't want kids? Well, surprise!' He'll be so utterly relieved."

Bronwyn straightens. The stance strikes Alice as defensive, squaring up for a fight. "I wouldn't have asked you to come if it wasn't important."

"You didn't exactly ask."

"Yeah, well, if you want a sorry for that you can fish it out of your ass."

"Nice language."

Bronwyn pounds her fist onto the steering wheel, and the honk makes Alice jump. She bangs her funny bone against the car door and swears as the pain zaps up her arm. "For one minute, stop fighting with me. There's some shit I need to tell you before—" The space between Bronwyn's neck and collarbones floods red with anger. "Before I bring you into my home. There's shit Ryann doesn't know, and we can't talk about it in front of her, all right?" Bronwyn looks so similar to Gisele in that moment it's as if they've traveled back in time and Alice is nine again, waiting for Gisele to wallop her, any answer to any question being the wrong one. In a show of good faith, Alice quiets. Bronwyn flicks the stub of her cigarette out the window and leans forward, and Alice throws her arms up to protect her head.

"For the love of—I'm not going to hit you. I would never fucking hit you, Beau." She places a hand, feather light, on Alice's forearm, and Alice flinches.

"Don't touch me. Please don't—"

"I'm not going to hit you," Bronwyn repeats, firmly this time. "I wanted you to listen. I'm sorry. I didn't mean to scare you."

Alice drops her arms to her lap. Her hands appear to be shaking, and she can't quite fill her lungs.

"Shit." Bronwyn leans forward again, very slowly, one hand raised placatingly, toward the cup holder. She fishes out another cigarette, but instead of lighting it, she taps the butt against her knee. "This happen often?"

"Not as much anymore." Alice's voice sounds far away, as if she's standing inside herself, shrunk behind some recess of space.

Bronwyn rakes a hand through her hair. "I was like that, too, for a while. After."

"After what?" asks Alice's body. Alice herself is studying the pumps, wondering what type of gas Bronwyn feeds this junker.

"After Killian came back to the Little House." Bronwyn inspects her thumbnail. "It was about two and a half years after you left, five months after I moved back in with Gisele." The words sound practiced, as if Bronwyn rehearsed this story while Alice slept.

There's something important here, Alice thinks. Something Bronwyn doesn't know how to tell her. But it's hard to focus. Her mind keeps jogging loose from her body. She studies Bronwyn's face, trying to center herself.

"Frank had a stroke, less than a year after you disappeared. He didn't make it. At the funeral, Beau, I swear to you she was different. Gentle, even. It felt like maybe losing all of us had changed her. And when my boyfriend and I were heading out, she pulled me aside." Here's a difference between her sister and their mother: Bronwyn's eyebrows soften when they knot together. Less cruel and more perplexed. "She noticed my bruises and told me to come home. I thought real fucking hard about it—stuck it out with that piece of shit for more than a year—but when push came to shove, she'd noticed and cared enough to throw me a lifeline. I was dead broke and so fucking overwhelmed. It felt like a way out. And for a while, shit was great. She really loved Willow and Ryann in a way she never loved us."

Alice doesn't want to hear this. She wants out of this car, wants to grab fistfuls of her hair and tear them out. But she doesn't move—she can't. She's tied down by her seat belt, or perhaps Bronwyn has her pinned in place like a butterfly to a corkboard. "She showed you the tiniest bit of kindness, and you thought she was healed?"

Bronwyn jerks back, shoulders flattening against the car door. "Yeah, I suppose that's fair. I guess I deserve that. I thought maybe it was the twins, that maybe they'd made her want to start over. I was only twenty-two. I thought a lot of things. Maybe I was just trying to will it to be true." Bronwyn stares up at the building's bright green bands, and from the set of her chin, Alice realizes she's trying not to cry. It disgusts her. She clenches her fists in her lap, reining herself in. "We had five good months, but when Killian showed back up? It was like a switch flipped, and she was right back to the old Gisele again."

"What do you want from me, Bronwyn? Some pity? An apology that you had such a hard time? You knew exactly who she was." Alice crosses her arms and digs her nails into the meat of her biceps. The pain jolts her, but it doesn't ground her the way it normally would.

"I'm trying, Beau. I'm really trying here. Let me get this out, all right? Fuck, I've been trying to get this out all fucking day, and I keep getting sidetracked. How do I—" Bronwyn massages her eyelids. "It started with little shit, at first. Lights flickering all the time, cold spots. Then, we'd wake up to shit flying around the house. He'd destroy furniture, tear up the carpets, mutilate the walls." She trains her eyes on the gas pumps over Alice's shoulder. Bronwyn never could meet your eye when she talked about the hard things. "The worst part was the quiet times, when he calmed down. Sometimes for a day or two, sometimes a few weeks, and I'd just sit there, scared shitless, waiting for him to lose it again, worried the girls would get hurt in the cross fire. And there was nothing I could do. I had nowhere to go. Gisele threatened to file for custody if I left, and I was young and dumb enough to believe she'd get it. She'd pull out her tarot cards, cool as anything, and tell me in specific detail what she'd say to make the court believe I was an unfit parent, referencing court precedents that didn't exist, making shit up about grandparents' rights. Because she needed me to stay. She didn't have anything else and I think she still hoped I'd be able to find you.

So we were stuck like that. Killian destroying the house, and all of us petrified. Then, one day, he started lashing out at Gisele. He really made her suffer."

"Good," Alice says. No amount of suffering would ever be enough to atone for Killian's pain. She thinks of all the times she woke up to Killian standing over her, his figure blackening at all his pink parts, reaching to slip inside her. Begging her again and again, "We need to go back to the Little House, Beau. We can fix it. If we get our hands on the knot, I know we can."

For a while, they'd had a schedule in place—times when Alice would surrender her body to shelter him from the death itch. Gradually, he'd begun to stretch those times longer and longer. Sometimes he stole her body for days at a time. By that point, he was having more bad days than lucid ones, the only relief coming when he possessed her. Then came the time he'd stolen her body for two and a half weeks. A handful of days after Alice had gotten her body back, she'd hidden from him in the bathroom and cast a banishing spell to fling him from the apartment. When it was done, she'd stuffed every door and window ledge with salt and cut her shadow out. Cut her brother out too—entirely, forever.

But you did more than that, didn't you, Alice? You bought yourself your freedom with something far more precious than even that. The thought stops her in her tracks—because what Alice did to her brother after the shed is so unspeakable, she cannot face it. She cannot touch it, not even in her own mind. Her fingers jerk in her lap as she struggles to push the memories away. *I am sitting in Bronwyn's car*, she thinks. *I will not think of that night in Midland. I will not touch it. I'm cold. I miss Eli. I want to go home.*

Slowly, as if soothing a frightened animal, Bronwyn touches Alice's shoulder. "What happened to Killian isn't your fault, Beau."

"Of course it's my fault." Alice's laugh is laced with bitterness. It's her fault more than Bronwyn could even know. "Who else swore that damn oath?"

"Gisele," Bronwyn says firmly. "She twisted us up inside until all we had were nooses to hang ourselves with. But we don't have to let her keep winning. We can be better than her. Better parents, better to each other."

Something in Alice's center tears open, the soft butter of a wound she thought had healed scar-tight, and suddenly she can't bear the weight of Bronwyn's hand on her shoulder. She shrugs her off. "You want to sit there and talk about how we can be better to each other? Then why the fuck did you show up at my fucking house and blackmail me into coming to Cleveland? Do you have any idea what she did to me? What she did to Killian?"

This shuts Bronwyn up real fast. Finally, she nods.

"You knew about the fucking shed?"

In Alice's clothes, Bronwyn looks like Alice had she lived a different life. When they were children, people frequently mistook them for twins. If Alice hadn't left, would they still? No, Alice suspects. Isabeau wouldn't have made it to Bronwyn's age. Isabeau would have died at eighteen either way. "Not for a long time. Not for years." Bronwyn's voice buckles and Alice feels a satisfaction in that. She hopes Bronwyn crumbles under her shame.

"You knew, and you threatened to bring her to my door anyway. So don't sit there and lecture me about being better. Don't ask me to feel sorry that Gisele didn't become the perfect fucking grammy for your kids. She made me a meat puppet for Killian. She put me through hell, and I took it for years while you went out partying and then you ran away."

"You really want to play the 'who had it worse' game?" Bronwyn barks out a laugh. "What about the fucking beatings I took for you? Where were your black eyes? Where are the belt scars on your fucking back, Beau? And when Killian came back, guess who she wanted to find? Everything she threatened to do to me, to the girls—and I still kept you safe. I made sure she never found you, you ungrateful bitch."

"You don't get to play that card, Bronwyn. Not when you made the decision to bring her back into your life and keep her there."

"You're such a goddamn martyr. She may have chained you up but then you got out—she didn't have to put chains on me. No, she had my babies. She could *take* them. Pack them up in her car and leave for days at a time, and I couldn't do a fucking thing because she could ruin my life with a phone call. No one ever fucking protected me. You're so ready to blame all of us. Gisele was the monster, and me? Frank? Killian? You hold us all guilty by association. Alice fucking Haserot in your big fucking house with your rich fucking boyfriend. Aren't you so fucking special."

"You're the one who wanted to talk about the Little House. And so far, I don't see what Killian has to do with your daughters."

"Killian has *everything* to do with it." Bronwyn bends her head to the steering wheel, her shoulders rising and falling in slow steady breaths. When she looks up at Alice again, her face is steady. "He kept lashing out. Only at Gisele, at first. Then me. I guess it pissed him off that I wasn't helping him—not that there was anything I could do. Bruises, rooms tossed, then punches, our shit broken. One day, he threw a frying pan at Gisele, when she was standing in front of Willow's high chair. He missed and it hit Willow instead. She had a scar, right here." Bronwyn taps the left side of her mouth, above the Cupid's bow, as she stares at the ground. "That was the day Gisele finally let us leave."

"Gisele let you leave?" When the implication of this clicks in, Alice's head begins to spin. She thinks back to seeing Bronwyn in the grocery store, when she had asked, "Do they know where I am?" And Bronwyn had said, "Who?"

"You don't talk to Gisele anymore, do you?"

"Not for over ten years. Gisele's still in the Little House, if Killian hasn't killed her yet."

If Bronwyn hasn't spoken to Gisele in that long, Alice seriously doubts she'd risk contacting Gisele just to sic her on Alice. Which means that Bronwyn lied. Not only lied, but manipulated Alice into coming here on a threat that Bronwyn never intended to make good on, while Alice reeled with terror. But what else should she have expected from her sister? Gisele had raised them both without mercy. Let Alice be merciless now. Let her pull all her hardness back out. She throws the door open and leaps from the car, storming toward the ice-locked road. It's colder in Mentor than in Saginaw, and the wind lashes tears from her eyes. She's made it past the pumps by the time the other car door slams, but it isn't difficult for Bronwyn to catch up, to grab Alice's wrist and hang on to her as Alice slides along the ice. "Fucking Christ, Isabeau. Do you have to do that? With the running? Why always with the running?"

Alice rips her arm from Bronwyn. She'll find her own way home. She'll hitchhike if she has to. She'll figure it out. She's done so all these years.

Bronwyn keeps pace with her. "Where are you going?"

"Anywhere else."

"Beau, stop. Please."

Alice throws her arms up. "You lied to me. You *manipulated* me."

"I never lied. If you thought I'd actually turn you over to her—that's your own damn fault."

"And that's not manipulation?"

"Beau—"

"No, it's been a real trip, but I'm not interested." As she turns back to the road, Alice's foot skids out from under her and she lands with a hard thump on the ground. In the street-lit darkness, Bronwyn strikes her as soft and broken and powerful all at once.

Bronwyn kneels and brushes a knuckle against Alice's temple. The tenderness silences her. "Ryann's a Medium. Willow's trying to force Ryann to channel her." Alice's body numbs. "I know what a poltergeist haunting looks like firsthand, Beau. I've seen it, and I'm telling you, it's happening. Willow is trying to steal Ryann's body. Ryann's trying to be brave, she's trying to fight it, but she doesn't know about Gisele, or Killian, or the Little House. She doesn't know how bad it can get. The other day she asked me, 'Would it be so bad if we shared my body?' You know what that leads to, Alice. You know." Bronwyn swallows. "I don't want that for my daughters. I already lost Willow. I can't lose Ryann too. So, please. Come back to the car. Help her. I don't care what you do after that but help her now."

A tear breaches Bronwyn's cheek and she smears it away. Alice glimpses again the girl Bronwyn once was, wrapping their mother's scarves around her hair like a turban and painting glitter on Alice's cheekbones. Sharing cigarettes on the roof of the camper. Bronwyn, selling love spells to her friends, sneaking Alice into parties, protective of her favorite skirts. Bronwyn, drawn thin in the twilight when they buried Killian's ashes.

Alice grinds her heels into the ice. And here, too, there is a choice. Here, there is a teenage girl named Ryann living with her sister's ghost. Here is a girl with Alice's gift, and Alice can save her from the pain of being possessed by the person she loves most. Here is a chance to put things right. And if Alice can save this girl, if Alice can save Ryann, then perhaps—but remember, Alice, there will be no baby.

The snow melts through her jeans, freezing the denim to her skin. Alice wants to weep, but the most she can manage is a whisper. "Why didn't you tell me?"

"Why did you run out of the damn car?" Bronwyn offers her hand and Alice accepts it. Bronwyn pulls her off the ground, and then Bronwyn wraps her arms around her. Alice grasps Bronwyn's shoulders, hard, but she doesn't realize she's crying until Bronwyn cradles the back of her skull. "It's okay."

"I'm sorry."

"Sorry yourself. We have sorrys all across the board today, don't we? Ryann can't do this alone and I can't do this without you. But if you still want to leave, you can. I won't stop you."

Alice bites the tip of her tongue until her mouth fills with wet-sour pain. "I'll stay," she says. "I'll do everything I can to help."

FIFTEEN

ALICE EXPECTED THE HOUSE to look more like Bronwyn—she'd pictured loose siding and rotting shutters, a dog in the front yard howling, a structure as crooked as the Little House if not the Little House exactly. But the place is small, neat, painted lilac. Ornate bird feeders hang above empty planters on the porch, while suncatchers dangle in the windows. If the house didn't belong to Bronwyn, Alice would be inclined to call it homey. Bronwyn parks beside a shockingly well-maintained truck, draped in snow. The house and the truck itch at her—both so carefully tended as opposed to the hatchback, which is not.

Through a large window Alice sees a TV playing a sitcom. A slim dark-haired girl rises from the couch in front of it, then darts from view. Ryann, Alice realizes. The dark hair surprises her. She'd been picturing another redhead like her and Bronwyn. All at once, Alice understands this is not a hypothetical. There will only be one girl on the other side of that door. Her other niece has died, and all Alice has is a mouthful of promises. And really, what had her promises ever been worth?

Bronwyn cuts the engine. "So, this is home."

"Cozy."

Bronwyn quirks an eyebrow. "Is that Rich Girl for small?" This time, Alice can tell that the ribbing is meant kindly.

"If you think Eli's house is big, you should see his mother's summer cabin."

As if on cue, Alice's phone vibrates. Eli again. *Alice, I'm losing my mind.* She returns it to her pocket, then looks back to her sister. Bronwyn arches an eyebrow.

"What?"

"Call him."

Alice shakes her head. Why does Bronwyn still not understand? "This isn't Frank we're talking about. He wouldn't believe me. Eli isn't like us." *Us*, Alice thinks. Yes. One day, and she's already part of that "us" again. No matter what she does, she will always be Isabeau Glass. Somewhere deep down, Isabeau Glass pounds on the coffin Alice buried her in, smelling of ozone, trying to claw her way back into her body.

Bronwyn shrugs. "He's a man. He'll be relieved you aren't off fucking your trainer, or whatever it is rich people do when they run off."

It's pointless to argue with Bronwyn—Bronwyn hasn't met Eli, and Alice isn't convinced her sister actually believes people have gradients. The Bronwyn Alice knew didn't. But then again, that Bronwyn wouldn't have lived in a house like this one either. "Consider it under advisement," Alice says.

The front door bangs open, and Alice peers past Bronwyn's headrest as a woman steps out of the house. She's rocking a bad dye-job and a baggy t-shirt speared with cigarette burns, but there's an openness to her that Alice likes. She seems like the kind of woman who carts over soup for her sick friends. Bronwyn jumps from the car and pulls the woman into a tight embrace. Bronwyn doesn't introduce her, so Alice stands behind her open car door, shifting from foot to foot.

"Hey, good trip?" the woman asks.

"Yep. Thanks for bringing Ryann home. She behave?"

The woman snorts as if this is a long-standing joke, and Alice smiles, too, out of a sense of obligation. "She baked you welcome home cookies. I also left you some beers."

"You're an angel." Bronwyn hugs the woman again. This Bronwyn who gives hugs and calls people angels chafes against Alice's memories. Her sister didn't have this ease when they were younger. The woman waves as she sets off down the driveway to a car parked in the street. Alice finally shuts her door with a thunk. Bronwyn jumps as if only now remembering her. "Old friend." Bronwyn nods toward the other car. "Her dog is an escape artist, and she's come to me a few times to help find him. That's how we met."

"I didn't realize you were still doing that."

"A little. I was a PI for a while."

"You?"

"I went through cop academy and everything." Bronwyn shoots her a grin. "But it sure as shit didn't stick. Did learn some handy things about court documents. How else do you think I tracked you down? The gift?"

"Yes, actually."

"Like you said, my gift gets unreliable at a certain distance. Court documents, though? Not so much."

It occurs to Alice that she really doesn't know this woman. Should Alice smile? Be impressed? Should she walk around to the trunk? Unlock it? In the end, she only manages to stand there, waiting half helplessly, until Bronwyn steps past her to grab the duffel. Alice reaches to take it from her, but she sidesteps out of reach.

"So." Bronwyn sets her shoulders. Funny that after all she's done to bring Alice here, Bronwyn now needs to steel herself. "I guess we better drop this off." She opens the front door into a burgundy kitchen, decorated with paintings of food and utensils. The house smells like the cookies on the counter, which almost, but not entirely, mask the smell of something musty and familiar underneath. Alice can't quite place it. Some sort of incense. Not angelica, but something in the banishing family. There's an oak table on the far left side of the room, and dust in the corners, but the laminate gleams white. It possesses a rough domesticity, the appearance of a well-loved, busy home.

She can imagine a mother here. Not Bronwyn—a different woman who shepherds her kids to soccer practice, who distributes top-heavy backpacks and lunch boxes filled with carrot sticks to her children every morning. Who knows? Maybe this is exactly the sort of mother Bronwyn is.

Bronwyn breezes through the kitchen, and Alice, obedient, follows. Most of the living room is robin's-egg blue, but on the far wall, there's a mural of a castle, surrounded by swirling impressionistic peonies. A scrawled signature near the bottom of the moat tells her that Willow painted it. When Killian died, Alice couldn't enter the living room, where his gaming controller was still perched on the arm of a recliner near the TV, his headset abandoned on top of a folded blanket. Mementos untethered from the person to whom they'd once belonged.

Alice forces her gaze to Ryann, who rises from the couch, the TV flickering off. Physically Ryann has inherited nothing from

Bronwyn except the dove gray of her irises and the slender slope of her nose. In this girl, with her curly dark hair, wide cheekbones, and heart-shaped face, Alice does not see the daughter she could have—she sees Killian instead. The exactness of his features in her face is uncanny. She'd always thought Killian looked mostly like Frank until she had Ryann to compare him to. Alice's mouth dries, as she considers for the first time birthing a child with her brother's face. It'd serve her right, a daily atonement.

But when Alice looks at her again, Ryann is only a girl. Not a threat, not a ghost. She hasn't spent much time around sixteen-year-olds, but Ryann looks extraordinarily young. She wears pajama pants and a punk band t-shirt that clearly used to belong to Bronwyn. Her hair needs to be redyed, the red creeping in at her roots—the fact that her dyed hair matches Killian's is incidental. Her wrists are thickly wrapped with handmade friendship bracelets. Bronwyn sets the duffel down, and Ryann hugs her mother tightly, rocking them from side to side. "You're home." Then she pulls away and wrinkles her nose. "You've been smoking."

There's real warmth in Bronwyn's shrug. "Maybe a little."

"There's nothing little about chain-smoking, Mom. Like, definitionally."

Mom. This is another thing that Alice didn't expect. She's unsure why—maybe since they never called their own mother anything other than Gisele. Alice imagines the term applied to herself, tests it out, pictures stepping into the skin of motherhood. But then the wistfulness rises in her chest, and she pushes the thoughts away.

"How was your time at Shauna's, baby?" Bronwyn tucks a strand of Ryann's hair back behind her ear. "You have fun?"

"Better than staying here, on the set of *Paranormal Activity*." When Ryann sees Bronwyn's wry expression, she adds, "We watched a lot of horror movies."

"You already do all your homework?"

Ryann rolls her eyes. "Yes, Mom, all the homework is done."

"Even the English paper?"

"Especially the English paper. Shauna checked it for me." After a moment, Ryann looks Bronwyn up and down and frowns. She still hasn't acknowledged Alice, and Alice is unsure if Ryann is just shy or thinks Alice unworthy of her attention. Maybe both. "What are you wearing?"

Bronwyn laughs, and Alice rounds her shoulders—those are her clothes after all. "Your aunt made me shower and change before we left Michigan. I didn't exactly smell like orchids by the time I found her." For the first time, Ryann looks at Alice and the corners of her mouth cautiously tip up. Shyness, then. Something else that Alice wouldn't have expected from Bronwyn's kid.

Alice extends her hand, which Ryann grazes instead of shakes, her touch featherlight and cold. "I'm Alice."

Ryann glances between Alice and her mother. "I thought your name was Isabeau?" Ryann tucks a piece of hair behind her ear, exposing multiple studs and a pair of neon blue plugs.

"I changed my name after I left home."

Ryann's eyes widen and she tilts her head. Her mannerisms are a softer echo of Bronwyn's. Alice wonders if this is deliberate or natural. She's a gentler, younger sixteen than Alice remembers being. "Do I finally get to know why you ran away?"

Alice blinks, and Bronwyn is swift to interrupt. "You can chat her up later, kid. Let's get her settled first." She sizes up Alice's duffel. "We'll put you in Ryann's room. She's sleeping on the couch tonight. Also did you pack for the fucking apocalypse? How did you even manage to get this thing down your stairs?"

Ryann's room is plastered with magazine women and boy bands, notebook paper with quotes from song lyrics, and bubble-eyed cartoon animals. Fairy lights drip from the ceiling. The effect is something rather like stepping through time—it looks almost exactly like Bronwyn's room when she was a teenager, except the walls are eggplant purple, not custard white. There's no sign of another inhabitant—either Ryann erased all traces of her sister, which seems unlikely, or Willow's room must be upstairs. Bronwyn follows her in and shuts the door.

"I thought you said Ryann didn't know anything about the Little House?" Alice hisses.

"She knows some shit." Bronwyn sits on the bed and picks up a threadbare stuffed bunny perched on the pillow. She holds the bunny on her lap, absently petting its balding head. "Willow and I decided it would be best if Ryann didn't know about Killian or too much about how Gisele was. We thought it might spook her—my girls didn't grow up easy with their gifts."

"But you told Willow?"

"You try keeping secrets from an Empath. Better to be honest because she could sense it if you lied." Bronwyn's smile fractures.

Alice hesitates. "Is there anything else that I need to know? If I'm going to try to help, you can't keep springing shit on me."

"No. That's it. I swear."

The child who inhabits this room is so ordinary, so full of innocence. Was Alice ever as young as Ryann? Did she ever love a stuffed animal to bald fur and chipped buttons? At sixteen, she'd already sold all her old toys at a garage sale or passed them along to Killian. It's a testament to Bronwyn that her daughter still has her childhood. "Have you trained Ryann?"

Bronwyn divots the bunny's belly with her thumbs. "I did what I could, but magic never clicked for me the way it did for you. The girls picked up a few things—luck spells, glamours. But Ryann doesn't do séances. If that's what you're wondering. She doesn't have 'clients.'"

"Good."

There is a knock at the door, and Ryann pokes her head in, her cheeks a bright red. "I forgot Pumpernickel."

Bronwyn stands and tosses Ryann the bunny. She catches it with one hand. "Why don't I help you make up the couch? We should let—Alice—settle in." Bronwyn closes the door behind her, and then Alice is alone for the first time in hours. She sits on the bed for a moment, then retrieves her phone. So many missed calls and texts.

I'm sorry. A lot to process right now. Will call when I can, she types. Then she erases it. She tries, *I'm at my sister's house, fell asleep in the car*, then, *I have a niece, and she is so beautiful, Eli, but she looks like my brother and seeing her made me miss him so much*, and even, *Nothing makes sense here except that it does and all day I thought I was walking into hell and I haven't and I'm so ashamed*.

All the texts open with *I'm sorry*, and none of them are adequate, because really, this isn't a conversation for text message. She should be calling him, but she can't do that now. Not until she decides how much to tell him and she still doesn't even know where to start, much less where to end.

A ghost. Her poor dead niece. How is she going to deal with her?

Finally, she writes, *I'm safe, and I miss you, and I love you. Please don't worry. I'll call when I can, but it's been a crazy day. I promise we'll talk when I'm home.*

A moment later, her phone vibrates again—a picture of a pregnancy test with twin lines. *Alice. Call me.*

SIXTEEN

ELI ANSWERS ON the second ring. "Hi, there." His voice is softer than Alice expected, given the circumstances.

"Hi," she says.

"My mom found it." Then, a beat later: "She says it was an accident, but I'm pretty sure she dug through our trash."

"That tracks. I buried it under about half a roll of toilet paper." Alice imagines him hunched over on their bed, his body vibrating with stress. She wishes she were there, but selfishly she is also glad she doesn't have to witness how much she is hurting him in the name of keeping him safe.

"You didn't want to tell me."

It isn't a question, but Alice treats it like one. "No, I didn't."

"But why wouldn't you—" He cuts himself off. "Do you want to keep it?"

"I—my family—there's a genetic condition, a bad one. In boys, it's always fatal." Alice's jaw burns and with some effort, she opens her mouth so she won't clench it so tightly. A nerve in her throat spasms. "My brother died from it when he was ten."

"Shit, Alice. I didn't even know you had a brother."

"I don't like talking about him." On Ryann's dresser, a white teddy bear hibernates with its face pressed against the mirror. It's Valentine's Day themed if the red paws and clutched pink heart are any indicator. Killian inherited most of Alice's stuffed animals. His favorite was her stuffed antelope, which he'd loved from relatively new to ragged. Its felt horns were worn to matted nubs and holes were opening in its belly and neck, but even to the end, he'd slept with it tucked under his chin. She still has it somewhere, in storage probably, crushed between knit blankets and old cardigans.

"Alice, when are you coming home?"

"I'm in Cleveland." The city tastes strange and forbidden in her mouth. "It's a long story."

"Cleveland?" His voice buckles and Alice flinches.

"There's an emergency with my older sister. Her daughter—one of her daughters—it's complicated, Eli, and I can't hash it out right now."

"No. That's not a reason, and for my own sanity, I need to hear one." And then, as if assessing the firmness of the boundary, his voice quiets. "Please, Alice."

Alice's first instinct is to be furious, to cry out that it isn't fair, that she's never lied to him without a good reason—as if that's any comfort—but she tries another route. "My niece died, and my sister needs me."

"From the genetic condition?"

"Different variant, but yeah." Then, because why not, she's already said too much, she adds, "There's a treatment for girls, but the operation doesn't always work, and you can still die from the side effects."

"Jesus. Jesus Christ, Alice, I am so sorry." He pauses. "I don't want to make this about me, I really don't, but—"

"Say what you have to say, Eli."

He's silent a long time, and from his side of the line, she hears a door closing. "You don't trust me. And that's hard to accept because you've seen me so vulnerable. I want to be understanding and respect your privacy, but these are huge things for you to keep to yourself. Not that vulnerability is a quid pro quo, but I thought we were building this life together, and it turns out I barely know you."

"Gods, of course you do. All the important parts."

"I didn't know you had a sister, much less a dead brother. I didn't even know you're pregnant. Those are massively important parts, Alice. And I understand there's a lot of trauma there. I really do. I won't push you if you aren't ready. But if you don't trust me even that much—what are we doing together?"

Alice swallows down the sobs welling in her throat. Is this what it comes down to? That if she doesn't tell him, she will lose him? She cannot lose him. He is the good at the end of a long day. He is home after a hard life of running. And she is so very exhausted by the keeping of so much from him—the girls and their gifts, the boys and their graves, and all the consequences she's carried for so long, alone. It's too much to hold. She needs help and besides that he's right. She owes him more than fragments of the truth. So, she will tell him. But not now, not sitting on her niece's bed with her sister waiting for her in the next room. She must be discerning, kind, she must find the right words to tell the story, she must make herself ready. "I love you. And when I come home, we'll talk about everything. Promise."

"When?"

"Soon. As soon as I can."

"Alice." His voice cracks, and he clears his throat. "Are you leaving me?"

"No," Alice says. "Hey, no. Never. I love you, okay?" When he doesn't respond, she adds, "Are you leaving me?" And it is supposed to be one of those things that people say, a small plea for reassurance that everything will be all right, but Eli doesn't answer. He has to think about it. Alice presses her fist to her mouth.

"No," he says finally. "I don't think so. But there's a lot to talk about when you come home."

"I'm sorry. I didn't mean to hurt you."

"I want to tell you it's okay, but it really isn't."

"I understand." She tells him she loves him again, and he hesitates before he says it back. After she hangs up, she clutches the phone to her. Her eyes are heavy and she aches to cry, but the tears refuse to come.

Bronwyn knocks on the door, then opens it before Alice can answer. She studies Alice and winces. "You tell him?" When Alice doesn't answer, Bronwyn clicks her tongue. "Sorry."Alice lets it sit between them, filling the space in the room. Then she nods toward the door. "So, are we doing this tonight?"

"Ryann hasn't seen Willow around lately. She must be somewhere in the house, but she's been keeping quiet. You sense anything?"

"No." Alice's mouth tastes like ashes, a mix of fear and anticipation. "But I wouldn't anymore."

"Well, Ryann baked cookies. Come hang out with us. Try on your new auntie hat. She's amped to meet you properly."

"Okay." Alice manages a smile. She means it. "Just give me a minute."

When Bronwyn closes the door, Alice lies back on the bed, breathing deeply, calming her heart rate by counting to fifty, a hand resting gently on her stomach. When she catches what she's doing, she yanks her hand away, and starts the count again.

Downstairs, there are three glasses of milk on the kitchen table. Ryann sits with one leg tucked under her, the other in a gymnastic position that wouldn't be comfortable for anyone but a sixteen-year-old. She glances up when Alice walks in, then resumes inspecting her nails. This avoidance would have annoyed her from Bronwyn, but it's strangely endearing on Ryann. She scoots her chair so Alice can sit next to her.

Bronwyn brings the cookies from the counter and sets the tray on the table with a flourish. The effect is ruined when she proceeds to immediately stuff one into her mouth with an exaggerated chomp, making Ryann giggle.

Alice tentatively reaches for one herself. The cookies have cooled now, but they're still soft, the chocolate melting on her tongue. "These are really good, Ryann. Did you make them from scratch?"

Ryann deliberately turns toward her mother. "Do I have to go to school tomorrow?" So much for being "amped" to meet Alice.

"Yes."

Ryann fiddles with the bracelets on her arms. "But I want to be there. When you talk to Willow."

"We can figure all that out tomorrow." Bronwyn licks chocolate from her thumb.

"I deserve to be there. I deserve to get to say goodbye."

"You will," Alice says and takes a sip from her glass. It's whole milk, which Eli hates and won't buy. Quite sharply, Alice longs for home. "Convincing a ghost to pass is tricky. It won't happen overnight."

"When will it happen, then?"

If you didn't already know it, you'd never guess a ghost lives in this house. There are tells, but they are small. The windowsills lined with salt, the picture frames and paintings askew on their hooks. "Have you asked Willow why she's stuck?"

Ryann tilts her head, perplexed. Her gestures are so reactionary, so transparent. No one's ever told this girl to guard her expressions. Alice can practically read her every thought. Bronwyn clears her throat. "Her gift isn't exactly the same as yours. Ryann can't talk to them."

"I can," Ryann corrects. "Sometimes. If I listen really hard. It's like someone turned the volume all the way down on the TV."

Bronwyn adds, "We think her gift came in at four." Early, then. Not a strong Medium.

"What do the ghosts look like to you?" Alice asks. The words come stiffly, a forgotten language, but beneath the hesitation, Alice can taste her own curiosity, the way the word "ghost" makes her blood sing. She doesn't like it.

Ryann gnaws on her thumbnail. "People, I guess? Just a little blurry. I can make out the faces, when I squint." Bronwyn touches Ryann's elbow and Ryann drops the hand she's been chewing on. Ryann shakes her head.

"And Willow never talks to you?"

Ryann drums the table. She's a jittery kid, can't seem to sit still. "Sometimes she yells."

"I'm sorry. It can't be easy, watching this happen to your sister."

"Twin." Ryann's lip curls. "Willow was my twin." It reminds Alice, acutely, of the way she used to call Killian her baby.

"Hey. Easy, kid." Bronwyn gently shakes her daughter's shoulder. "This is all new territory, okay?"

"I'm tired of people being sorry, this shit that's fucking obvious. We didn't even like each other." Bronwyn stiffens, straightening as if to say something, but Ryann shrugs her mother off. "It's true, Mom. We weren't friends, we didn't hang out. I was a bitch to her. And now she's dead, and she's hurting so bad, and I can't help her, and it fucking sucks." Ah. There's the Bronwyn in her.

"Of course, it does," Alice says. Impossibly Bronwyn looks like she might cry. "Because what's the point of your gift if you can't do anything to help? But you don't know what to do. She's stuck, so you're stuck, too, and nothing you do makes a difference. It just makes you want to tear your skin off."

When Ryann asks Alice, "How did you manage for so long with such a shit gift?" Bronwyn pretends to ignore them, picking up crumbs from the table with the pad of her fingers. She's listening, though. Her body is tense as a wire.

"You've done real well for yourself," Bronwyn had said back in Alice's kitchen. "I didn't expect that." Willow is dead, and died of a bad gift, and didn't Alice also have a bad gift? Weren't they blessed with gifts that came too late and therefore too strong? Hadn't the gifts always given them trouble? *How come Willow died and you're still here?* That's the crux of it. Alice's bind runes raised right and Willow's didn't, and that was the difference between a dead girl and a live one. But she cannot say this to Ryann. Bronwyn shakes her head, almost imperceptibly, as if she can follow Alice's train of thought.

"Talismans," Alice lies. "But they were never very good."

"You'll have to teach me." Ryann's eyes flash. "I can make an okay banishing bundle, but I want to learn everything. I want to do everything you can."

No. Alice shudders. She really doesn't.

"Well, that's enough for tonight." Bronwyn stretches out her arms, tipping back in her chair. "We've had maybe the longest day of my life. Go forth. Sleep, child."

Ryann tries to protest, but Bronwyn silences her with an arched eyebrow. "Brush those teeth and wash that gorgeous face. And don't forget your vitamins. Go on. Shoo."

Ryann groans but shuffles off in the direction of the bathroom. As soon as she's out of sight, Bronwyn slouches at the table with her head buried in the crook of her elbow. Alice hesitantly reaches out to touch her shoulder. "You okay?"

"I think it's bedtime." Bronwyn blows a piece of hair out of her eyes. "Tomorrow is going to be as long as a rooster's cock."

SEVENTEEN

BY THE TIME ALICE closes the door to Ryann's bedroom, her body hums with static. Kneeling stiffly, she rummages through her duffel bag for a sleep shirt, but she forgot to pack one. The shirt she's wearing will have to do. As she pulls her arms from the holes to maneuver off her bra, she spots a bruise forming on her side—purple and large as a book, probably from her fall at the gas station. When she presses on it, she hisses in pain. She tries to muster the effort to dig out the wipes from the bottom of her bag, but after eyeballing the chaos, decides to sleep in her makeup instead.

Alice peels the comforter from the bed and slips under the sheets. She considers calling Eli again, but it's past midnight now and she doesn't know what else she could add to the conversation. By herself, Alice occupies too much space in Ryann's bed. The last time she slept without Eli's solid warmth beside her was months ago. She misses the deep huffs he swears aren't snores, that when she wakes in the middle of the night, he tucks the sheets around her and settles her in the warm shell of his arms, her back to his chest. He runs hot in his sleep and sweats when he dreams. The sweating sometimes annoys her, the slickness of his hand on her thigh or the dampness of the sheets, but tonight she craves his weight beside her.

More out of habit than anything else, she curls up on one side. The sheets smell like Herbal Essences shampoo and peach body mist. Tomorrow, as Bronwyn said, will be a long and difficult day. Sleep then, Alice, or try to.

Alice tosses and turns, her mind roiling through flashes of snow, and cranberry cans, and Killian's dead body. She's not sure how long she's been asleep—or if she's even slept at all—when she hears the drip of water. It's intermittent, at first. A drop at a time, the gap between each long enough to convince herself she imagined it. But then the next one comes and confirms, yes. Something is dripping.

She's dreaming or maybe hearing things. Sometimes, in the night, she hears the house settling and mistakes it for the garage door. Anxiety transforming the benign into a threat. This is no different. But then another drip. She's sure of it. A ghost lives here. What else could it be?

Alice shifts, the sheets rustling. She sits up straight. Listens.

The dripping comes faster, rhythmic now, insistent. It's not coming from the direction of the kitchen. It's coming from the other side of the wall, where the bathroom is. Then the water eases into a steady stream. Alice swallows and her throat sticks. Her pulse thumps in her ears, and she wishes it were silent so she could better hear the water.

It's nothing. Alice's brain is playing tricks on her. Ryann's probably thirsty, and didn't want to wake her, forgot to shut the faucet of the sink off all the way. But why didn't Ryann go to the kitchen?

It isn't a poltergeist, no matter what Bronwyn thinks. It isn't Willow. It can't be. No spell has been cast to make her one.

The water shuts off, and Alice buries her face in the pillow. She's jumpy tonight, of course she is. It's been a long day. Her muscles have been balled up tight since Bronwyn grabbed her at the grocery store. Alice releases her grip on the pillowcase and relaxes her hand across the soft fabric. Now her neck. She stretches out her shoulders. Tenses and releases her arms. Her bruised side throbs.

The water turns back on. Not a faucet this time, but a shower head. Accompanied by a soft sound, like a child's whimper. Alice sits up again, muscles taut.

Then, all at once, it stops.

Alice wills herself to stand, but the sudden silence immobilizes her. *Move*, she thinks. It's impossible for Willow to be a poltergeist. She's sure. But is she willing to stake Ryann's safety on it? Alice puts one foot to the ground. She waits.

When Ryann screams, the sound cuts through her. There's a crash upstairs—Bronwyn. Alice leaps from bed, throws open the door, and sprints toward the living room, toward Ryann, slipping on the hardwood. It's only because she slips that the lamp misses her, whirling past her and shattering against the wall. Alice lands hard, but then she's up again, feet scrabbling to propel her to where Ryann sits upright on the couch, the blanket bunched in her hands, screaming. Alice tries to focus on Ryann's shape, her outline in the bluish dark moonlight. It is so horror movie that Alice would laugh under different circumstances. *This is happening*, she thinks. *This is real. There's a poltergeist in this house.*

She's almost reached Ryann when a picture frame lashes free of the wall and flies over the couch, denting Willow's mural. The shatter of glass and the wooden crack of the frame. Behind her, she hears a thump from the stairwell—it sounds like Bronwyn has slipped down the last few steps. Alice doesn't look back. She reaches Ryann and lifts her from the couch, blanket and all. The girl is hyperventilating and tugs painfully at Alice's hair. Alice half-carries, half-drags her toward her mother.

"Where's Willow?" Alice asks.

When Ryann presses her face into Alice's neck, Alice shakes her. Ryann must be her eyes. It's unfair, this demand from this untrained child, but life is unfair. "Where is she?"

"It's not—" Ryann groans, and Alice struggles to hold her weight. Her arms burn. "By the bathroom."

Alice jumps as Bronwyn careens into her. "This isn't normal." Bronwyn rocks back on her heels, wild-eyed. "Willow's never been violent before. To objects, yes, but never to us."

"Take Ryann outside."

"Willow's never done this before—I didn't grab my bundles from upstairs," Bronwyn is saying. A banishing bundle. They can't deal with a poltergeist without one. Something Alice would have considered when she heard the first drops of water, if she hadn't been busy convincing herself the dripping wasn't real, couldn't be a goddamn poltergeist. She's out of practice. She's been safe for too long, and it's made her sloppy.

"Where are they?" Alice shakes Bronwyn by the elbow.

"I have some," Ryann says. "My room, in the dresser."

"I'll get the bundles." Above them, the ceiling fan stirs to life. "You, go." Alice pushes Ryann, firmly, toward her mother, and Ryann's grip briefly tightens on Alice's shirt before she lets go. Alice pushes them outside and slides behind the couch just before the light bulb in the ceiling fan explodes. The whine of the light bulb echoes in her ears and her vision buzzes in protest. She struggles to acclimate to the dark.

In order to reach the banishing bundle, she has to pass the bathroom. Where Willow is. She can hear herself panting and she steels herself before she gets up off the floor. She moves quickly toward the bedroom and is almost there when something grabs her collar and yanks her back. By some instinct she throws her hand out, so that it absorbs the force of the impact from the floor instead of her skull. Her wrist rings with pain, and her body wants to curl around it but she pushes herself up. There's no choice.

A light flickers to life above her. She turns to see a glass candle jar levitating in the center of the living room, its flame sparking and dying, casting strange orange shadows down the hall.

"That's enough." It surprises Alice to realize that the words come from her. Quiet first, and then firm. "Settle down. You're angry and confused, but you don't want to hurt them. Can you hear me?" The candle's flame dances but the jar stops rotating. A good sign. Alice raises to her feet, one muscle at a time, as if soothing a skittish animal. "You're scaring your mom and your sister."

She steps toward the bedroom, experimenting. The candle stays lit, its flame shivering on the wick. "I can help you, Willow," she says. "I know you don't want to hurt them." A few more steps, and she'll be there. "The gift burned you but acting out won't fix that. I don't know what happened to you, but I'll find out. I can help."

The candle flares again, rotating in a circle. Every so often it jerks, as if Willow is gearing up to throw it, as if she's enjoying the way Alice keeps flinching. A shiver of cold ripples its way down Alice's right shoulder blade. Two more steps. One. "Willow, don't do this."

Then Alice is in the bedroom, and she manages to slam the door shut as the candle whips toward her, the jar shattering on the wood a moment later. She stumbles toward the dresser, yanking drawers out as she goes—upending sweaters, t-shirts, jeans. Where the hell would Ryann put them? Finally, her fingers close around a dry juniper branch. But where's the lighter?

She upends the last drawer, but no luck. Of course not. Ryann isn't trained. Why would she know to keep a lighter with her bundles? Alice could have told her that last night if she'd known. Out of practice idiot. How could Alice have forgotten to discuss precautions?

The door swings open, the creak deafeningly loud. Without considering what she's doing, Alice throws herself through the doorway. Her skin ices as she passes through the poltergeist, and then she's in the hallway again, bolting for the kitchen, shielding herself from the flying paintings and airborne coffee mugs. It feels like Willow is everywhere—in the bathroom, in the living room, chasing her through the halls. That preternatural poltergeist speed disorients her, but there's no time to consider that. The cookie plate bounces off her arm and cracks against the tiled floor. Alice gasps as the pain blossoms through her shoulder, but the important thing is to keep moving. The back door beckons, just feet away. Another mug goes flying over her shoulder, shattering against the doorframe, just above an herb bundle that

Alice notices for the first time. There are two of them, hanging on either side of the entryway, nailed at shoulder height. The location suggests something that would protect the threshold, and the pointed aim of the coffee mug hints to Willow's wanting to interfere with them in some way, but Alice doesn't have time to contemplate this. She needs to get to Bronwyn and Ryann.

And then she bursts outside, panting, her bare feet howling with each step across the icy driveway. The hatchback's engine is running, and Alice beats a fist against the window. Bronwyn jolts for the door handle, almost slipping in her haste to get out of the car, and Alice steadies her with a rough hand under her elbow. "Lighter," Alice says. "We need a lighter."

"I don't know how to cast a banishing ritual." Bronwyn's words come out strangled as she pats down her pockets. Alice snatches the Bic from her hands. "I've never done one."

"I have," Alice reminds her. She could cast a cookie cutter banishing spell in her sleep. She focuses her attention on the bundle, but the flame won't light. Alice flicks again and again but the damn flint scratches and scratches and comes up empty. Then, Ryann stands in front of her, lifts the bundle from Alice's hands, and grabs the lighter.

"No, not you." Bronwyn grabs for the bundle but Ryann takes a step back, out of reach, quickly flicking the lighter to flame. When the bundle catches in Ryann's hands, Alice almost cries in relief. "Give it here," Bronwyn snaps, but Alice holds out a hand.

"She needs to know how to cast a banishing spell," Alice says. "It's mandatory for a Medium's safety."

Bronwyn frowns and crosses her arms, but steps aside.

Ryann holds the smoking bundle tentatively in her hands. "What do I do?"

"Like this," Alice says, and pantomimes the broad strokes of the banishing ritual. Ryann watches, mimics, wields her power for them both. The movements are rough-hewn and awkward, and it's only then that Alice realizes there's a problem. The banishing ritual she knows is meant for someone who understands the metaphysical theory of movement, of words corresponding to action. Ryann cannot rely on that structure because she hasn't been taught magical theory, not under Bronwyn's tutelage. Bronwyn was never taught the subject herself. Alice will have to dumb it down for Ryann. She exchanges a glance with Bronwyn, who immediately seems to understand.

Bronwyn stands behind Ryann's shoulder, lifting her arm up into smooth gestures. "Focus as hard as you can," she says to her daughter. "Imagine white light filling up the whole house. And say the words in rhythm to the way you move your arm."

Ryann throws Alice a panicked glance. "Words?"

"Repeat after me—by juniper and salt, I cleanse this air," Alice chants. "No poltergeist is welcome here." Alice cringes at the oversimplification of the ritual, the triteness of the rhythm, but she's gotten the essential in there. It'll get the job done.

Ryann's voice wavers, but Alice's voice is steady, and Ryann repeats the lines carefully as Bronwyn puppets her arm. When Ryann releases the spell, the smoke raises up, thick and dark, and although Alice knows it's impossible, it seems as though she senses, rather than sees, the weight lift from the house. Ryann sags against the car, then slides to the ground, her head in her hands.

The house is a house again and not a vessel. It won't hold Willow off forever, but it'll buy them some time. Time to better figure out what's going on with this ghost that can't be a poltergeist but somehow is—how the haunting could have escalated so quickly, from burning trash cans to this frenetic attack. Even when a poltergeist's lucidity ebbs, it's a slower decomposition than this. The sweaty smell of angelica hangs heavy in the air, smoke threading its way through the brittle cold.

A hysterical laugh rips through her lungs—she helped, actually helped, banish a poltergeist, a proper poltergeist, when she is not this person anymore, not a Medium, all those skills dormant and untouched, and how can the night be this calm, the sky with its scant feathered clouds above her, as if nothing in the world were wrong? Who can sleep through the world being upended and rummaged through like a thief through a purse? Though of course she knows it's only her world, her carefully wrought identity as Alice, that's imploding. Nothing to see here.

Ryann makes a small sound, and it startles Alice. She looks down to see Ryann is crying, and a lick of tenderness shudders through Alice. *Oh, little love*, Alice wants to say, *I was only a little older than you the last time I cried for a ghost.* A memory comes to her then: the image of Gisele standing beside a younger Alice, teaching her how to do a banishing spell. It makes her chest ache. The difference, she reasons, is that she and Bronwyn had no choice but to teach Ryann—it is for her protection, not exploitation. She must cling to this thought. It's the only way she can absolve herself of the guilt.

"Alice." Ryann's voice is raw, her teeth chattering. "Alice, who the fuck was that?"

Bronwyn stands beside her daughter, immobile, her knuckles whitening as she clenches her fist as if that action is the only thing pinning the world in place. Around them, an awful resounding quiet sinks its mantle over the night. The whisper of wind over snow. The hush of a car in the distance. Alice's breath puffs out in clouds.

"That kid." Ryann tightens her hold on her elbows. "The boy."

"What boy?" Alice asks.

From the corner of her eye, Alice can tell Bronwyn hasn't moved. She doesn't turn to look at her face though. She's afraid it will resemble her own yesterday—only yesterday—when Bronwyn grabbed her arm in the grocery store. Behind her, the kitchen door creaks open and shut with the wind.

EIGHTEEN

ALICE'S FIRST SEMESTER at hair school was a lonely one, with friends out of the question because sometimes Alice needed to talk to thin air and sometimes, Alice wasn't Alice at all. Besides, Alice and Killian used all their downtime to scour occult books, trying to find a way to undo the spell that had turned him into a poltergeist. They spent whole afternoons curled on the floor of the technical college attached to her hair school, heads tilted against the flimsy shelf of the occult aisle because it felt sacrilegious to bring those texts into their normal-life apartment. Killian would absently flip through the pages beside her, fully absorbed.

Alice would read with her nails dug into the meat of her neck or rubbing her wrists against her jeans until the fabric chafed the skin raw to ward off memories of the shed.

One evening, Alice decided to revisit Aleister Crowley's work, specifically his depiction of the Abramelin rite. The rite promised a variety of magical boons, but it required the caster to cloister themselves away from the material world for six months of ritual prayer. Killian had argued hard for it, but they'd ultimately dismissed it as impossible—they were too broke to go that long without a job. This particular night, Alice was cross-referencing it against an older grimoire she'd come across at a library online that referenced something called the Thymos ritual, which, as far as Alice could tell was the Abramelin rite, accelerated into a significantly more promising three-week timeline, albeit with much harder to get ahold of ingredients, such as ritual meals prepared with rabbit hearts.

One evening, Killian had been lying beside her on his stomach, flipping through an old grimoire, when he suddenly sat bolt upright. "Wait, listen to this." He read directly from the grimoire, his finger hovering in the air above it as he stumbled over certain words. "'Certain necromantic spells, such as those that force spirits to stay on the earth, are inherently unstable due to their fundamental reliance on the energetically drained spirits. This can be remedied by two components. The first is to bind the dead to the living. Blood works best, particularly that of the deceased, taken while they were living, but consuming the remains will work to a lesser effect. The second is a physical object to work as an anchor to hold the spell steady, usually in the form of a rope knotted with intention. It is imperative you take great care with the anchor, as anything that disturbs the knots will destabilize the spell and unwind the binding.' Did you hear that, Beau? I think this is the blood oath she used." His eyes were bright with excitement. "It couldn't be that simple, could it? All we'd have to do is destroy the knot."

Of course he would be the one to find the answer with that vibrant determination of his. She's missed that about him. His absence feels like a cyst deep in her kidneys, her gallbladder. It's the jagged stump of an organ severed, the hollow gap where her magic lived. She missed him, and she damned him, and now he is back, and he is angry, and all of this is her fault.

In the aftermath, Bronwyn refuses to return to her house.

"We need to sleep," Alice says, knowing her body will fail her if she doesn't manage a few hours. "It's safe. I promise."

"Fuck that."

"Do you plan to stay in this car all night?"

"If I have to."

"Bronwyn, come on."

"Not happening," Bronwyn says, nodding toward Ryann. "I'm not risking it." Because they don't know how Killian found his way in, because a poltergeist as far gone as Killian can slip into a Medium's body like a hot knife through butter. Why hasn't he already?

This is how they find themselves at the all-night Denny's near the airport at four in the morning. And what a picture they make—Ryann with her fluffy penguin-print pajama pants and Bronwyn in an oversized t-shirt and sweats. Alice herself looks the most ridiculous, shivering in a turtleneck and gray shorts, her leg hair bristling with goose bumps. The only other people in the Denny's are a rowdy group of drunk kids, one of whom keeps smacking a sausage link across his friend's face. By their waitress's dead expression, this is a standard Monday night shift.

"I think Willow was trying to warn us, with the faucets. Maybe even when she tried to possess me," Ryann says while she mechanically bites through a stack of pancakes piled with bananas and chocolate chips. Alice sips watered-down, acidic orange juice. Alice would kill for a sip of Bronwyn's coffee, but when she reaches for the mug, Bronwyn slaps her hand away. Alice assumes it's out of concern for the fetus, which she considers exceptionally unreasonable, given Bronwyn's chain-smoking the entire ride to Cleveland. "When I woke up, she was standing in the bathroom door shouting at me. He kept circling the living room, touching our stuff, then he'd squat down and open his mouth as wide as it would go. Like maybe he was screaming so hard no sound was coming out. And the way he moved across the room? It was so fast. He'd be in the living room one minute, then in the kitchen a second later. It was creepy as fuck."

"Language."

"Mom, if any occasion calls for the use of the word 'fuck,' it's a poltergeist squatting in the middle of our living room and screaming, like, five feet from me."

"What I don't understand," Bronwyn says to her white coffee mug, "is how the hell he got in my house."

"Do you think it could be—" Alice wants to finish, but Bronwyn shakes her head. A warning—don't talk about Gisele in front of Ryann.

Across the room, the college students whoop. The boy closest to the window sits in blinking embarrassment, the runny yolk of an over easy egg sliding down his cheek. Who would Killian have been if he'd lived to nineteen? He'd always wanted to be a tattoo artist, spent hours sketching designs in his notebooks, then Sharpie-ing them onto his skin. Or would he have gone to college, majored in something like art history? Ridden a bicycle to campus, had coffee with his dinner?

They never had a chance, none of them. Not her, not Killian, not Bronwyn. Gods, she envies these drunk kids, theatrical in their joy, who have no concept of gifts and ghosts and blood oaths. She's worked hard to leave these things behind herself, so how has she ended up here, calculating the mechanics of a poltergeist again?

"It doesn't make sense." Bronwyn stares at the tabletop as if she can scry the answers off the sheen.

"We need to figure out a game plan," says Alice.

"Go on. Let's hear it. You're the expert."

"We have two separate problems: Willow not passing, and Killian lurking. He shouldn't be able to leave the Little House. Maybe it has something to do with me being back in Cleveland? But I haven't seen hint or hair of him in years, and neither have you. That means something's changed. We need to figure out what." Alice grips the hair near the base of her scalp, the pain settling her.

Ryann makes a small sound in the back of her throat, like an animal caught in a trap. "Killian," she says, testing out the name. "You've dealt with it before? How'd you get rid of it the first time?"

"Hey," Bronwyn says, "gentle. He's not some monster."

Ryann tosses her fork onto the plate. "That thing? I don't think it has enough human left to remember it ever was one. I've never seen a ghost that fucked-up before."

"Him. Not 'it.' Him."

"Fine. *He* attacked us. *He* trashed our house. *He* could have burned it down. Who is this *he* that you're defending him right now? Go ahead, Mom. Enlighten me." Her fear threads through her bravado. She wraps her arms around herself, narrows her shoulders.

"Don't worry about it." Bronwyn scrubs her face with her sleeve. "It's not your problem."

Ryann scowls as Alice rounds on her sister. It's a bad idea to interfere, but she can't help herself. "Bronwyn."

"Don't 'Bronwyn' me. That's my kid. You don't get a say here." As her voice crescendos, and the college boys stare, Bronwyn jabs at the table, whispers, "She won't get sucked into this shit. Do you hear me?"

"Ignorance won't keep her safe."

"Because all that hands-on experience worked out so well for you, right?" Bronwyn bares her teeth, and there's something vulpine about the expression. A fox that, though small, can still savage. "All that knowledge of yours kept us all so safe tonight, so protected that Killian ended up in the middle of my living room right next to my sleeping daughter."

"Mom, I'm not a baby. Quit treating me like one. I need to be able to help."

"Over my dead fucking body. You're not going anywhere near him."

"For fuck's sake who is he?" Mother and daughter stare each other down across the table, both breathing heavily. They'll fight until sunup, if Alice lets them. They don't have that kind of time.

"Our brother," Alice says.

Bronwyn beats her fist into her forehead. Alice pries her hand away. There's a moment of pressure where Alice thinks that Bronwyn will fight her, but she lets her hand drop.

Alice clears her throat. "So you know how some people become ghosts when they die? There's a way to ensure the dead don't pass. If you bind them to someone living." A deep breath. "Has your mother told you about the curse?"

Ryann puts her elbows on the tabletop, her mouth disappearing behind her sleeve. Her silence tells Alice everything she needs to know.

"There's a price for the gifts." The words stick in Alice's mouth. Handing Ryann this cruel inheritance is one more revolution of the cycle.

"The boys die," Bronwyn interrupts. "All our sons die before their nineteenth birthday, okay?" Her voice quiets then, straining into almost a whisper, as she speaks of the camper and the Little House, and their mother, and what was done to them in the name of love. "And here we are. Alice had to cut her shadow out—cut away her gift—to send him away."

"It wasn't his fault," Alice says, then she explains the shed, the possession, her impossible choice. She keeps an eye on the drunk boys. They are easier to look at than Ryann. Than Bronwyn. One of the boys has fallen asleep, his hand draped in the bowl of sugar packets. Another is pulling out a Sharpie.

Ryann squeezes her eyes shut. "I don't know if I'm understanding this right. What makes Killian different?"

"On a practical level, a poltergeist violates the rules," Alice says. "It's a ghost who has all this potential energy stored up from wanting to move on and not being able to. When I bound my shadow, it didn't undo the damage from the first spell—the one that turned him into a poltergeist. It only negated the blood oath that bound his death radius to my gift. Now, he should be contained to his original death radius at the Little House. He shouldn't be able to leave."

After a minute, Ryann asks, "What do we do with him?" Alice can see the fear in her eyes. Alice wonders if Ryann or Bronwyn has strung together the evidence yet. Willow cannot be a poltergeist, because it requires a spell. Willow cannot do the things Bronwyn described in Alice's kitchen—overflowing bathtubs and setting fire to trash cans. Willow cannot throw objects. Willow cannot possess Ryann for any length of time.

And if all this haunting isn't Willow, it means Killian's been the poltergeist in Bronwyn's home this whole time.

"We need to gather more information," Alice says finally.

"How?"

The answer hits Alice so squarely, she jolts, sloshing her orange juice onto the table. She lunges for napkins to mop up the puddle, bowing her head. *Willow*, she thinks. And there is only one way a conversation with Willow can happen. Even if Ryann could hear her sister well enough, Alice wouldn't let her take that on because if Killian has been haunting Bronwyn's house, Alice is responsible. This is a reality Alice can't run away from. And it's one thing for Alice to face the consequences of what she did to her brother, but Ryann is a normal girl, an ordinary girl who sleeps with stuffed rabbits and cries at banishing rituals, whose room is decorated in magazine cutouts, who calls Bronwyn "Mom." Alice will not allow what she did to Killian ruin this girl too. Then, with more certainty, she considers the exact amount of pain involved in peeling the scars off her heels with a knife.

When Alice doesn't respond, Bronwyn starts like a dog shaking off water. As if she understands, implicitly, what Alice intends. She turns to Ryann. "You up for school today, kid?"

"Not a chance in hell. But I don't want to go back home either."

Bronwyn sighs. "Okay. Soon as the sun's up, I'll call Shauna. She can watch you for the day."

It's a testimony to Bronwyn's parenting that Ryann doesn't argue, though judging by the set of her jaw, she wants to. How has Bronwyn accomplished such a healthy relationship with her daughter? It's a marvel how well she's taken to motherhood, given where they come from.

"We need to go back to the house." Alice puts up a hand as Bronwyn opens her mouth. "We need more banishing bundles, and I want to be in pants almost more than I want to be alive."

"We should switch cars too." Ryann gulps down her coffee. "It's supposed to snow later today, and the heat in Willow's barely works."

"Willow's car?"

"The junker Mom drove to Michigan. Willow bought it herself and absolutely trashed the thing." Ryann shrugs. "Mom won't let me drive it, says it's too dangerous."

"That's because it is," Bronwyn says. Leaning toward Alice, she stage whispers, "Ryann is a *terrible* driver."

As Bronwyn flags the waitress and mimes signing the check, Alice taps her thumb against the table. She strives to smother the plan coming together in her mind, begs herself to find any other way.

NINETEEN

AFTER THEY DROP Ryann at Shauna's, the drive to Bronwyn's house is quiet. A few houses on the block still have Christmas lights up, dim animatronic reindeer rotating on the front lawns, deflated Santa balloons flapping in the wind. "The house is safe," Alice says, because it bears repetition. "The banishing spell worked."

At a red light, Bronwyn rolls down her window and lights a cigarette, and Alice's lungs ache with jealousy. "Fuck this," Bronwyn says as she exhales.

"You were all forgiveness and understanding yesterday." Alice scrounges around her purse for gum. She's chewed through most of her pack. If Bronwyn keeps smoking at this rate, they'll have to stop at a gas station soon, so Alice can restock her replacement vice.

"That was yesterday."

"I've been thinking." Alice shivers and nestles deeper into her coat. The gum doesn't help her as much as she'd like—she still wants a cigarette. "Willow can likely tell us why Killian's here."

Bronwyn drives the car onto a side street, her brow furrowed. For a moment, there's only the sound of the turn signal clicking and the snow crunching under the tires. "Ryann can't hear Willow, but I'd be able to."

"Lot of good that does. Considering your bind runes and all." Bronwyn pulls into her driveway and kills the engine. When she turns toward Alice, her under eyes are a raw red, bruised and worn with sleeplessness.

"What if—" Alice pauses, steadying herself against the glove box—"I cut the runes off?" What is she thinking? Aren't there other ways to communicate with a ghost? But none are as effective as her. How can she leave all this trouble to her sister, this grief-scooped woman, who has already been through so much? When Killian's poltergeist is a problem Alice created? Bronwyn blinks slowly until her eyes close altogether. Her lips press together so tightly they disappear into her mouth. She's painfully thin, her sister. Was Bronwyn always this thin, or has the mourning whittled her?

"It would solve a lot of problems." Two days ago—only two days ago—she would have laughed at the idea. Just yesterday, it was an impossibility. Except now she's met Ryann, and the idea of teaching her, of making her do this, makes Alice feel dirty. All this mess—it's Alice's own fault. She's sure of it. *I will not think of Midland. Not now, when I have to get through this conversation.*

Bronwyn shakes her head, eyes still closed. Slowly, at first. Then decidedly.

"I can ask Willow why she's here," Alice says. "I can figure out what Killian's doing. We can keep Ryann out of the house until it's over."

"Stop talking." Bronwyn opens her eyes. She sounds furious, though what she's furious about, only the gods know.

"This is the Occam's razor solution." For a moment, she considers telling Bronwyn about the promise she made to Killian—about what she could do if she got her hands on the blood oath, but it's one thing to know that Alice cut her shadow out. It's another matter entirely to know what she did to Killian after she learned that information.

"Fuck Occam with his razor."

"Give me one good reason I shouldn't."

"You and your fucking martyrdom complex! Do you ever think about the consequences before you decide to do shit like this? Did you think about how pissed off he's going to be after fourteen years stuck in the goddamn Little House with Gisele? Or better yet, you think about how this might affect your baby?"

"I'm not having the baby."

"Did you decide that before or after you set your mind on being this stupid? You think you're going to go back home to your boyfriend, your feet all bloody, and say, 'Honey, I see dead people'? When you couldn't even tell him you were pregnant?"

"Don't act like you know me." Which, how stupid a thing to say, because of course Bronwyn does, better than anyone else in the world. "You asked me to help you—this is me helping. Or do you have another option?"

"Don't try to put this shit on me. I'm not asking for this."

"I didn't say you were. I'm choosing it." Alice knocks her knuckles on the dashboard. She wants to go inside, to wash her face and brush her scuzzy teeth, and she wants a pair of jeans over her freezing legs. She wants this conversation over, and even as she insists to Bronwyn she will do this, she's still praying for a way out, isn't she? *Tell me there's another way*, she wills.

"Un-choose it."

"Give me one good alternative."

"I refuse to let you be this stupid."

Not good enough. Alice unlatches her seat belt, resolved. She thinks of Ryann's terror last night, the awkwardness of the banishing bundle in her hands, and Alice knows she will do what needs to be done to keep that child safe.

Alice dresses in layers. Jeans over yoga pants, sweater over t-shirt. Her limbs thaw. She holds her contact case for an extra moment before deciding she's better off in glasses. A few splashes of cold water and a good brush of her teeth, and she feels almost human again. Ready, at least, to tidy the house.

She transfers the few remaining banishing bundles to her purse, then dumps the unearthed clothes loosely into the drawers. The house is a poor imitation of itself. The plate of cookies broken on the floor, crumbs and ceramic crushed together. Cabinet doors ripped from their hinges. Gouges in the drywall. Alice tries not to consider herself an omen of destruction.

On her way out, Alice stops to inspect the bundles hanging on either side of the back door, the ones she'd noticed last night. She lifts one from its nail. The herbs are tightly wrapped with twine, and Alice picks apart the knot. Bound together are some things Alice expects to find, like pennyroyal, a few dried shoots of a garlic plant, chamomile. But there are important herbs missing. No Saint-John's-wort, no hyssop. No angelica or juniper. And then some things shouldn't be there at all, like mugwort and wormwood. Used apart, they can keep spirits out, but together, they trap ghosts in place like fly tape. The person who made this bundle had no idea what they were doing. She jogs outside, the bundle in hand. "Who made this?"

Bronwyn sets her ice scraper on the hood of the truck, and squints. "Is that the one by the door? It's been up there awhile."

"Since before Willow died?"

Bronwyn frowns. "Maybe?"

"Is it possible Ryann made it?"

"Probably not. Since Willow started showing up, she's made a few banishing bundles, but spell jars are more her jam."

Alice rolls her thumb over the dried herbs, a leaf crumbling under the pressure. It smells sharply, for a moment, of rosemary. Store-bought rosemary is functionally useless in a banishing spell—too dry. "Did you bury selenite at the property corners?"

"Why would I do that?"

It's hard to hold her patience in check, but she shouldn't expect Bronwyn to know about ghosts. She didn't want her daughter to touch Medium work, she had no reason to learn. "Because selenite works like a no loitering sign for ghosts."

"Should we pick some up then?" Bronwyn picks up the ice scraper again, and chips at the back window. "There's a shop in Willoughby."

"I thought this was supposed to be a banishing bundle, but something's off."

"We can just fix up a new one, right?"

Alice drops the bundle into the snow. The herbs scatter like flakes of ash. "I think Willow made this."

Bronwyn stretches to better hack at the upper windows, her shoulders tense. "Willow wouldn't have needed a banishing bundle. No ghosts to banish."

"How much did Willow know about ghosts?"

"Nothing. Not a whole lot. I don't know," Bronwyn snaps. "What does it matter?"

"You're not listening to me." Alice grabs Bronwyn's arm, jerks her away from the car.

"What am I missing, Alice? What am I not hearing? Say a damn thing straight instead of talking around it. I can't read your damn mind."

"This bundle is the problem. It's been the problem the whole time. It has mugwort and wormwood in it. It traps ghosts. She's not passing because this bundle bound her here. What if the person who made it didn't know that? It isn't common knowledge. This looks like the kind of thing you'd throw together if you googled banishing."

Bronwyn's arm trembles in Alice's grip.

"Let's say Willow made this bundle before she died."

Bronwyn shakes her head.

"Who was she trying to keep out, Bronwyn? What ghost might she have been trying to banish?"

"She *wouldn't*." But her voice is loaded with the heat of denial, not the certainty of fact.

"But you didn't make it. And Ryann didn't make it. And Killian is in the house. That means Willow did. So Killian must have already been in the house before Willow died." Alice releases her arm. "Let me talk to Willow and find out why."

"I'm begging you not to do this. Not yet. We have other options."

"I don't think we do."

"You realize that if you do this, you're going to have a hell of a time going home? What are you going to tell Eli?"

"Why don't you let me worry about that?"

"Because you're refusing to."

Alice throws her arms up and stalks back toward the house. Behind her, Bronwyn starts up with the ice scraper again. Of course, there will be consequences if she does this. One of them: Killian will be able to follow her again. She imagines how the danger will begin. Slowly at first. Knocks on the walls and misplaced keys, Eli's overturned spice racks. Lights that flip themselves on and off. Then doors slamming, glitching cell phone, pots that throw themselves through cabinet doors. Cold spots despite the heating on blast, flickering TV sets, long red scratches down Eli's pale skin. Shadows in the hallway and echoing laughter and rotting fruit and dead mice in hampers of clean laundry. It'll begin with the things she can explain away until eventually explanation fails. And it will escalate and escalate until either Killian hurts Eli or sees Alice dead. If Alice starts down this path, she will have to see it through, she will have to do something to end it. Is she sure that she can manage it this time? She has to be. Killian is her burden to bear. She cannot leave him to Bronwyn and Ryann. She will not be able to run away from her brother again, no matter what comes next.

She flattens her palms against her thighs to stifle the shaking. She focuses on the muscles in her face, one at a time. Tip the lips up—not a smile, but a hint of one. Eyebrows angled down—aim for sheepish but also reconciliatory. She works harder at it than she used to—she's out of practice. "Is there any way you'd be willing to go to the gas station and pick up some coconut water for me?"

"Right now?" Bronwyn gestures at the truck.

"Pregnancy craving. Besides, you're almost out of smokes." Alice pulls out her wallet and presses a twenty into Bronwyn's limp hand. "Maybe some beef jerky? We could use the protein."

Bronwyn eyes the bill. "Beef jerky? At seven in the morning?"

"It's one of the few things I can keep down before noon."

"Weirdo," Bronwyn mutters, but tucks the money into her pocket. When she hesitates, Alice is almost sure Bronwyn understands what she plans to do. That she'll call Alice out—but perhaps she's successfully given Bronwyn the excuse she needs to let Alice do what she can't bring herself to condone. "Anything else you want, your highness?"

"Hand sanitizer, if they have it. And some chewing gum. I'm almost out." Alice's hand tightens around the nearly full travel bottle in her purse. "Maybe some apples?"

Once there was a girl without a shadow. No. That's not quite right. Once there was a girl who cut her shadow off. And then she lost everything.

In Ryann's bedroom, Alice touches the scars on her heels, tracing the shape of the bind runes, the raised straight lines, their brutal and elegant angles. They've been with her for more than a decade. Almost half her life. Alice doesn't even notice them anymore. The runes are part of her, like a freckle or a mole. She's crazy to think she can do this. She has to be crazy to try.

There are choices you cannot undo without great pain and great sacrifice. It'd been nearly impossible to carve the runes into her heels, but to carve them out? How can she consider it? How can she consider bringing back the twisted creature her brother has become? Is there even any saving him now? She has to try. Leaving him in the Little House isn't a tenable option anymore. If Ryann can take that banishing bundle into her hands and enter a world she should never have been forced to touch, surely Alice can face what she did to her brother in Midland.

Alice paces the bedroom, from one purple wall to the other. On the bed, the paring knife she took from the kitchen winks like a jewel in the morning light. What will Eli think, if she comes home a bloody mess? If doing this hurts the baby? The one she will not be having, the one she refuses to think about because acknowledging it at all means making a decision she isn't ready to make.

She shouldn't be thinking of undoing this spell. And for what? For whom? Bronwyn? Ryann? Ryann could find her own way. Alice did. Willow? A niece she's never met, who will likely pass on her own terms when Alice has destroyed those mangled bundles hung beside the door? It isn't too late to change her mind. Alice can help Willow without the gift, can't she? It would be hard, of course, but maybe not as hard as slicing the skin off her heels, as unleashing Killian. But Alice has atoning to do. She can't abandon Killian, not again. How exactly would that abandonment go? She will—what? Betray Bronwyn, damn her daughter, and take the bus back to Michigan? Show up on Eli's doorstep and tell him—what exactly? Don't worry, she fucked over her family again? Don't ask darling, it doesn't matter, darling, just forget it ever happened? Those secrets have already been unearthed inside her—there's no returning from this unscathed. Whether Alice likes it or not, Isabeau Glass twists inside her, resurrected.

How is it Alice hadn't understood—was it really yesterday—the way Bronwyn had reached for Alice's face in the car? What had she said? *You've done real well for yourself.* She'd thought Bronwyn meant the house. She'd thought Bronwyn meant her money. Gods, how stupid she'd been. She couldn't separate her sister from the expectation of her sister—the unwashed clothes, the missing tooth, Willow's car in complete disrepair. Alice hadn't understood it was grief, nothing but grief. *You look healthy.* Healthy as in, well, as in alive. As in, you survived this darkness, you survived your gift. Bronwyn doesn't want her to do this, to throw away her only chance to live without the ghosts. If she were here, Bronwyn would tell her, don't waste it. Because that's what it was really about, all that protest. Even through all this, Bronwyn wants her to be safe. *Breathe, Alice*, she tells herself. *You have to breathe.*

What about the logistics of bending over to cut the skin off her heels? All the consequences aside, is she physically able to mutilate herself like this? Alice could call Ryann. "Help me," Alice could say, "I have to do a very brave and very stupid thing, and I cannot do it by myself." And then she would—what? Give a sixteen-year-old girl a kitchen knife and say, "Please cut the skin off my heels"? No, gods no, she cannot do that. Alice will not do that. Alice is not her mother, a grown woman who forces a child's participation in bloody magic.

Alice drops to the bed and the knife shifts and slides toward her. It's a sharp knife, well-kept. She closes her eyes. She is here. She is present. There is a knife, its plastic hilt in her hands. The keen blade, the perfect tool for what she must do. She presses her heels into the rug below her. She has done so very much running in her time. But she will not anymore. Whatever she was before, she's no longer the child in the trailer and she's not the girl in the shed and she's not the woman from two days ago with the festering wound where her memories should be. Now, she can choose. In the end, it's a simple decision because it's the only one she can continue to live with. It's just a matter of holding the knife precisely right and biting the pillow, screaming into stuffing and linen.

Alice thinks she will pass out after she finishes the first foot, but she doesn't. She hopes the second one will be easier. It isn't.

And when it's done, she lies on the bed weeping so hard she makes no sound. She reaches for her magic, feels the heat traveling her veins, her back arching as it floods the seat of her spine. The taste of dirty pennies fills the back of her throat. At the tip of her forefinger, she calls a witch ball the size of a dime. It flickers and sparks, before holding steady, its round energy bright and silver. Her magic, her power, her gift. Her veins ache as it comes flooding back in.

She doesn't know how long she's lain there when she smells it, cutting through even that rusty scent of blood. Like lightning but a touch sweeter—a ghost, not a poltergeist. And her eyes well again because it smells exactly the way she remembers. In the haze of her blood loss, she expects Killian to appear, murmurs his name, surprises herself with the force of her need to see his face—but of course it can't be. The banishing spell would have cast any poltergeist from the area. A ghost however could stay, and the one who emerges gradually, like a lens coming into focus, is a teenage girl. She looks like a rusalka, her hair a longer golden echo of Ryann's curls. Her eyes are a pale mint green, the sclera around them shot through with light gray threads. She sits near the dresser, chin to her knees, a hand clamped over her mouth to muffle whatever she's chanting.

"Oh god." That's what she's saying. *Oh god*, over and over again.

Willow,
Four Months Ago . . .

YOU SHOULD NOT *be in this place.* This is what Willow thinks as her car grunts up the driveway—impossibly long and winding—to the house set back in the woods, the place her mother called the Little House, though in truth, there's nothing little about it, all this wood, all this land. There's ivy twisting its way up the brick facade and paint flaking off the shutters. The front lawn, a mess of tangled husks—the skeletons of wildflowers dying en masse in the fall frost.

Willow rubs her chest. Her pulse is pounding with an emotion she can't place. Could be that someone in the house is scared—good possibility given who the house belongs to and what lives there. Could also be the sense memory of the spine-cold horror her mother experiences whenever she speaks of Gisele. Could be her own sense of intimidation. Or it could belong to someone else altogether. A neighbor. A dog walker. A delivery driver.

The gift has been less reliable since Willow tried binding it. Sometimes there's only empty space inside her, but other times, the volume cranks so high Willow can't hear her own thoughts, can only curl into a ball and breathe until it passes. With her gift malfunctioning, Willow's lost her sense of balance, her compass.

As she parks, she spots the weatherworn shed in the backyard. "I should've known she'd do something to trap Beau," her mother said, balled with a guilt Willow has never been able to soothe despite her best efforts. In front of the building's carapace, in the long yellow grass, a wooden door lies half obscured by leaves. It must have fallen. Or someone pried it off. Either way, no one has bothered to reattach it. "Later, when Gisele wanted me to track her, I said no, and she put me in that shed too. Killian cracked her head open with a tree branch. She bled so much, I thought she'd died. She let me out and never tried that shit again."

Willow wasn't expecting to see the shed—or maybe she hoped she wouldn't have to. It's hard to pinpoint, these days, where her own emotions live under the mangled bind runes. A place that is no place. A flutter of fingers beneath an avalanche of snow. It's too late to question the wisdom of being here.

She closes the car door and locks it, follows the front walk to the Little House's faded green door. But she waffles on the step, toeing a leaf, as she considers the cracked orange light of the doorbell. If Ryann were here, she'd tell Willow to hurry up and press the button already. Ryann is the impatient twin, the impulsive one, eternally done with Willow's caution.

Entering the house will be the ultimate transgression. Willow tries to picture her mom's betrayal when she tells her, all the hot, screaming, throat-clenching depths of it. Willow's mom already blames herself for the failure of the ritual. But Willow wouldn't be here if she had any other options. Hers are unlivable: continue with the stuttering, mutilated, unpredictability of the gift now—or remove the bind runes and return to the way things were before. If anyone knows of a third choice, it's this woman.

Though she's yet to ring the bell, deep in the house, a light shudders on. She can still leave. The scabs on her heels ache—she's been standing too long. As her knuckles graze the door, it opens. Willow considered this possibility before she left home. That by even making the decision to drive to the Little House, Gisele might See her coming. The old woman braced in the doorway still surprises her.

The top of Gisele's braid is very white and the bottom very copper, as if dip dyed. She isn't really old, not by any reasonable stretch—early fifties, if Willow's math is correct—but Gisele holds herself like she's ancient, slumped forward, as though something inside her is broken. Willow recognizes the stance. This is the way she holds her own body too. But it's more than that, isn't it? Gisele carries an incessant worry that gnaws the edges of her lungs as if a physical pain—ah. She's ill. Something nasty, or it wouldn't worry her quite so much. She thinks she's running out of time. But for what?

"You're letting all the warmth out." Gisele's voice comes out as a hoarse croak, and she sucks in air after the sentence. Whatever the illness, it's in the lungs. Willow bites her cheek and nods, but doesn't move. "Your tea will get cold."

"In how many futures do I come in?"

Gisele makes an impatient noise in the back of her throat. "Now that you're already here? Every future but three."

"What happens in those futures?"

"Would you like to leave and find out?" Gisele arches an eyebrow, and an emotion twinges in Willow's chest, something that might be excitement or perhaps despair, but it dissipates so quickly that she can't place if it belongs to her or Gisele. She peers into the dark of the house beyond and hesitates.

"He isn't here," Gisele scoffs. "I threw up a banishing spell for our chat. He's in the forest—he can't leave the property, but it does keep him out of the house."

Willow nods, and she walks past Gisele into the house of her mother's memories—now a chaos of broken glass, missing floorboards, and broken furniture. This is what a poltergeist is capable of. Worse than she expected.

"The kitchen is through here," Gisele says as she walks ahead. "Don't gawk. You'll sprain your ankle gaping at the walls."

Entering the house is like swimming underwater. Willow places her steps exactly after Gisele's. She tries to imagine her mother living here, walking at this angle, her feet exactly where Willow steps, but it makes Willow sad to picture her mom in the midst of the thick dust and hole-ridden carpets.

In the kitchen, Gisele walks her to a small central table. It's illuminated, barely, by a damaged light fixture above. The bulb is crooked and the cords exposed, nearly ripped from the ceiling. In the middle of a stained tablecloth, Gisele has set out two cups and a porcelain teapot, pale blue interwoven with twisted veins of gold leaf. Preposterously delicate pieces, given the rest of the house.

Each wall of the kitchen is a fortification of banishing bundles, stapled in a line around the room. "The kitchen can be the most dangerous room in the house, if it isn't warded," Gisele says over her shoulder. "Too many knives." Gisele gestures for her to sit, and Willow does, one foot crossed over the knee to give her aching heels a rest.

"My mom said you couldn't See the future unless you touched someone, or used the cards, or whatever. How did you See me coming?"

"I might not be able to read your future, little love, but I can read my own."

The teapot is heavier than expected, and the tea smells strangely musky. "Mugwort?" Willow pours carefully, an equal amount into each cup.

"Call it artemisia. That's the proper name and a better one. More elegant." There's a hint, Willow thinks, in the upward tilt of Gisele's chin, of the woman she used to be, the woman her mother described. "Drink."

Willow stares at the murky liquid in the teacup. A few mossy chunks have escaped the strainer and float on its surface. This situation demands an awareness she won't be able to manage in an induced trance.

"It wasn't a suggestion. Drink." The words sound forced and practiced, impatience flickering somewhere beneath Gisele's diaphragm. Willow suspects Gisele has rehearsed this conversation many times before today, already knows Willow's every move, wants to skip to the end. It required so much certainty to make this tea, to set out these cups. If she could see the future so clearly, then why had she suffered through all that disaster? Willow wondered.

"No. I didn't See it coming, not the way you mean, with that accusatory little frown." Gisele's mouth curls, but Willow can sense her amusement. No, not amusement. It's more like gloating. It doesn't align with Gisele's expression or her words, but if Willow focuses, she can sense that sullen blossom unfolding its violent petals. "No, little miss, the Sight is not that simple.

There's a calculation involved, possibilities and percentages. The occurrence of this particular future was infinitesimal when I came to Kirtland. I had a son in one singular thread out of thousands. A small enough percentage that I didn't even consider it a risk. But it's brave of you to ask all the same, given all the ghastly stories I'm sure Bronwyn has told about me."

"But I didn't—"

"Ask? Not yet, but I know why you've come, and I'll save us both some trouble. You did a very brave thing very stupidly, and your mother can't fix it. You're hoping I've uncovered some secret she never learned." As Willow starts to interrupt, Gisele raises a hand. "I've Seen every possible version of it, and I find it irritating that you are making me verbalize this because you're smarter than your mother, and you know better. Bronwyn couldn't reckon up from down and didn't retain anything worth a damn about magic. You're also here, whether you want to admit it or not, to satisfy a curiosity you've been denied your entire life. *What happened?* you're wondering. *Who are we? Where do the gifts come from? Is it true she trapped her own daughter in the shed?*

"So many questions waiting to slip off that tongue. And not only do you think you deserve answers, but it has yet to occur to you that some mysteries are better left that way. I'll try not to hold that against you, though I despise stupidity in a young woman—young women already have too much working against them. But I won't sit here and be interrogated by a child who came to my doorstep desperate for help. We aren't equals, girl, and I've spent too many years of my life trying to coax stupid and stubborn girls into their best possible futures. If I tell you to drink the tea, it's because you'll need it."

At the end of this tirade, Gisele breaks off into a coughing fit. She presses a napkin to her lips, and when she pulls away, it's flecked with blood. She emerges red-faced and triumphant, but beneath everything, calmer. Less lonely, Willow thinks. Together, they are buzzing with Gisele's joy. Willow taps the teacup's handle with a nail. "I'm not afraid of you."

"Oh, but you are, little love. That's why in most futures, you leave now. You walk out the door and drive away and try to forget you ever came here. It doesn't matter though." Gisele's smile is unsettling and Willow senses she's coaxing herself to be gentle against all her instincts, because Gisele truly fears whatever it is that she's trying to prevent, and that fear makes it difficult to be soft. "Because in any future you choose, you live unhappily and die young."

The words are horrible, said bluntly and without kindness and though they send her reeling, Willow also finds herself empathizing with Gisele. They are both terrible at the social dance of knowing too much and pretending they don't, floundering as they navigate the subtleties of the secrets and denials people use to protect themselves. Though this doesn't make Willow trust Gisele, it does make Willow understand her better. "Can you at least tell me why?"

Gisele drums her fingers on the table, and frowns. "It's hard to weave the threads on a tense client. If you want my help, I need to See what to do."

It feels like the truth, so Willow drains the cup in front of her down to its chalky dregs. Gisele grants her a pleased nod, then folds her hands onto the table.

"Why haven't you started chemo?" Willow allows herself a meager satisfaction that she, too, can play this game.

A beat passes before Gisele blinks. "No point. My web ends only one way."

"You're dying."

"Is that meant to be some profound declaration? Do you have any other such obvious observations to make? Next, you'll tell me the sky is blue, or that mugwort and wormwood are an essential combination in banishing ghosts." Anger morphs Gisele's face into a porcelain mask of false indifference, as if she were contemplating how best to flay the skin from Willow's muscles. Then, fractionally, Gisele relaxes. "My apologies. I thought I was beyond my sensitivity over this."

"In my mother's stories—" Willow hesitates. It strikes her as sacrilegious to talk about her mom in this place, to the woman who abused her, but if Gisele knows anything and is willing to give her answers, it's worth Willow's discomfort. "You promised Killian that you would never let him become a poltergeist. Did you ever mean it? Did you know what would happen?"

Gisele shrugs. The question discomforts her. Good. "When I was young, my four older brothers died. I tried to stop it, but nothing worked. They always died. My mother tried to save them too. She was a Healer. She could manipulate bodies, fix them, but she paid a price. She swallowed the illnesses in a way, underwent all the pain and horror and gore herself to heal them. Everyone in her stupid little coven said, 'Your mother—she's such a good woman. So caring. So helpful. What a saint.' She mended my brothers so many times it almost killed her. Imagine that."

"I'd rather not." Willow has sensed people die before, though thankfully always at a distance. It's not a place Willow lets herself touch, all those neurons firing. Euphoria and pain and panic and fear and relief all at once.

"When my middle brother died, my mother gagged me. I mean that literally. She could manipulate flesh and blood and skin and not just for healing. I kept telling my horrible truths about what the future held and she kept finding ways to shut me up, until my saintly mother sealed my mouth. And once I couldn't scream, she tied me up and bound my shadow. I expect she didn't realize I'd be enterprising enough to cut the runes off. She wasn't a terribly clever woman." The flash of hate that rips through Gisele makes Willow gasp, bracing herself against the table. Even though she knows the danger this woman poses, she did not feel it in her bones until now. But then it flickers and is gone, Willow left panting and empty.

As Willow collects herself, Gisele rolls her shoulders, grimacing. "I grew accustomed to playing the dumb girl after that. And when I had my daughters, I thought, I'll never be like my mother. I'll spare my little loves from every horror, every hurt. Don't we all start with the best intentions?"

"Then why did you put your daughters in the shed?"

"You're missing the lesson here," Gisele says, drumming her fingers on the table. "The shed is irrelevant. Bronwyn and Beau are irrelevant."

"If Beau was so irrelevant, why did you try to use my mother to track her down? Why not use the cards?"

"Because my gift doesn't work like that. Bronwyn's was better suited." Gisele glances up at the chandelier, and impotent frustration floods Gisele's body. "To read the threads, I have to see patterns. Killian threw a wrench in things—I can't See the actions of the dead. They have no patterns, no energy for the tarot to read, and he kept changing Beau's future in ways I couldn't anticipate. When I read a future, I run through all the possible scenarios, every possible future, then narrow it down to the most likely ones. The best I can do is direct small actions to shift the course of what comes next down one of these threads. Killian made Beau's future too unpredictable to track. Then, when he returned home, after Beau cut her shadow, there wasn't a single thread where I succeeded in bringing her back here. She would rather have died." Gisele smooths down the ruffles in the stained tablecloth. "I never should have told them that damn story."

"Can I ask you something?"

Gisele's posture stiffens. A suppression of exhaustion, though this might belong to Willow herself. "Why did I teach them about binding their shadows in the first place?"

Willow nods.

"I meant to impose a lesson early—the opposite lesson, in fact, than the one they learned. They were meant to understand that it is almost always better to live with the gift than to deny it. That it is a vile thing to sacrifice your specialness for the sake of the ordinary nothings that walk around in the outside world. But that, my dearest love, is not the question you came here to ask."

Willow tries to focus, to pack away the questions she'll ask her mother later. "What are my options?"

"Well, if you insist I state the obvious—you live like this or you live with the gift. You knew the risks when you tried to bind your shadow. Don't whine about it now. It's unattractive."

Willow nods through the sting of disappointment, though it's hard to track her own emotions with Gisele bursting across the table. How long has it been since Gisele spoke to another living person? How has she survived for years alone in this ruined house? "And if I cut the bind runes off?"

Gisele reaches into her pocket and removes a deck of tarot cards, bound with stiff black cord. She pats the deck before picking the knot apart, and as soon as the cards are free, the top card slips to the left. Gisele shifts it back into place with the tip of her pinkie. The way she shuffles the deck is halfway to a caress. It's gentle, intentional. Innate. She picks three cards from the top, flipping through them so quickly that Willow doesn't have time to see what they are. The one time Ryann bought tarot cards from the bookstore, their mom had burned them in the firepit behind the house. Willow has never even seen a deck up close, but she can tell this one must be handmade.

"If you bloody yourself a second time? In your longest life, you die at thirty. The gift becomes unbearable, and you move to a mountain town, population twenty. You think it's better like that, to disappear. Ease your mother and your sister's pain, since you don't want them to watch you suffer, to worry the way they do. But you're lonely, Willow. At first you talk to your mother and your sister often, but it hurts too much to speak to them when you can't be with them, so eventually you stop answering. You go for a walk one night—night because it's the quietest, the only time you can. You aren't expecting the drunk driver who comes barreling down the road, but you freeze because it's been so long since you sensed that much of someone else so close by. You don't jump out of the way."

The mugwort warms her belly and her vision softens at the edges, dizzies her thoughts. Willow's never liked the trance—it blurs the lines between her and other people even more. "And if I stay here?"

"You die in months. Maybe weeks. Depends on your choices." Gisele pours Willow more tea, then glances out the porch door.

It's such a quick gesture, Willow almost misses it. But the gift retreats—it's been unusually consistent till now—and there's no corresponding emotional flare to interpret the meaning behind the gesture. "It'll be a kinder death, if you die young."

Willow doesn't fight the tea this time, though she drinks it slowly. It tastes different than the mugwort her mother makes for magical workings. It must be a matter of ingredients—it's clear that Gisele uses fresh herbs where her mother always uses store-bought tea bags. "There's nothing I can do?"

"No."

"So that's it, then." Willow feels very small and outside her body, because it's impossible that she should be sitting here, in this house that smells like stagnant water, dark and rotting. She has a feeling that the mugwort is preventing her from feeling the full impact of her impending death, and for the briefest moment, she's grateful for Gisele's forethought. Gisele was right—this news would have hit her much harder if not for the trance.

"But it's not all bad news," Gisele says. "You have a chance to accomplish something bigger than yourself." Though her face stays calm and level, her anticipation thrums through Willow's body, their hearts skipping a beat. "A small chance, if I've timed this right, and I'm sure I have. But first, I need something from you."

"What?"

Gisele presses the deck down on the table, spreading the cards in a long line. Then she gestures to Willow. "Pick one."

"In any particular way?"

"Whichever calls to you first."

Willow inspects the cards, waits for some sense of deliberation to fill her, but they are only inert, laminated drawings. Nothing special.

"By all means, take your time," Gisele says dryly. As Willow finally reaches for them, Gisele's hand shoots out, knocks it away. Gisele smiles apologetically. "I'm out of practice reading for other people. I almost forgot—you need to say some words."

This was not part of her mother's stories, and unease curls around Willow's spine. However, the mugwort makes it hard to hold on to the specifics of that fear. "Words?" she repeats.

"Nothing elaborate. I guess Bronwyn wouldn't have mentioned them to you—it was all so normal to the girls." Gisele waves a dismissive hand. "But if you're that fussed about it, you're free to leave at any time."

Willow grapples between her fear and her need for certainty. "What are the words?"

"What was lost to the past will be bound to my future, may I drink in this burden and accept what awaits. Eyes open, mouth wide, may this gift that has withered thrive once it's tied to my fate." Gisele says it once, and then Willow repeats it. When the last word is out, Willow feels the magic trickling through her and become a hard wrench in her chest. She winces, rubbing away the pain. Gisele gestures her toward the cards. "Go ahead."

Willow grabs a card at random from near the middle and flips it over. It is upside down. A woman huddles in the corner of a boat, face twisted in a scream, with her arms wrapped around her child's shoulders. A man wearing a plague doctor's mask steers them through turbulent inky water. A grotesque card, so much terror in it.

"The Six of Swords," Gisele says. There's a palpable heat to the stare she turns on Willow. "Did she tell you that you were my favorite?" Gisele leans forward and lowers her voice. "When you were little? I loved you very much, before Bronwyn stole you from me. You and your sister used to call me Jelly and you screamed when she ripped you out of my arms that last time. I'll even admit, little love, I cried. Not where that wretched daughter of mine could see, but later. In secret." Gisele shakes her head as if to clear it, and her voice raises again. "I did hope you would come sooner, Willow. And I'm very sorry, but I have one more question for you—can your sister speak to them?"

"What?"

Gisele hardens, quick as lightning, her grip clamping onto Willow's arm. Willow cries out in pain. It will leave a bruise.

"Don't play dumb with me, girl. Does Ryann speak to the ghosts?"

"No." Unease prickles the nerves in Willow's neck as joy trills in the bottom of Gisele's belly. "She was an early bloomer. Her gift is pretty weak."

Gisele's eyes flicker closed, and she releases Willow's arm. "I worried you'd waited too long to come here. That I'd be gone before I had the chance to see you all grown up. I'd hoped you'd bring your sister too—that all this preparation would be unnecessary—but at least I got to see you again."

As Gisele speaks, a cold watchful presence forms in the corner of the room. Catlike, almost, predatory. Its anger rips Willow's breath from her in one big gust, and her fingers numb. But despite her terror, Willow finds herself grinning because Gisele's love is so warm and fierce, stronger even than the fury in the room. Willow hasn't held joy like that inside her in so long. Then, a realization. "What did I drink?" Willow lowers the cup.

"His ashes."

The bile rises fast and hard in Willow's throat, and she retches.

"I know, little love. But the binding ritual is already done." Gisele soothes, her face sad and tender in the dull light. "And there was no other way to transport him to your sister. I won't leave him to rot in this house when I'm gone." She stands from the table. "It was truly a pleasure, dear, to see you one last time."

TWENTY

"A MONTH AFTER THAT, I died." "

By the time Willow drops her interlocked fingers into her lap, the pillow under Alice is wet. *Sweat*, she thinks, though it could be tears. It wasn't enough for Gisele to destroy Alice's life? She had to destroy Bronwyn's too? Killian hadn't even wanted to live like this in the first place. How could she? Did her selfishness know no end?

And a coven—Gisele's mother had belonged to a fucking coven? All this time, there had been other witches, just like they'd hoped, but Gisele's silence and lies ensured they'd never have any sources of knowledge other than her. It burns Alice all the way through. She tries to move and ends up flopping back onto the bed, her body too weak to do what is demanded of it.

This is the true nature of their curse. It isn't just the boys dying. It isn't just being fated to love and protect and grieve their whole lives, doomed to repeat the same mistakes every generation under the guise of not knowing better. No, the women had a curse of their own. To seek power over happiness. Control at all costs. To rot from the inside out. But enough is enough. Alice will choose a different way. Alice will pick happiness. She will pick it every fucking time.

Alice takes a shaky breath, tries to press those thoughts away for now. She feels weak, wants to weep, but she holds herself steady. There are questions to ask. They will not be comfortable, for her or for Willow. "What happened then? After you left the Little House?"

Willow kneels, bringing her to Alice's eyeline. A thoughtful gesture since Alice is beyond movement now. "You've lost a lot of blood, Alice."

"I'll manage." Alice forces a small smile. "Don't worry about me."

"We should wrap your feet, at the very least."

"I can't stand," Alice admits. "But your mom will be back soon and this can't wait." And at any moment, Killian could appear. Where is he? Why hasn't he come?

"You know what happened." Willow rounds her shoulders, making herself small. It masks her resemblance to Bronwyn, who's always been all limbs and wild horse eyes. "I killed myself."

If Alice could, she'd spare this child her dignity and let it be. But the necessity of the answers outweighs the cruelty of the questions. "Before that."

Alice wants to reach out, her fingers twitching before she remembers she cannot touch Willow. For a moment, it embarrasses her. This has always been a flaw of her gift. The ghosts come to her fully formed, entirely present, yet wholly unmaterialized. She hasn't tried to touch a ghost, since she was a child. Willow doesn't notice the slip.

"It was stupid," Willow says quietly. "What I did. Why I did it. I don't want my mom to know."

"I'll make sure she understands."

Willow shakes her head. "No. She'll blame herself. She already blames herself for everything. If you want me to tell you, then you promise. You only tell her what I say is okay."

Alice considers pushing back—it's a bad promise, a flawed one—but already, they're pressing up against time. Bronwyn's return is overdue. "I promise."

Willow settles back on her heels. "It's my fault that Killian broke into the house." She hesitates, glancing around the room as if she can find support from the magazine girls taped to the wall. Or perhaps she's searching for him, waiting for him to appear. "That he tried to take Ryann's body."

"Not your fault," Alice corrects. "Gisele's."

Willow wipes a hand across her mouth, like she's barricading it. "I drank the tea. That was my fault, and of all people, I should have known better."

"She's tricky like that."

"Do you want me to tell you or not?"

Alice mimics locking her mouth and tossing a key. Willow waits another beat, testing the silence. "I'm sure you guessed some of it—I can't tell what though. I can't access your emotions now that I'm—well. Like this." It's the careful way she avoids saying *dead* that makes Alice want to cry. "The quiet is too loud sometimes."

Willow considers the carpet for a long time before her shoulders soften. Then she nods. "The words she had me say, and tea I drank, made me a vessel for Killian. He got tied to me. Not like how he was tied to you."

"It was probably weaker because it came from ash instead of blood," Alice thinks out loud. Her mind moves sluggishly, each thought languid where she needs it sharp.

"Well, it was enough that he could follow me home. While I was still alive, I could sense him. Here and there, in flashes. And then weird things started happening—he would mess with me sometimes, flicking the lights on and off in my room. Or writing in my sketchbook. He'd leave me these horrible creepy smiley faces. And if I didn't do anything back, he'd break things in my room, or ruin my artwork. He started messing with Mom's makeup drawer and breaking all her eyeliner sticks. But then he started fucking with Ryann. And that scared me because I knew he could possess Mediums, and I was worried about Ryann. I'd done enough to ruin her life. I couldn't let that happen to her too."

The despair in Willow's face takes Alice by surprise. "Willow, you didn't do anything to ruin your sister's life. I'd know a thing or two about that."

"You don't understand." Willow shakes her head vigorously. "My gift made me feel so sick. I couldn't go to parties, ever, so we never had big birthday parties growing up. And Mom worried so much about me so we spent a lot of time together. I'd try and make sure Ryann was included, but Ryann felt like I was pitying her. And every time I tried to talk to her about it, it got so much worse, because then she'd scream at me to stay out of her emotions, that they were hers and she didn't want me in her head, too, when she was already stuck with me in every other way." Willow pauses, fumbling over the words. Alice thinks of her own brother, of her own moments where she wanted Gisele to love her better, and how it would have destroyed her for Killian to know she felt that way. She understands Ryann more acutely than she'd like to acknowledge. It makes her long very much to have known Willow in life. "She loved me, but she didn't like me very much. And—this is so shitty to say, but—I didn't like her very much either. Her emotions were hard to be around. But she was my twin, and I would never, ever let Killian take her. So I tried for a while to fix things. Made the banishing bundles with mugwort and wormwood, just like she said, but they made things worse. I must have put it together wrong."

"Mugwort and wormwood?" Alice asks sharply. "Not juniper and angelica?" Willow shakes her head, her eyes wide. "It's juniper and angelica that are mainly used for banishing. Hyssop, too, and Saint-John's-wort, if you're being thorough. Gisele told you mugwort and wormwood?"

The well opens deep inside Alice as she realizes what Gisele has done. What a calculated and cruel thing to do. Gisele must have rehearsed that conversation with Willow a dozen times, a hundred, to guide her step by step into this outcome. To coax her to drink the tea with Killian's ashes and bind them together. To incite Willow to put up the bundles with the wrong ingredients, trapping both her and Killian in the house. And Gisele knew all the players so well. This time she had assumed beyond what the cards could predict and done so correctly—Killian's escalating haunting, Willow's death. That only this would be enough to make Bronwyn track Alice down and bring her within Killian's reach. Gisele has wanted her here—to what purpose, Alice does not yet know, which terrifies her.

Willow is staring at Alice, who swallows thickly. With the loss of blood, Alice's mind is moving too sluggishly to think it through. But she must continue, so she turns her attention to the matter of Killian instead. "How was he?"

Willow's face twists with pity. "Hopeless. Desperate. He did a lot of hating." She quiets. The thought of Killian still suffering hurts more than she would have expected. "I haven't seen him since I died, though I know he's been around."

This isn't surprising. Alice has never met a ghost who could see another ghost. "Has he been here since you met with Gisele?" And when Willow nods, Alice asks, "Why didn't Ryann see him until yesterday?"

"He doesn't want her to, I think. I asked Ryann a few times, when I was alive, if she felt something off in the house, but she told me to fuck off. Ryann's gift isn't very—" Willow pauses. "She'll never admit it, not ever, but she barely sees them. It takes all my concentration, screaming as loud as I can, for her to hear me. One time, I had to slam into her so hard I almost possessed her."

This echoes Alice's own private assessment. "Why didn't you tell your mom?"

"Because Mom couldn't have done anything—or at least I didn't think she could. I didn't realize hunting you down was even an option. And it would've hurt her so badly to hear what Gisele said." Willow pauses, looks down. "I fucked everything up, and she would have been so, so disappointed in me. I didn't want to know exactly how much. There's this thing people do—I don't understand it. They'll feel something so deeply and then deny it and deny it. Like with my mom—I knew how it'd go. She'd tell me it was okay, and that she loved me, and we'd work through it, and the whole time I'd be able to feel her screaming inside. I just couldn't do it."

"It wasn't your fault, Willow."

Willow rushes on. "But it was. I messed everything up. Every single thing I did was wrong. Like I did my best to keep him away from Ryann. I even sewed some dill into Pumpernickel—that's her stuffed rabbit. But it just made him angrier. And then one day, I came into the kitchen, and found Ryann standing at the counter jamming fistfuls of ice cream into her mouth. When she looked at me, her eyes were completely blank, and I knew it was him. I could feel all that hate and rage just crammed into her and so I thought, all right if I'm how he got into the house, then I'm how he gets out of it. If he's using my body as a vessel, then—" Willow cuts herself off. "I thought if Gisele was right about the rest of my life, at least my death could be noble. I thought he'd go back to the Little House when I died. But it didn't even matter. He still couldn't leave." Willow fixes Alice with a miserable look. "This is the part you can't tell my mom. That I thought I was going to save them. That I fucked that up too."

"You didn't fuck anything up, Willow." Alice's hand curves around her stomach. She wants to protect herself from the reality that this girl is dead. She's dead, and she died because once upon a time, Beau promised to keep her brother safe but wasn't brave enough to die for him. Yes, she can trace a direct path from her blood oath to this death. "I'm sorry," Alice whispers. "I'm so sorry."

"It's odd, being without the gift. I didn't realize I'd miss it. Did you?" Willow tugs the sleeves of her cardigan, wrapping it around herself.

"After I bound my shadow, a guy I had a crush on disappeared from campus," said Alice. A young man with a red backpack who rode the same bus as her every Tuesday morning. Every week, Alice had steeled herself to speak to him, but never garnered the courage. He'd never stepped close enough for Alice to catch the smell of ozone. "I didn't realize what it meant for weeks."

"I keep thinking—I wanted this, right? I wanted it to disappear. But still." Willow lifts her palms then lets them drop back into her lap.

"If I had to quantify it, I'd say it isn't really that I missed it exactly. I'd never want it back," Alice says. Willow arches a brow. "Or I *didn't* want it back, I guess."

"You didn't answer my question."

"Yes. I missed it." It hurts to admit it. "It's like—I spent my entire first year of hair school avoiding Park Street because I didn't want the poltergeist in house thirty-four to realize I could see it—because if it knew I was a Medium, it might try to possess me. It was weeks after I bound my gift before I realized that I could just walk through. That muscle memory doesn't evaporate overnight. My whole way of walking through the world changed. It felt as off as—suddenly not being able to see purple."

"When did you stop? When were you able to move on?" Willow stares up at the ceiling and shakes her head. "I guess it isn't going to matter for much longer, is it?"

"Willow, honey. I have to ask you something." When Willow nods, Alice swallows. "How badly has it started hurting?"

Willow tilts her head as if she doesn't quite understand the question. "Not very much. Sometimes, it feels like my bones are itching." She scratches absently at her collarbone.

"That's good, honey. That's really good." When Willow's brows furrow, Alice forces a smile. "We'll get you out of here before it gets worse."

Willow jolts, following the direction of a sound only she can hear. "My mom's back."

"What in the red hell did you do?"

Bronwyn stands in the doorway, a plastic grocery bag in her fist. Alice tries a smile that comes out more like a grimace. A thud as the grocery bag drops to the floor, lolls in the threshold, an apple rolling out onto the carpet. Willow jumps back, slipping through the dresser as Bronwyn rushes past. Old habits, perhaps. It isn't as if Willow actually needs to move. Bronwyn stops at the foot of the bed, out of Alice's view. She hears Bronwyn make a sound, and she tries to push herself up to make out her sister's expression, but her ears ring, her limbs buoyant. Alice gives up, mid-wriggle.

"Fuck," Bronwyn says. Then again, with more venom, "Fuck."

"It'll be fine," Alice mumbles. "But I couldn't find your first aid kit. Could you please find me some gauze?"

"Find you some fucking gauze." Bronwyn kneels. There's a featherlight touch on Alice's big toe, as Bronwyn tips her heels to survey the wounds.

Alice flinches, even though the touch doesn't really hurt. "I said please."

"You stupid bitch." Then Bronwyn jogs out of the room. Alice hears her footsteps, choppy and quick, on the stairs.

"She doesn't like blood." Willow hovers in the doorway, peering after her mother. "Not since she found me."

"She didn't tell me that she found you." Alice suddenly finds it hard to swallow, her tongue almost too large for her mouth. With the adrenaline draining from her body, it's becoming harder to keep a handle on herself.

"You can't tell her, Alice. How I tried to save them, okay?"

"I won't." Alice shuts her eyes. Only for a minute, she thinks. She won't fall asleep. "But you need to understand it isn't your fault—what Gisele did to you."

Willow's voice sounds as if it is coming from very far away. "Will you tell Mom I'm sorry?"

"I can do that." Talking grows more difficult, all of Alice's concentration focused on moving her mouth. "But I want you to leave, once we take care of this."

"When he's gone." Willow nods, and it sounds like a promise.

"That's good. The leaving. You don't want to become something like him."

"I won't."

"I'm sorry," Alice tells her because there's nothing else to say. "You deserved more than this."

Willow is quiet for a long time, and then Bronwyn storms back in, cursing. "So did you," Willow whispers. Then there's wet fire trickling down Alice's feet and she yelps. She tries to thrash but Bronwyn pins her knees.

"It's rubbing alcohol, you damn pimple. Stop moving."

Her muscles twitch of their own volition as Bronwyn wraps the gauze around her feet, and then there's only the soft sound of fabric unspooling as Alice slips into sleep.

Alice wakes again when the room is blunted with the brightness of afternoon sun poking through the blinds. Bronwyn's reading a magazine on one of the kitchen chairs, which she's dragged to Alice's bedside. A banishing bundle lies across her lap, a lighter balanced on her thigh. Her form is blurry, and Alice realizes that at some point, Bronwyn must have taken Alice's glasses off and set them on the table.

Though Willow is absent, Alice can still smell lightning. Somewhere close, then. Alice's neck is stiff, her brain swaddled in a fuzzy thickness. But she can taste the copper electricity of the gift behind her teeth. "What time is it?"

Bronwyn glowers over the top of the magazine. She returns to the article she's reading. "Three."

Alice pushes herself into a sitting position. It's easier now that she's rested, though she must roll onto her back very carefully to avoid grazing her wrapped feet against the bed. "Did you sleep at all?"

Bronwyn doesn't answer, but she doesn't flip the page either. Alice watches her chest rise and fall, the rhythm too quick.

"It'll be a long night," Alice says. There's a glass of water on the bedside table, and she drains it all in four gulps. "We've got work to do."

"The hell we do." Bronwyn snaps the magazine shut. "The fuck were you thinking?"

"It was the only way to get answers."

"I told you not to. I didn't actually think—"

"You dragged me here to talk to Willow. So, I—"

"No, don't you put this on me. I wanted advice, guidance for my kid. But *this*? I would fucking never—" Bronwyn cuts off mid-sentence and lobs the magazine as hard as she can across the room. It slaps the door and tumbles to the floor in a muffled hush. Bronwyn leans forward, head in her hands.

"I saw her," Alice whispers. "I've talked to her." There's a point at which, when you've survived so many bad things, any new tragedy, any new hurt becomes a cruel cosmic joke. You're inoculated from the full, painful brunt of it because a thin protective layer of chitin whispers, *Can this really be happening again? How hysterically, unbelievably impossible it is that things can get worse?* This is the place Alice goes to as she tells Bronwyn what happened to her daughter. That ash, too, can work as a binding reagent, not as strong as a blood oath, but enough that it opened a crack for Killian to squeak through. That Willow's banishing bundle trapped first Killian, then Willow herself, in Bronwyn's house, all orchestrated by Gisele. And that Killian had been escalating slowly until Alice walked through the door, triggering all the rage and betrayal that hung between them. Alice leaves out the reasons Willow died—Bronwyn doesn't need to hear these, and Alice has learned her lesson about keeping promises. "We need the knot I swore on. We need to burn it."

"Can you even break blood, Alice?"

For the first time, Alice notices threads of gray in Bronwyn's hair. They've been apart so long. "We'll figure out the logistics of breaking the spell later," she says, as if she doesn't already know. But she can't explain this to Bronwyn without explaining what she did to avoid doing exactly that. She will not go back to that night in Midland.

"Because that's not an absurd plan. And how are we supposed to get it anyway? Waltz right into the Little House?" The exasperation in Bronwyn's voice doesn't quite conceal a note of hope.

"Maybe not waltz but think about how far we could make it with a good set of jazz hands," Alice says dryly. Then, more serious, she says, "If we want the knot, there really isn't another choice. We go back."

"And do what exactly? Show up, saying, 'Oh, hey, Gisele, don't mind us, we decided on a quick jaunt in the woods. No worries, not trying to banish dear old Killian or anything.'"

"There's always the possibility she's expecting us."

"Possibility, my ass."

"Well she can't have Seen it at least because Killian and Willow are involved. And she might be too weak to do anything about it," Alice says, tentatively, and Bronwyn meets her eyes. Neither of them are ready to breach the implication that their mother might be dead. "Terminal lung cancer, four months ago."

Bronwyn snorts. "She doesn't have to be physically strong to fuck with us. And who knows what she might have done to the Little House in those four months." The possibilities are daunting. Gisele could prevent their rituals from taking effect, or their magic might not work at all on the perimeter. But it's a chance they'll have to take.

Willow slips through the doorway, and plops on the ground, legs crossed. As Bronwyn talks about Gisele's foresight, Willow asks. "Can I talk to my mom?"

Alice puts a hand up, and Bronwyn freezes. "Is she here?"

Alice nods. To Willow, she adds, "Do you want to slip in?"

Every tendon in Bronwyn's body tightens as she glances between Alice and the door. She's checking every corner of the room, as if she can pinpoint the spot where Willow is sitting if only she focuses hard enough.

Willow rises, cat-smooth, and sits on the bed. Alice expects it to shift with Willow's weight and it surprises her again when it doesn't. "Not if it hurts you. I just want her to know I'm sorry."

When Alice repeats the words, Bronwyn stiffens. Alice points her toward Willow. Bronwyn smiles gratefully before she kneels at the foot of the bed. "Baby, what're you sorry for? There's no reason to be sorry." Bronwyn's voice is an animal keening, holds a grief too private for Alice to feel comfortable serving as Willow's intermediary in responding.

"Willow," Alice says. "It's okay. I'll hold you as long as I can." She reaches out, palm up. "Come on, honey."

Willow glances between Alice and her hand, hesitating. When Alice gestures again, Willow tentatively interlocks their fingers.

The shift of Willow into Alice's body lurches her vision—the cold douses her, sending her into violent jerking shudders, her throat raw with the desire to scream even as she can't. It is every horrible thing Alice remembered, yet somehow worse. As Alice's vision goes dark, as she fades away to let Willow speak, Bronwyn's arms close impossibly tight around her, and in an intonation entirely unlike her own, Willow whispers, "Mom?"

TWENTY-ONE

THE BANISHING BUNDLES are strong magic, though they have to be refreshed every twenty-four hours or so to keep the banishing intact and keep Killian at a safe distance in the Little House. Alice is careful to structure the spell in such a way that it doesn't cast Willow out too. Her magic feels weak, but the hot rush of it sings inside her again. The return of the gift is like nothing so much as the first day of waking up without a head cold. Her mind moves agilely from thought to thought. She sleeps deeper. Her body is still a wreck from the blood loss and pain, but this gradually passes until the only thing remaining is the pain from the physical wound.

Bronwyn sways around the house, solemn and wan. She can't settle, won't sit still. She checks every room for the essence of her daughter—rattled by the reality of Willow as an actionable entity rather than a hypothetical one. She runs errands to collect crystals and borrow New Age spell books from the library, busies herself repairing Killian's damage to the kitchen.

The first night, they empty Alice's duffel and use it as storage for the spells they prepare. Alice enchants points of raw quartz and tourmaline for protection until sweat beads her upper lip and dampens her hair, her arms numb from the electricity inside her, then passes the pieces to Bronwyn to be wire-wrapped into amulets. A piece of polished black obsidian hangs in the middle of each, intended to repel any scrying from Gisele. "We would've gotten into so much trouble, if we'd thought of this as kids." Bronwyn smiles to herself.

They grind pieces of tourmaline to sand and dump the grains into a mixing bowl with two containers of kitchen salt. The mixture is meant to repel ghosts. Bronwyn retrieves glass ornament balls from her attic. "Willow liked to paint them," she explains, as she hefts the box onto the kitchen table. "I bought them in bulk every winter." Outside, they test the shatter, lobbing an ornament against the hard-packed snow, where Willow stands as their test subject. The ornament breaks satisfactorily and sends Willow sprawling ten feet, so they fill the others, then fix them to infinity scarves. Glittery gold bandoliers of ghost repellent.

When they finish the spirit bombs, they build more banishing bundles, proper ones, which Alice fortifies with blood. There's no absence of it, with her oozing heels. The scabs keep breaking open as she walks.

They study their newly assembled poltergeist kit in the first rays of sun poking through the windows as the second day dawns. Bronwyn puts an arm through Alice's, holding her steady. Their preparations might not be enough. "We have to do something to cut off Gisele's magic," Alice says grimly. "I don't see another way."

Bronwyn gestures to the books on the kitchen table. When their spines are not black and swirling red, they are opaline pastels. "'An ye harm none, do what ye will,'" she intones. "We won't find anything on witch-binding that actually works. Not in those books."

They both eye the stack. "She never taught us curses," Alice says, quietly. "Nothing baneful, nothing spell-breaking—did you ever notice that?"

Bronwyn runs her fingers through her hair. "Yup. Controlling bitch."

Alice picks up a pink book from the top of the pile, flips through its pages without reading it. "I wonder how much she kept from us."

"*You*," Bronwyn corrects. Her gaze skates over the half-packed duffel by the front door, the clippings of fresh rosemary thicketing her place mats. "She didn't give a flying fuck about my magic. Half the shit I learned came from books like that." She takes the book out from Alice's grip, tucks it under her arm. "I'll keep looking."

When Bronwyn's search for baneful magic turns up empty, they settle on rubber banded bunches of dill shoved inside their bras to soften any direct casting. None of these are precise rituals, but for once, Alice decides they don't have to be. She works on instinct.

They sleep through most of the second morning in that collapsed exhaustion that follows so much casting. It leaves a satisfied exhaustion inside Alice. She doesn't dream.

When Alice wakes, she counts four tensely worded texts from Eli that leave her too ashamed to call. They ask how she is doing, how her sister is. He tells her that he hopes she is well, that she will come home soon. It is his way of telling her he misses her, that he's worried, while still respecting the wall she's raised between them. An unacknowledged understanding is arising between them: that until she comes home, until they have that serious talk and Alice gives her explanations, they can have conversations no bigger than this. *Are you well? Yes, I am.*

In that ominous silence from its father, the baby decides to make its presence known. Little things—a metallic taste in her mouth that won't go away, a staggering nausea that leaves her near incapacitated around 3 p.m. But this is perhaps as much from the blood loss as the baby. A reminder of what she will have to sacrifice to see this done.

Bronwyn does not allow her daughter to return home until they're absolutely certain Killian can't get back in. When Ryann does return, she stomps past her mother to her room, slamming the door shut. She doesn't reemerge for the rest of the night, and though Bronwyn offers to evict her daughter, Alice insists on sleeping the remainder of the day on the couch.

It is almost dusk on the third day by the time Alice and Bronwyn finish readying their stores for their attack on the Little House. Three bundles for the three days of preparation before Gisele's three cloven children meet again by moonlight. There is a satisfaction in this triplicate. A sort of fairy tale to it. It smacks of Gisele's bedtime stories when they were children. If it were—in what ways would their mother choose to mutilate them? *Once there was a mother with two furious daughters and a poltergeist for a son.* Alice would've preferred a daytime excursion, but night will offer a more practical cover for their trespassing.

Ryann and Willow hover in the small kitchen, watching Bronwyn pack a duffel bag. They stand as mirrors of each other, despite Ryann seeming unaware of it. As Bronwyn hefts the bag over her shoulder, Ryann plants herself in front of the door, blocking it with her body. "I'm going with you," she says, decisively.

And though Bronwyn can't hear her, Willow also whispers, "You can't let her go with you."

Ryann is dressed as her idea of a heroine. A *Vampire Diaries* meets *Supernatural* couture—black jeans, shredded at the knees, and impractical heeled booties. A leather jacket, two sizes too big for her narrow frame. She keeps rolling it up to her elbows so her hands won't vanish into the sleeves. Today, Alice has longed for velvet and tulle, craved the slim point of a liquid eyeliner pen. The costume that once granted her strength. She itches to knot a braid, to slip flower stems in her hair.

"For Christ's sake." Bronwyn grabs her daughter by the shoulders and tries to push her back into the house.

Ryann digs her heels in, refusing to budge. "I can help." She reaches for her mother's elbow, and a spiked bangle glitters on her wrist, the points sharp as weapons.

Bronwyn glowers. "Move."

Ryann searches out Alice over Bronwyn's shoulder. Willow shakes her head.

"Tell her, Alice. You need me there. I can help," Ryann says.

Alice flinches. They could use another Medium—all of Alice's magical instincts have gone soft, the muscle memory returning to her in instants too late to be truly useful. But the Medium she needs is not Ryann. Even if Ryann were as experienced as Alice, she would never let her niece come with them back to that place. Before Alice can respond to either of them,

Ryann grins victoriously. "I knew it! You need me." She plants her hands on her hips. "If I can help, take me with you. It's stupid if you don't."

Alice doesn't have to make eye contact with her sister to sense her glare. "This isn't something you should be a part of," Alice says. "I promise."

"You're wrong," Ryann says. "I want to be there. I owe it to Willow."

Willow, behind Ryann, makes a noise of protest.

"Willow disagrees." Alice touches her hand briefly to her mouth, to the chap of her lips, the divot where her teeth broke through the skin the night she sliced the bind runes off her heels. "And even if she didn't, there are some things you don't come back from, Ryann. You can never be the person you were before."

"I'm not a child, and you don't have to protect me. I want to be there when you put that *thing* down."

Despite everything, Alice still cannot think of Killian as a monster. No matter what he is now, he was a child when he died, was once a boy she'd do anything for. Bronwyn recoils as if Ryann has struck her.

"This," Bronwyn says, jabbing a finger at her. "This is exactly why you're staying."

"It's his fault that Willow died." Ryann's chest heaves as if she's trying to squeeze every last particle of air from her lungs. "I want him gone. I want to be the one to do it."

There have been many times that Alice felt exactly that—that she wanted Killian gone and parceled away, that she wanted him to suffer—but to hear Ryann say it makes the nerves in Alice's spine ring like struck glass. In the part of Alice that can stand at a distance and consider such things, she marvels at the irony of being in the position to justify Killian's humanity to someone else, when she knows better than most how inhumane Killian can be.

"This isn't about revenge." If anything, in Alice's center, there is a morsel of holiness, a plea for absolution. "I understand that right now it seems like there's a whole lot of right and a whole lot of wrong, but it is so much more complicated than that. A mother tries to save her sons, the girls suffer for it, and the boys still die. And then the cycle continues. And so we have the hardest job—of breaking this cycle so the same damn thing doesn't keep happening over and over again."

Ryann sinks into herself, deflating. She pulls at the sleeves of her leather jacket until they cover her hands again. Bronwyn leans back against the wall, glancing between Alice and her daughter with a chasm of grief yawning in her eyes. "But my twin died," Ryann says finally, trying one last approach. "And that makes me part of this, whether you like it or not."

"This isn't a TV show, Ryann. It's not a fucking anime." Bronwyn slaps the front door, just to the left of Ryann's shoulder, and the sound echoes around the kitchen. Both Ryann and Alice startle. When her daughter still doesn't budge, Bronwyn throws up her hands and stalks toward the living room. Willow bites her lip, hesitating, before she hurries after her mother.

Without Bronwyn, the kitchen grows quiet. It's the first time Alice has been alone with Ryann and suddenly, it feels too intimate. Alice isn't sure what she's meant to do. The role she's being asked to fill feels too tight, itchy at her neckline, is too long in the sleeves. She steps back, needing the added space between them so she can think.

"What she means," Alice says, "is that we are about to do an incredibly difficult thing, and even if everything goes right, we're still losing something. Maybe we'll heal from it. I hope we do. But I don't think that me or your mom are going to be okay. Not for a long time."

"But I—"

Alice cuts her off. "There's no happy ending here. There's only the least bad outcome."

"But what if I can't live with myself for staying behind?" Ryann closes the distance between them, puts her cold hands on Alice's arms.

Hesitantly, Alice strokes the crown of Ryann's head, lowers her voice to a whisper. "It's okay to hate us for this. But if you can't stay for yourself and you can't do it for us, then you have to do it for Willow. Because she needs you to help her pass, and then she needs you to go into the world and live a full life. To be better than we were, Ryann. Staying here is braver than you know."

They are nearly the same height, their eyes nearly the same color. Ryann leans into Alice, presses her forehead against Alice's shoulder, and Alice chokes with the love in her chest. Maybe not even for the girl, but for the idea of her surviving. "I will hate you for this," Ryann whispers, even as she hugs Alice tighter.

TWENTY-TWO

BRONWYN HESITATES, the key in the ignition. "Sure you're up for this?" This is the fourth time she's asked, the fourth time Alice has nodded—even though her throat's dry, her fists balled to stop the shaking. Yes, she's ready. Yes, it's time to end this. Yes, it must be done. Yes, Bronwyn, start the car.

"Your feet okay?"

"Bronwyn." Even though Alice softens her voice, Bronwyn flinches at the sound of her name. She tries to cover it by shrugging. "Are *you* ready for this?"

"Yeah, sure." This would be significantly more convincing if Bronwyn had started the engine by now. She taps a staccato rhythm against the steering wheel. "What if she's expecting us?"

"We've been over this."

"It's been months since Willow visited her. What if she's dead?"

"We have to assume that she isn't." Alice stifles the urge to reach over and start the damn car herself. "It's the safest assumption to make."

Bronwyn presses her lips together. "We can always be pleasantly surprised, I guess."

"See?" says Alice. "That's the spirit."

Bronwyn snorts, chewing her lip. Drums the steering wheel again. "And Killian?"

"There's no other place he can be, at the moment."

Bronwyn makes a sound halfway between a laugh and a sob. "Are we ready, Alice? Will this actually be enough?" She gestures to the duffel in the back seat, which admittedly seemed much more substantial with its contents spread out across Bronwyn's kitchen table.

"It'll have to be." And because this isn't terribly reassuring, Alice adds, "It's now or never. We don't have much of a choice."

Alice cannot fail. Failure means losing too much, too many people she loves. Eli, who she cannot return to until she sees this done. Bronwyn, heartsick between her daughters, living and dead. Ryann, untrained and eager, who will insist on taking up the mantle if Alice can't fix it. Willow, who refuses to pass on, even with the banishing bundles removed, so long as Ryann is in danger. And Killian—the chance to finally do right by him. To keep her promise and finally grant him peace. Urgency thrums in Alice's bones like a bass guitar.

Bronwyn raps her knuckles on the dashboard and eases her forehead against the steering wheel. "I'm scared shitless," she admits. "Of what we'll find out there. Of what—of how she'll be." Alice hasn't forgotten the day Killian died—the wooden spoon in Bronwyn's hand, the blood welling around Gisele's nostrils, the red imprint across her cheekbones.

"I'm scared too. But she's dying. What great magical workings can she be capable of now? That kind of magic takes energy she doesn't have."

"Yeah, well, you know what they say about cornered animals."

Bronwyn reaches for her cigarette pack in the cup holder, but Alice snatches it out of reach. "Your daughter will walk out here any minute, and she won't let us talk her into staying a second time. You want her to prance into that house like she's goddamn Dean Winchester? Let's go. Now."

Bronwyn's fists curl. Uncurl. Curl again. Finally, the key turns. The engine starts. "Give me one. To calm my nerves," Bronwyn says. Alice fishes a cigarette free and passes it over. The click of the lighter suspends between them, under the whisper of the engine and the wind from Bronwyn's cracked window. And then they are heading home—heading to Killian, just like he asked her to so many years ago.

There was an afternoon, maybe a week before Alice bound her shadow, fourteen years ago, one of those lazy fall afternoons that gathered all its warmth for a last hurrah before the Michigan winter descended.

"Is this what you had in mind when you told me we could share your body?" Killian had asked.

"No," she'd said after a moment. "I never thought it would be like this. Not this bad, but not this good either."

Their new life was caught between two extremes—the horror of watching Killian lose himself set against an evening of a wonderful TV show ordinariness. Most nights, Alice folded herself cross-legged to lean over the armrest of her battered but comfy sofa, to better angle her newest true crime book under the singular standing lamp. On Sundays, she swung by the laundromat near the bar where she worked and scrolled through

Tumblr on her laptop while she waited for the spin cycle. They watched sitcoms together on a small TV Alice bought at a garage sale. Killian was especially partial to *How I Met Your Mother*, and sometimes when the pain crescendoed in Killian's body, she distracted him by coming up with new addendums to their own personal Bro Code. They bought a beta fish and named him Gustav, and loved him to an absurd degree before he died as a casualty of one of Killian's episodes. Other days, Alice sat on the floor beside Killian as he screamed from the pain of the death itch, as he relived his death over and over again, and wept for it to be over.

It was on one of those days that he first brought it up. "Gisele wouldn't have been able to fix it," Killian said, referring to the death itch, which was overcoming him more and more often. He rested his forehead against his knees, angling to fix her with a stare. "You know that, right? If we haven't figured it out, she wouldn't have either."

"Maybe there isn't a way." It was hard for Alice to admit.

"If we could only get our hands on the blood oath," Killian said. "Do you think that would work? That if we burned it I could pass?" He'd been fixated on the idea ever since they'd read about the necromantic rite in a book at the library three months before.

"Maybe." Alice paused, bowing her head. In her lap, her hands seemed small and useless. The magical principles had felt right, and Alice was almost certain if they burned the knot, it would release him. But burning the knot meant first getting through Gisele, and that wasn't something Alice was sure she could do. "But we're making do, aren't we? We've built this life, and it's a good one." *Tell me*, she was thinking. *Tell me I've built you a good life. Tell me you don't want to leave.*

Killian's lip curled into a snarl. "The only thing I've ever wanted was to pass, Beau. I've given it a shot; I've tried. I really have. But it has to stop. How can you not want more than this? How can you not want more than splitting a body?" Alice couldn't shake the sense he was aging in death, more like the thirteen-year-old he was supposed to be than the ten-year-old he'd been when he died. His voice dropped into a low urgency. "We'll go back to Kirtland. I'll keep her busy—you have no idea how creative I can be—and while I distract her, you'll search down that blood oath. Then we'll burn it, and I can finally go. It hurts, Beau, how much I want to pass. Just let me, let me, let—"

"I can't go back there." Alice's voice cracked, and she rubbed her wrists against the fabric of her jeans, trying to banish the sensation of the handcuffs, her nose filling with the reek of lilies and her own unwashed body. Gisele would break her. Returning to Kirtland—Alice would freeze, she would disassociate, she would try to gather her strength for him, and she would fail, and then they would both be trapped again. She was sure of it. "I'm so sorry, Killy, but I can't do it. I can't go back."

"Yeah," Killian said after a moment, his voice laced with bitterness. "Of course not. Why risk yourself for me, huh? Gisele was right, you don't love me nearly enough."

It knocked the breath from Alice's chest. "That's not fair."

"It's not fair to live like this—not for either of us." Killian turned, putting his back to her, and nestled down. Alice almost offered her hand—their symbol for the times it was okay for him to inhabit her—but dropped it back to the fold of the couch. And that was the end of it, for a time.

But then, he brought it up again. And then again, and again, and again. Weeks of pestering her to return. And when Alice didn't comply, he started taking her body without asking. A child throwing a tantrum. Proving a point, and Alice could allow him that. Until he'd gone too far. It will never leave her body—the horror of coming to, realizing that two weeks had passed without her knowing, without any means of stopping it. That with Killian around, she'd never again be able to trust she had control of what happened next. That her own body wasn't fully hers.

She doesn't want to touch what happened next. She's spent so long avoiding it. But the memory rises again unbidden as they get closer to the Little House. As they get closer to him.

It was almost three weeks after Killian returned her body. They'd both had a particularly rough adjustment to Killian's separation from her body. The death itch was always worse for Killian after he had sheltered inside her, and the more time he claimed, the weaker Alice's body became. The two-week possession had left her shaking and vomiting on the bathroom floor for two days. But the worst part was the feeling of violation, the terror that it would happen again and that she was helpless to prevent it. Even as her body grew stronger, Alice couldn't eat or sleep, and though she had to inhabit the same house as Killian, she couldn't stand to be in the same room as him. Finally Alice had made the decision that this could not go on. That she could not let it happen again.

Killian had been watching squirrels quibble at a bird feeder out the window when she approached him. "I'm ready," she said.

Killian whipped around to look at her. "What?"

"You were right. We can't keep living like this. I'll go back with you to the Little House." Alice had already made the banishing bundle, placed it and the saltshaker under the bathroom sink. "I have class this week, but I'll buy the bus tickets to Cleveland after school on Friday. I'll burn the blood oath for you."

The way his eyes lit up. The grin tipping across his face. "Really? You'll really do it?"

"Yes," she'd said, swallowing down the grief, the guilt. "I don't want you to suffer anymore."

"You have no idea how much this means to me," he'd whispered.

"I promised I'd never leave you," Alice said. "I'm with you, now and always."

And Alice used the rest of that week well. She prepared a banishing bundle, gathered all the ingredients she needed to cut her shadow out, and when Friday came, she told Killian to start packing their clothes while she gathered her toiletries. "Go get the duffel bag," she'd instructed him. "I'll be there in a minute."

Once he was distracted, she'd grabbed the bundle from under the sink, then she'd banished Killian from the apartment. Only then had she cut the bind runes in.

I didn't have a choice, she reminds herself. *I couldn't have gone back there. Not then.* Not when she'd still be so damaged, so susceptible to Gisele's ways. Every choice had been a bad one. She'd been choosing Killian her entire life—and this time, this worst and most horrible time, Alice had chosen herself.

In the aftermath, she'd wake three to four times a night, unable to breath, from nightmares of the shed, or of her brother reliving his own death, or of her brother begging her not to leave him alone in the Little House. She'd be sitting on the bus to school and spot a child with his mother a few rows away, then find herself locked in a flashback of resurfacing from her last possession, hyperventilating in place. She worried, obsessively, about whether or not she had made the right choice. And finally, after months of this, when she'd become a shell of herself, in order to survive, she'd bisected herself. Those memories belonged to Beau, and Beau was dead, and so she became Alice. Alice didn't have those memories. Alice was normal. Alice had never had a family like that. Alice had never been forced to make that choice. Alice would never have been so selfish as to save herself.

But now, after hearing what Gisele had done to Willow in the name of giving Killian a life—Alice knows there was no other choice she could have made. Gisele would have done whatever it took to ensure Alice never left the Little House again. That it can both be her fault, and the only option she could have taken. If she'd gone to the Little House with Killian when he'd wanted, they would have failed. Back then Beau was still a prisoner to her panic. It would have immobilized her and Gisele would have bested them.

Beau could not save Killian then, but maybe Alice can save him now.

Alice has made this drive a thousand times in her dreams. Right on Chardon Road, past the quiet dark of the Historic Kirtland buildings, the white house on the hill that hasn't been the Carriage House in a very long time. Now the Penitentiary Glen, the crystalized and bare-branched trees twisting up the hill onto

Regency Woods Drive, and the houses there, brighter now and newer than the Little House.

The night is clear, the moon nearly full. She wishes for thick fog hovering over the road, clouds slung low in the sky, a moon like a jagged tooth, a crackle of thunder. No matter what they told Ryann, she wants the comfort of a clean narrative. The expected story because with the expected story comes the expected ending—the overcoming. The clean severance. The night's beauty sets her on edge. If Eli were here, he'd calm her—place his hands on her shoulders, hold his forehead against hers. There are good reasons why she hasn't told him about this place. She can't currently remember what those are.

As Bronwyn reaches the turn, she cuts the headlights and steers carefully up the rolling driveway, fighting to keep the sliding car steady on the ice, until the Little House comes into view. It's even bigger than Alice remembers and she chokes. Her skin flashes hot then cold then hot. She doesn't want to die here. *Breathe, Alice. You're sitting in a leather seat, the seat belt strapped tight across your chest. Put your hand on the window. It is cold. You are not safe, but you will do what you need to.*

Bronwyn parks in front of the garage door. When she cuts the engine, the only sound is the wind skating over the ice through Bronwyn's cracked window. One of the garage lights burns dimly, on its way out. The other is entirely broken. It's too dark to see the yard, and so Alice can't make out the shed, and this is such an unexpected mercy that Alice manages a ragged breath. Is the path to the clearing still there? Alice wonders. Have the woods reclaimed it as if it had never been? Is the red ribbon marker still tied over Killian's grave?

Bronwyn hops out of the car before Alice can bring herself to and nearly slips, slapping her hand against the car door to keep her balance. "Black ice," she mutters. "The whole driveway's totally unsalted."

Unsalted suggests absence, suggests Gisele may not be here. Alice grits her teeth. She eases herself from the car, babying her heels, which scream in pain as they accept her full weight. Bronwyn skates her way to the truck's pickup bed and retrieves a shovel, then slings the duffel over her shoulder. The ghost bomb bandolier glitters ridiculously around her torso.

The outside is still, calm, the air cool. Nothing but the fresh smell of snow, no sulfur on the breeze. But he's here somewhere, even if she can't see him. It's the only place he can be. Alice shivers.

"Anything?" Bronwyn asks.

"No." Alice walks around the pickup, keeps her eyes planted on the driveway. She will not look behind the house, to where the shed stands, its mouth yawning open and trying to swallow Alice back inside. Where even in the black nothingness, she knows the shed is waiting. She hazards a glance to the Little House, landing on the damaged siding. How different it looks from that very first day, the way Gisele clapped her hands over her mouth and cried, "What a darling little house!"

"Are you okay?" Bronwyn touches her elbow and Alice shakes her head. This isn't the Little House, not really. This is a silent husk. She wants her mother to be there. She prays her mother is dead.

"I don't know why I was expecting her to hold the fucking door open for us." Bronwyn rests the shovel on her shoulder. "Should we let ourselves in?"

"I guess so."

When Bronwyn tries the front door, it opens easily. The hinges keen. Bronwyn leans in, tries the entry light. Nothing happens. Alice points overhead. In the front room, all the overhead bulbs have been broken in their sockets. Farther in, a gap in the kitchen door offers a dim and sickly glow.

Bronwyn moves to step in, but Alice grabs her wrist, nearly upsetting her own balance. "Willow said there are holes in the floorboards."

"Right." Bronwyn swallows. "That's fantastic. Really just stellar."

"Witch ball?"

Bronwyn hands Alice the shovel before she summons a ball of light the size of a silver dollar. It flickers grumpily on her index finger before settling. Bronwyn tosses it into the air, where it hovers above her head. "I don't have to point out that this is the part in the horror movie where the first idiot dies, do I?"

Alice scowls and passes the shovel back. The sisters peer inside, the hallway gradually taking shape in the dim light.

Even with Willow's warning, Alice isn't prepared for the damage. For the Little House, which has always been dusty and a little strange, to become its own haunting. Holes in the drywall, the carpet torn to shreds, the dusty staircase. Half the banister hangs onto empty air, straining against the few remaining nails. And on the walls, line after line of furious scrawls. *YOU DID THIS*, one says. *I WILL RIP YOUR LIVER FROM YOUR BODY AND WEAR YOUR MEAT AS A HAT*, says another. Below it, a dripping smiley face: *COME OUT TO PLAY, MOTHER*. Then, on the other side, a set of sentences repeated from floor to ceiling: *MOTHER. I HURT. KILL ME.* She reaches for Bronwyn's hand. Bronwyn squeezes.

Alice feels a sudden longing for her mother, for arms wrapping Alice's shoulders and a *hush now, hush now, all is well, little love*. But this is followed immediately by deep, shuddering revulsion. The moments where Gisele could be that mother were never worth the moments she wasn't.

"I almost feel sorry for her. Almost." Bronwyn's grip tightens. "I don't want to go in."

"We—" The bile rises in Alice's throat, but why the hell have they come if they refuse to be brave now? "We have to." Alice tugs Bronwyn forward, and they pick their way carefully through the debris. Glass and pebbles and god knows what else crunch under their boots until they reach the kitchen.

Here, too, Willow's warnings fall short. The kitchen contains a different kind of horror. The walls are a dense foliage of banishing bundles, stapled to the walls, the ceiling. There's a makeshift throne of throw pillows assembled in front of the oven, and a sleeping bag stretches along the pantry door beside a veritable pharmacy of pills. It's barely warmer in the Little House than outside it, and there's a strong possibility the pipes are frozen. Alice debates testing the faucet, to be sure. Alice nudges Bronwyn and points at the threshold, which has been lined with salt. Another salt line, on the other side of the room, demarcates the kitchen from the living room. They carefully step over the lines on their way into the kitchen.

A shoebox sits on the coffee table, its glossy red stark against the disintegrating yellow tablecloth. There's a Post-it note on the lid. When Alice reads it, her throat dries. She unsticks the note, holds it out for Bronwyn: *To My Little Loves*.

"Should we open it?" Bronwyn whispers, though it's clear Gisele isn't here. There are no other lights on, no other sounds—the house is empty. Except for them, of course. And, somewhere on the grounds, their brother.

Alice sets the duffel bag on the table and, before she can talk herself out of it, in one quick gesture, flips open the lid. Inside are three items: Gisele's will, notarized twenty-five days ago; that damned tarot deck, bound in black cord; and a single folded piece of paper.

Bronwyn pulls the tarot deck from the box. She runs her thumb over the knot of black cord and lifts the cards close to her mouth, almost as if she's about to kiss them. Then, without warning, Bronwyn lobs the deck against the wall. Alice flinches. She expects them to burst from their thread, to explode around them into myriad impossible futures, but the cards thump harmlessly onto the sleeping bag. Bronwyn closes her eyes, concentrates on her breaths.

Alice lifts the will from the box with shaky fingers, flips through the pages. Even in death, Gisele still manages to surprise her. "She left it all to Ryann. The house, the land, all of it." There's too much detail for Alice to take in now. She'll deal with it later. "You and I each get one penny." A tactic to ensure that neither Alice nor Bronwyn can contest the will.

Quietly, Bronwyn says, "I need you to read it." For a moment, Alice thinks she means the will. But when she turns to her sister, Bronwyn is transfixed by the folded piece of paper. The only thing that remains in the box. She jabs Alice with her elbow, points. Her voice comes out in a whisper. "Please. I can't."

Alice lifts the piece of notebook paper and reads.

My darling daughters,

It will already be over by the time you read this. You are coming, be it in days or weeks, but in every thread, far too late. I'll be dead by the time you arrive—run off the road picking up my groceries, my purse thrown from the window, the paramedics still yet to find my ID. Cleveland General will have my mortal remains. There's no need to watch for my ghost—you can rest assured that I have no intention of loitering at the side of the highway.

It does disappoint me that I won't see you again. Maybe it's better this way. What have we left to say to one another? Very little, I reckon. Yet, I still find myself writing.

My mother told me once that to mother is to garden a wayward plant. That in order to grow straight, the plant must be corrected, bound to a twig. If so, I've been a poor mother. I know you will not forgive me, and I do not hold the leaving against you. I ask only that you understand I did the best I could.

Your final gift is one of absolution. Your brother has suffered so much these last two decades. I've done what I could to ease his condition, but he was never meant to be trapped the way he was when Isabeau cut her shadow off. I beg you, Isabeau, as a last gift to me, do the kind thing. If you cannot let him have you—let him take Ryann instead. Stay out of his way. Let him live.

Your Mother

TWENTY-THREE

EVEN IN HER LAST WORDS, Gisele picked herself over all of them. Alice scrunches the letter up and tosses it onto the table before collapsing into a chair. It creaks but holds her weight. The scabs on her heels crack with the sudden movement, blood warming her socks. All the adrenaline empties from her body, leaving Alice exhausted and aching and numb in every one of her limbs. This, too, is part of Alice's legacy. Gisele was a bad mother who had a bad mother; found herself with an inopportune child; tried softness, found herself lacking. Who is Alice to think she can do better? She wraps her arms around herself.

Bronwyn snatches the paper, flipping it over. "This can't be it."

Despite what she told Ryann, Alice feels she's owed some closure, some finality. In every story Alice has ever read about trauma, there's always *something*. It's not always tidy, not necessarily clean, or even positive—but still, there's some sort of resolution. Why not for her? Why must she be left with this sorry excuse of a letter and a penny and a deck of cards?

"She has to be here," Bronwyn says as she paces the room, the broken glass crackling under her boots. "She can't have died. Not before we got here."

"Why did we expect anything else?"

"She was supposed to be here, Alice." Bronwyn kneels to the ground, her arms wrapped around her knees, and starts to howl. Alice tries to force herself up to reach her sister, but Bronwyn says, "Don't fucking touch me. Don't."

Through Bronwyn's keening, Alice recognizes in her sister that grief particular to mothers, and Alice closes her eyes to it—she wants to join in, to howl, too, because this feeling isn't rational. It is deep-bellied, it is blood song, and in this moment, Alice is mourning the death she could choose to birth, the flawed motherhood that would be all she could manage, and which her child would not deserve. *That lead in your bones, Alice—that is certainty. You will not have this baby.* All her life, she's been running from that mother's grief, only to find it inside herself now.

These deaths and gifts and births and curses, this game of girls and chance. It's for the best that they didn't find Gisele in this house. Neither she nor Bronwyn would have survived the things they were capable of doing to their mother if they'd found her.

They've been sitting maybe ten minutes, cradling their silence, when sulfur creeps its way into the kitchen. Alice reaches into her pocket for the banishing bundle and Bronwyn's red Bic lighter. She tests the spark wheel. Blessedly, it lights. He will not catch her unaware this time. If the salt lines fail.

"Bronwyn," she says. Her sister is still kneeling on the floor, crying quietly. "Bronwyn, he's here." Bronwyn doesn't move.

Alice clutches the table to support her weight, then pushes to a stand, ignoring the urgency of the pain. Pain must come later, after. Because it's coming closer—the sulfur and then the rot, the wrenching pongy decay. The house is cold, yet Alice is sweating through her coat. She crosses the distance between them, yanks on Bronwyn's arm, and Bronwyn finally stumbles to her feet, clutching Alice's elbow. "I can't." Bronwyn's teeth are chattering. "I can't do it, I can't."

From the front of the house, a mechanical shriek: the front door, opening. It can't be Killian. A poltergeist wouldn't need to use the front door. Bronwyn and Alice exchange tense glances as footsteps make their way toward the kitchen. A neighbor investigating after spotting Bronwyn's car? Police would announce themselves. A trap set by Gisele? Meanwhile, that smell of decay draws ever closer. Alice clicks off the flashlight. Her rabbit-quick breaths sound riotously loud in her ears.

Then, the footsteps stumble and a horrifyingly familiar voice yelps, "Fucking ow! Shit!"

"Ryann?" Bronwyn makes a noise halfway between a scream and a whimper, launching herself toward the hall, but Alice manages—almost too late—to grab her wrist. Bronwyn tries, briefly, to shake her off, but Alice won't let her sister cross the salt threshold, this most powerful of their safety measures.

"Hey, Mom." Ryann limps into view, using the damaged walls to support her weight. "I think—" She swallows, a flush rising up her throat. "I think I broke my ankle."

Foolish girl. But there will be time to deal with her anger, later. When the house doesn't smell of rot and death. "Get into the kitchen. Fast. And be careful not to touch the salt line."

Bronwyn has stopped struggling, but is rubbing her eyelids with two fingers, muttering, "Grounded. Grounded until she's thirty-four. No, for the rest of her fucking life."

From the other side of the living room, a wet retching sound. Alice's heart thumps once. The Little House quiets again. The ice machine in the fridge lets out an exhausted gurgle, as if it has startled awake. Bronwyn shivers beside her. The ornaments in her bandolier clack where they meet Alice's own.

"Ryann, you have to hurry."

"I'm trying." Ryann is hopping toward them, but not fast enough. The sight seems to trigger something animal in Bronwyn, and Alice locks her hand around Bronwyn's elbow this time, barely a moment before Bronwyn lurches toward her daughter. Bronwyn strains forward, but Alice holds steady.

"Do not cross the salt line. It's the only thing that's keeping us protected in this room. He's almost here."

"I can help her across," Bronwyn snaps.

"She's going to make it, but crossing the salt threshold weakens it. You know that. And if it gives, all three of us are fucked," Alice says, but Bronwyn doesn't want to listen to her logic. Alice barely manages to restrain her.

And then it happens—a black and bluish blur rushes at Alice and Bronwyn from across the living room, stopping short at the salt threshold. Alice releases Bronwyn, holds out the bundle, flicks the lighter, touches flame to herb till smoke curls, as she takes in this ghost of bloated and melting purple skin, this black-eyed child in the vaguest shape of her brother. This boy whose bruises she kissed and scrapes she bandaged, who saved her from their mother, who is so very dead and yet, here. Here, again. "Oh, Killian," she breathes.

"You came," Killian says, a note of awe in his voice, as if he has spent very long imagining them and now can't quite believe they're there. He hasn't seemed to notice Ryann yet, and from behind her back, Alice gestures for Ryann to stop moving. Alice swallows, looks at Bronwyn. She needs to buy Ryann time. "Both of you."

He's lucid, Alice realizes, and she presses her hand to her abdomen in shock. It would be easier if there were nothing left in him but the death rage. The hate. Mind too gone for recognition. Another confrontation like the one in Bronwyn's house, all thrown lamps and broken dishes and the adrenaline of dodging killing blows. Not this gentleness. This desperation. The guilt-infused love that rocks through her. So does the fear—if he's an active threat to Ryann now, how much more so now that he's lucid.

Killian looks around, notices that he's stuck in the threshold. "Afraid of me, Beau?"

"The last time I saw you, you wrecked Bronwyn's house and could have seriously hurt us in the process." Alice shifts her weight to the other foot, trying to redistribute the pain. "Of course, I'm afraid of you." It relieves her to say the words, to stop feigning bravery.

"The last time you saw me isn't the last time I saw you." Killian clucks his tongue, and it surprises Alice. It seems too adult, too coherent for the body Killian inhabits. He's been trapped alone in this house with their mother for years, unable to speak except through his taunts on the walls. Is this return to lucidity a result of Alice cutting off her bind runes, of being seen for the first time in over a decade? Alice decides yes, because the alternative—Killian trapped and writhing in pain alone, in a horrific kind of solitary confinement, for over a decade—is too horrific to consider. "Perhaps I overreacted. But to see you at Bronwyn's house with her girl—the black-haired one, not the dead one—you came for her, didn't you? No, don't lie," Killian says sharply, cutting Alice off before she can deny it. "Gisele told me that you'd come—and for a girl you'd never even met. Was I not good enough to play hero for?" There's almost a teasing tone to his voice, but his face is surveying, eyes hard on her face. "Was I not worthy of saving? She must be something so special for you to come all this way, considering how you banished me and mutilated yourself rather than come back for me. Was I so unlovable?"

"That isn't fair." Alice tries to keep her voice measured. To keep him distracted. She releases Bronwyn's arm, takes a step forward. Slowly, she hobbles to the other side of the room, well within the bounds of the salt lines, to guide his eyes away from the hallway. "Of course I loved you. Of course I wanted to save you, but I couldn't. I couldn't come back here, Killian."

"You're here now." Killian shrugs. There's guile in the gesture, wrong and adult on his childish body. The fury contained and manipulated. "Kind of Gisele, to leave the house to the black-haired girl. Are you aware how weak her gift is? I could crater her out of that body and make it my own. Are you here to play messiah, Alice? Save the girl from the big bad poltergeist?"

"I couldn't come back then. I wasn't as strong then. I couldn't face Gisele or the shed or myself. And if I'd hesitated in front of her, if I'd broken, we'd never have gotten away again. I know you were just a kid, but so was I. I'm so sorry I couldn't do it then. But I'm here now. I'm strong enough now." Alice tries to take another step, but the pain in her heels locks her in place.

She grits her teeth. She spots Ryann receding into the hallway from the corner of her eye. "I came back."

"No." Killian clasps his hands. He almost seems to be enjoying this. "That's not good enough. You let her trap me here, and then you left me all alone. You promised me you'd save me, Alice, and then you locked me away in this miserable cage of a house, alone with her. I trusted you, and you damned me to save yourself. And what's worse—you did it on purpose."

"What's he saying?" Bronwyn whispers, her eyes darting back and forth across the empty space. Alice prays she's not looking in Ryann's direction. "Does he hate us?"

"Hate you?" When Killian laughs, it shows the purple mottling and rot in his throat. "Of course, I did. For a long time. Years, even. But I don't hate you now. Hate is exhausting, Alice. You aren't worth the energy to hate. And having spent all this time now, in the Little House, I understand. I would have damned you, too, had our roles been reversed."

"I'm glad." Alice tries to smile. Fails. "That you don't hate me."

"Are you?" His eyebrows arch, an alarmingly Gisele-esque gesture. "You shouldn't be. Because I have no intention of forgiving you. I want you to understand that for all these years, you've been my monster in the dark."

"I never wanted to—"

"What? Hurt me?" Killian makes as if to slap the salt line threshold, and even knowing he can't touch it, Alice jumps. "When you swore that blood oath, and then when you bound your shadow. When you *lied* to me about coming back to Kirtland—you've never had a problem hurting me."

"I didn't know it would be like this, Killy." The nickname tastes strange in her mouth, webbed with disuse. Alice moves closer, and Killian retreats, eyeing the bundle in her hands. Bronwyn grabs Alice's arm, tugging her back.

"Don't you dare say that. It hurts. It hurts all the time, and you knew, and you left me alone. What did you expect would happen?" He rolls his shoulders as if cracking his neck to relieve tension.

"I was twenty, and I was scared. I was having panic attacks twice a day. I couldn't have helped you then the way that I can now." Alice softens her voice. This is how she used to speak to ghosts as a child. Make herself gentle, beguiling. She is thankful that he never saw her tricks at the séance table, that he doesn't know just exactly how convincing she can be. "If you help me find the blood oath, Killian, I can set you free."

Killian opens his mouth, but pain grimaces across his face. This is the only warning before he buckles, back arching impossibly, folding back until he's snapped shut like a spider in death throes. The scream that comes out of him—Alice claps a hand over her mouth. She'd forgotten. One by one, his fingers snap backward. Then his limbs. The crunch, audible. The pain, mirrored in Alice's own joints. He thrusts himself up, briefly levitating, before his body slams back into the ground. His arms, pretzeling. His calves, perpendicular from his thighs. The force of it reverberates through the floor, sending the half-attached overhead light spinning on its wire. Bronwyn gasps, jumping away. Alice only becomes aware that she has been chanting, "No, no, no," when Bronwyn's nails dig into the soft flesh of her upper arm.

Pond water, thick with algae, leaks from their brother—gurgling from his throat, the rotted holes of his ears, the creases of his fingernails. She wants to run to him, aches to help. Bronwyn's bruising fingers are a tether. A thread of water runs toward them, diverts into a hole in the wood. *I did this. It's my fault.* It goes on for minutes. Hours, maybe. Each convulsion a beaded string of eternity. And then it passes. Killian's mangled body eases on the floor, panting heavily. Slowly, he pulls himself back together. One dislocated limb snapping back into place, then another. A series of sickening crunches. *This is my fault, I did this, this is my fault, I did this, it's your fault, you promised me, you promised me, and then you left me, you left me alone, this is my fault, I did this.*

"You said you're here to help, Beau, but what if I don't want your help anymore?" There's a hint of petulance in the set of his jaw. "I've spent a lot of time in this house, and I've had time to think and consider and *miss*. I miss living. I miss Mountain Dew, and I miss skateboarding, and I miss being hugged. I miss the taste of berries. I miss Goldfish crackers, and the smell of snow in the winter." The water still leaks down his cheeks, a poor cousin to tears. "I was supposed to die. You promised me. Gisele promised me. And if I couldn't die, if that was so unthinkable to all of you—" Killian crawls forward, along the edge of the salt threshold. He tests it with his fingers, almost comically, mime-like as he pats the air. "Maybe instead I'd like a body of my own."

Then, in the hallway, Ryann falls with a terrible thud, whimpering as she goes. Killian freezes. "What," he says, "was that?" He disappears then materializes at the other salt line by the hallway door, standing above Ryann. She opens her mouth to scream, but no sound comes out—there's no time. Like lightning, Killian puts a hand on her chin and a hand on her forehead, and rips his way inside of her.

Alice has never known what a possession looks like from the outside. If forced to hazard a guess, she'd assumed it wouldn't look like anything at all. But with her gift restored she can see him, a mottled shadow, under Ryann's skin.

Ryann—Killian—holds up an arm, marveling at the movement. "That's better," he says. "We can all talk, now."

"Ryann?" Bronwyn's throat is raw. "No, you can't do this. Please. *Please.*"

"I could've taken her at any time, you know. I thought about it. Testing out if the principles of our oath would hold. If she could be a sanctuary. If being in her skin could stop it from hurting." Killian shakes his head. "I even tested it out once or twice. It was so easy. Weak gift, no training—she didn't even know she *could* fight me."

Bronwyn moans, collapses to the ground. "Please, Killian. Please let her go. Don't do this, don't—"

This is my fault, I did this, this is my fault, I did this. "It isn't her that you want. You know that." It slips out before Alice can hold it back. "You want me."

Killian jerks back, hissing at her like an animal. The contortions of Ryann's face shift, fierce and vulpine. "I don't need to *split* a body. Not when I can have this one."

Think, Alice. Stay calm. Breathe. Block out Bronwyn's tears. Block out the wind rattling the windows. Killian spent four months trapped in Bronwyn's house. He could have stolen Ryann's body at any time, could have found solace from pain, chose not to. "But you don't want to hurt her," Alice says. This gambit, this logic, it has to work. She must pick her words carefully. "You aren't a monster, Killian. You let her be for months."

Killian's lip curls. He's scratching at Ryann's flesh—leaving long red marks along the white skin of her arms. Alice flinches, both from seeing the damage inflicted on Ryann's body and the knowledge that Killian's death itch must be so bad that this gesture is now an ingrained habit, because he cannot still be hurting so badly in Ryann's body. "Aren't I?" he says. "If I'm not the monster, who is?" Bronwyn murmurs something unintelligible, and Killian cups a hand around his ear. "Speak up."

"I said," Bronwyn snaps, "Gisele was the fucking monster. You—*you* are better than this."

"Maybe once, but I spent sixteen years dreaming of the hurting coming to an end. And now, I have her, a way that won't hurt. I've tried her out. She fits like a dream."

"But you don't want her." Alice moves forward again. She can feel the sweat on her palms soaking into the banishing bundle. "She's not a good fit. Not like me. I was made for you. You can take my body anywhere. You can't do that with her. You'd still be trapped in this house."

Killian seems to consider this, cocking his head. "Riddle me this, Beau. Do you think it makes you a good person that you finally came?"

"No," she says. She thinks of his pain, and the shed, and the twin lines of the pregnancy test she spirited away, and the unanswered texts on her phone from the man she hasn't loved nearly well enough. "I don't think I am."

Killian nods, his jaw settling. It's grotesque, the bruised mottling of him under Ryann's skin. "I could keep her." He crawls forward, and before Alice can jump to stop him, he sweeps the salt line aside.

"But I won't," he says softly, and then Ryann is gasping and clutching her throat as Killian slips out of her skin. Bronwyn throws herself across the room, pulling Ryann tight into her arms.

Then, he's standing in front of Alice, that little boy she loved so much, just out of reach of the banishing bundle. The rest of the world fades, except for the two of them. "If I give you the blood oath, you'll set me free? This isn't another trick?"

"It isn't a trick. I swear." And even though she knows her promises mean little, Alice says it as firmly as she can. Alice's hand begins to shake around the banishing bundle, smoke spurting up in unsteady patterns. She drops it to the floor, stomps on it with her bad foot to extinguish it despite the pain. "See?" she says. "Now I can't stop you.

When he touches her face, Alice freezes so she won't flinch. A lick of cold trails down her cheeks. Up close, the smell of rot is acrid. Underneath, almost sweet. A cloying decay. Alice grits her teeth. His skin is pocked with putrid yellow welts, the flicker of an eyetooth visible through the gaping muscle. "And what if it doesn't work?" Killian asks.

"Then you can take me."

"Liar," he snarls. "You wouldn't."

"I would," Alice confirms. "If it doesn't work you can have my body."

"Alice, stop it. No." Bronwyn is still clutching Ryann, who is sobbing. "Don't do this."

"It's going to work," Alice says, because it has to.

"I'll never give the body back. You know that?"

Alice nods, shakily. "Yes."

"Then we have a bargain. I'll be back. I have to go dig it up." Killian moves so fast, his body blurs. For a few long minutes, the three of them are alone.

"Close the salt line," Bronwyn urges. She tries to stand, but Ryann cleaves to her. "Now, Alice, before he comes back."

Alice shakes her head. "Trust me."

"If this doesn't work, he'll take you. Please. There has to be another way. Close it. Close it now." Bronwyn's throat sounds raw. And Alice understands clearly that if this fails—if she cannot fix this and Killian takes her body—Bronwyn will blame herself. Bronwyn will take on the guilt and the responsibility for bringing Alice back to the Little House.

"Promise me you won't stop him," Alice urges. "It isn't your fault. I swear to you. It was always going to end like this, Bronwyn. I was always going to end up here. If it doesn't work, I accept the consequences. I know the choice I'm making. But you have to believe me. It's going to work."

"Alice—"

But then, from the darkness of the living room beyond, something skitters across the floor. Bronwyn tenses, tightening her grip on her useless bandolier. The knot. It flicks through the gap in the salt barrier, coming to rest against Alice's shoe.

Alice scoops it off the floor and soil spills into her palms. She traces the threads with her thumbnail. They are stained dark with both their blood, gruesome against the grayish pink of Killian's baby blanket, withered herbs laced throughout. There's a grit to the texture that might be ash, and Alice bites down on her tongue until her mouth floods with pain. She never did get a good look at it, back then. It was in her hands and gone so fast she never saw the ingredients Gisele had used to compose the spell. It's the cleverest binding she's ever seen—the correspondences exceedingly simple in design. It fits exactly into her suspicions, just what she'd read in the library in that book in Midland. She's never felt so hollow, everything that makes her human scooped out and twined around this terrible knot. Killian was right. All she has to do is burn it.

Killian's grim smile matches her own. "You see, Beau? I waited for you. I was always waiting for you." And it's like the moment an argument sputters and dies, and she is left winded and unsure of her footing. She came here expecting to fight him, came here ready to pry this knot from the earth while throwing dill and salt in the air—in cutting the bind runes off, she's already bled for this moment. And now that, too, rests between them—that she ever considered that his refusal to forgive her would trump his desire for freedom.

When she rolls the knot between her fingers, the soil feels cold and dry under her thumb. Her throat is raw. Her limbs, trembling. "Killy, I'm so sorry."

"I hope you are. I hope you're sorry forever." He pushes himself up, the limbs still cracking and strange. And as Alice repositions the knot in her hand, Killian's face hardens.

She wants to say more. Wants to tell him about Eli and the baby and cutting off the bind runes, because he is her brother, and because she has missed him. She wants and she wants, but Killian has been subject to other's longings for long enough. And the truth is, there would never be enough. There would never be an end to it, no catharsis, no closure to make her ready.

Bronwyn is saying something, but Alice can't hear her over the ringing in her ears. She waves Bronwyn off. "It's okay," Alice says. And then she walks into the living room, comes to a stop in front of her brother.

They stare at each other. She doesn't want to let him go, but the one gift she can give him now is a painless passing. A death with no itch. So like she did so many times when he was a child, Alice opens her arms and he unravels into her. When the cold overwhelms her, Alice barely has a chance to scream before their body buckles.

His lungs ache until he remembers at last to gasp down a breath. Alice's body is strange, with the heaviness of meat and the warm pound of blood, yet quiet, painless. Even having so recently inhabited Ryann, Alice's body feels different, roomier. All those bind runes on her joints made her a more comfortable fit. He experiments, flexing her fingers, her toes, flinching at the contact of her torn heels to the ground. They are more painful than he realized. He's surprised she was still standing.

It's right, in the end, that they do it together in this body, he thinks. It feels correct. He lifts the lighter, but his attempt to use fingers is clumsy. He doesn't remember exactly how to make them work, begins to panic until Bronwyn appears behind his shoulder. She takes the lighter from him cautiously, as if worried he will lunge for her. He almost wants to, just to startle her, but he restrains himself. Flick. The lighter catches, it burns.

She holds it up for him. It's time. Oh blessed gods, it's finally time.

"Goodbye," he says.

"Goodbye," she says.

When he touches the flame to the knot, it lights, improbably, like kindling. The heat spreads like oil under his skin, and he's warm finally, finally right, and he is going—he is going at last. The knot goes up with him, dissolving into impossible ash in the air. As Alice's knees buckle, Bronwyn catches the body, pulls Killian tight to her. The contact with Bronwyn is comforting, eases the pain. He tilts his head toward the ceiling, and his smile is feral.

Then he's gone like ash on the wind. Slipping away from Alice with a clean, hushed roar. As if he'd never been there at all. She sways, then topples, dragging Bronwyn down with her, the brackish flavor of water on the back of her tongue. Only now can it finally be over. Only now can Alice, finally, live.

Epilogue

AFTER THEY CHECK IN at the front desk, the woman shows Alice and Eli to a claustrophobic waiting room. A violently pink humidifier sits on a table along the far wall, hissing out something floral that does nothing to cover the smells of antiseptic and anxiety.

The beige wallpaper is patterned with mauve seashells. The sheets overlap imperfectly. Someone, probably two decades ago given the state of these rayon seats, picked this wallpaper with an eye toward the soothing and nonthreatening. As if Alice didn't already know the dangers of motherhood, of what it meant to step foot in here. Her nails itch to peel the paper from the walls.

Eli presses a kiss to the back of her hand. "Still with me?"

"Mostly." Then, because Eli is watching her, she adds, "I'm thinking of Killian." She forces the words out. It still feels strange to say Killian's name into the open air, uncomfortable to push past her instincts for avoidance. Eli lifts an arm and Alice shifts so she can lean into him. He smells of sandalwood and soap and himself. It's the smell of home, this miracle of a man who loves her, even more precious because she could have lost him. Even now, this comfort between them is conditional on her continued honesty. She has promised to do her best, to work on herself. As Eli has pointed out, this is the contract of their relationship: He will support her through anything, but only if she takes the steps to heal. He cannot save her, cannot be responsible for her recovery. That is work she must do herself. He will hold her accountable to it, but he will not carry her. And this is as it should be.

Susan was gone by the time Alice returned to Saginaw. Eli had sent her home a few days early. Alice had expected to be greeted with crossed arms and maybe a little bit of hate, but when she walked through the door, Eli folded her into his arms, burying his face in her hair. "I love you," he said. "But it's time to tell me." And she had.

It had been so much easier than she expected to convince him of magic. He's approached it with the same clearheaded organization that he brings to every endeavor—making to-do lists for protecting against possession, researching the best occult shops in the area, arranging an appointment with a body modification artist who specializes in scarification to see if something can be done to remove the runes on Alice's joints.

This week, again and again, they'd sat cross-legged on the bed across from each other. "Show me again," he'd say, and Alice would comply, conjuring a witch ball the size of a silver dollar, which would bounce happily on her palm before settling on the tip of her index finger. She'd pass it to Eli, who'd reverently lift it from her fingers, then toss it into the air. When they'd had their fun, she'd sprinkle a saltshaker over top to extinguish it.

A few days ago, they drove an hour and a half to the nearest occult supplies shop and browsed the store with their heads bent toward each other, Alice whispering the correspondence of each herb and crystal Eli touched. They purchased an obscene number of supplies, but each one was necessary, Eli argued, despite Alice's protests that she never really used many physical supplies. Alice was starting over fresh with magic, must have the resources to practice, must be prepared if—when—she next encounters a ghost.

She still doesn't know how she feels about seeing the ghosts again, though she's yet to find one in Saginaw. The hair on her arms still bristles each time she thinks of her gift, and she's wondered, again and again this week, if it will ever come as naturally as breathing again, or if this is a part of her that Gisele excised and kept. This time, though, the gift belongs to her fully. She will use it any way that she likes, even if that means not using it at all.

Ultimately, she thinks, the next time she sees a ghost, she'll most likely turn away. She's spent too much of her life tending other people's grief. She deserves to cultivate her own happiness now. No one has the right to ask her for more than she's already given.

In the waiting room, she glances at Eli, who has been inspecting her carefully. "Are you really okay?" The wounds between them are still fresh, will take time to heal. This morning, he helped her schedule her first therapy appointment. Tonight, he will pack their suitcases. Tomorrow they will drive to Cleveland, and Alice will conduct the rite that will finally let Willow pass. She hopes Willow is holding on, hopes the itch is not hurting her too badly.

She waits to smile until she means it. "I will be. Soon."

He sweeps his thumbs in circles on the metal arms of the chair, hesitating. "If you want to reschedule, we can. I mean, not too long. But if you want to talk it through again—"

"We made a decision," Alice says. And even if her insides are turning to raw hamburger, she also knows it is the right one. "I'm ready."

When the nurse calls Alice's name, Eli grabs her purse and slings it over his shoulder. As she stands, Alice pauses to take it all in. The horrible wallpaper and Eli and the new life that waits beyond that door.

There will be no more Glass girls, not from her, and no more sons—but that doesn't make motherhood impossible. A child can come later, by adoption—if she wants it. If she chooses.

This morning, Bronwyn texted to wish her luck. When she opened the message, she saw a selfie of Bronwyn and Ryann sitting in the truck, each blowing a kiss to her. *We love you*, the text said. *You're going to be just fine, kid.* And Alice knew what Bronwyn meant was: We will help each other survive.

And they will. They are.

Acknowledgments

WRITING *GLASS GIRLS* has been the work of half a decade and the centrifugal force driving the latter half of my twenties. I am astoundingly fortunate to have so many dear ones to thank for the existence of this book.

First and foremost: to Topaz Winters. We have grown with and for each other in ways I never could have imagined—I would not be the person I am today without you. Our friendship has been my favorite song for the last decade. May we continue to love each other like this in every lifetime to come.

To Erin Wicks, my brilliant editor, who held the heartbeat of this book and worked with me to shape it into something beyond my wildest dreams. Working with you has made me both a better writer and better editor. May we have many more Paris adventures and someday actually make it to the medieval museum!

To Margaret Sutherland Brown for believing in this book from the first; for safeguarding my dreams, health, and sanity;

and for being an endless font of calming energy, enthusiasm, and wise counsel.

I remain in awe, as I did then, at my luck at finding a home for *Glass Girls* at Gillian Flynn Books at Zando. I've been awestruck and moved beyond words by the support and brilliance from every person who has touched this work. Thank you Gillian Flynn, thank you to the indefatigable Katie Burdett, thank you to the truly spectacular marketing team, and to everyone else who has worked so hard to bring *Glass Girls* into the world. You are incredible, stunning, brilliant people. I could not imagine trusting this book to anyone else.

To Kathryn Harlan and Michelangelo's Coffee House in Madison, Wisconsin, where we worked on the drafts of our books side by side almost every day for three years. I am eternally grateful for our writing days, horror movie nights, and endless discussions about the state of the world.

To Autumn Gielink, who loves this book almost as much as I do, who organized a personalized tour to refamiliarize me with Cleveland while I was writing the first draft, and who recreated the Little House on the Sims for me. You have been my biggest cheerleader for the last twenty-five years. Mylodya Lylian May.

To my brother, Nic, and my sister-in-law, Molly, and the way the three of us have made not only a family but a little Coven which has been the stabilizing force of my life. Thank you for making your home a safe place for me to rest and for holding onto me so tightly during the worst days. I love the two of you beyond measure, with all of the oodles.

To my loving partner, Jad Akhttou, who with unending tenderness and patience has gentled my workaholic tendencies by making sure I remain fed, hydrated, and get at least some sleep during my deadlines. There are hundreds of words for love among our four languages; the only one I will ever need is your name.

It takes a village to raise a writer, and I'm endlessly grateful for mine: This book would not exist without the love and support of the University of Wisconsin–Madison MFA program. To Sean Hayes, Em Binder, James Eberhard, and Angela Boyd, who read the early pages of this book with such patience and care. To Beth Nguyen, Jesse Lee Kercheval, Amy Quan Barry, Sean Bishop, and the rest of the incredible faculty at UW–Madison. A special thanks to Jaquira Diaz, who told me this was *the* novel I needed to write, and to Porter Shreve, who read every ugly duckling draft and without whose guidance *Glass Girls* would be half the book it is.

Immense thank-yous to Kit Pynes-Jaeger, Jesse Pierce, Annie Schoonover, Jordan Ryder, Kayla Wilson, and Tim McRoy for the number of eyes they loaned and sounding boards they provided. Thank you to my family for their baffled support and loving acceptance as I worked to realize my dreams, but especially to Ella, who is a bulldog when it comes to supporting me, even though I'm supposed to be the big sister.

Lastly, this book owes its existence—as I do—to my father, Steve Hay, who passed away in 2016. Some days, I only kept writing because of the force with which you believed in me, and it all turned out applesauce after all. I miss you every day.

About the Author

DANIE SHOKOOHI (SHE/THEY) is a graduate of the University of Wisconsin–Madison MFA program and the managing editor at Half Mystic. Her poetry and fiction have been published in the *New Ohio Review*, *The American Journal of Poetry*, the *Mississippi Review*, the *Cincinnati Review*, and others. She was raised a Michigander by her Iranian mother and American father, but in true wanderlust fashion, Danie's lived in five of the twelve Midwestern states. *Glass Girls* is her first novel. Currently, Danie lives in Paris. You can find her on Instagram at @danieshokoohi.